DADDY'S LITTLE GIRL

DADDY'S LITTLE GIRL

a novel by

BRITTANI WILLIAMS

Q-Boro Books
WWW.QBOROBOOKS.COM

An Urban Entertainment Company

Published by Q-Boro Books

ISBN-13: 978-1-933967-04-2
ISBN-10: 1-933967-04-8
First Printing February 2007
Printed in the United States of America

10 9 8 7 6 5 4 3 2 1

Cover Layout & Design—Candace K. Cottrell
Editors—Melissa Forbes, Tiffany Davis, Candace K. Cottrell

Q-BORO BOOKS
Jamaica, Queens NY 11434
WWW.QBOROBOOKS.COM

Being the heir to a drug empire doesn't guarantee the life of a princess . . .

PROLOGUE

Meet Giselle

What else could possibly go wrong? I thought as I sat in the dirty-ass jail cell, waiting for my lawyer to arrive and get me the hell out of there! I was tired and mad as hell that I even let myself get into the situation that I was in.

Basically, I let some nigga ruin my life. There was a time when everything was perfect. Then I let the only man I ever loved take away everything that was important to me.

After all that, I was stuck in jail on a murder charge while my children needed me. Why women allow men to change their entire beings to make them happy, I'll never know. When I love, I love hard, and I loved my husband with all of my heart. I got married very young, but I knew from watching my mother that it was very important to please your man. However, if that man had a plan, there was nothing that you could do to change that, and in my case there was nothing I could have done to make things any different.

I wished that I had known then, everything that I know now. I wish that I had someone to guide me along the right path, forewarning me of men like him. I was so in love with the outside that I never cared about what was inside. I thought I would be able to mold him into the man I wanted him to be. I thought if you loved someone with all of your heart and soul, they would have no choice but to do the same. I walked into my relationship blind. I bragged about snagging a prize but in reality, I lost. I was far from a winner, and the ups and downs that I had to go through to survive were much harder than I ever expected.

The longer I sat in the holding cell, the more annoyed I became. I could feel all the evil stares and in the mood I was in, I was waiting for a bitch to jump up so I could knock her ass right back down. My hair was a wreck, and I was feeling sick to my stomach since the cell reeked of piss. The one toilet that was available was the filthiest thing I'd ever seen in my life. I would have sacrificed peeing on the floor or on myself, for that matter, before I would ever think about sitting my ass on that toilet seat. I still had blood all over my hands and face since they wouldn't allow me to wash it off. I knew that if I ever made it out of there, I would make some major changes in my life and thank God for giving me another chance to make things right.

I decided to sleep sitting up straight that night and though I was extremely exhausted, I could barely stay asleep for more than a few minutes before I would jump up to make sure the females I shared the small box with knew I was awake and definitely aware of my surroundings.

My lawyer finally arrived the following day, and I was soon disappointed when she informed me that I could possibly spend months in jail before the judge would set a trial date. I didn't know much about the legal system, but I would have never expected that I would have to do possibly six months to a year before I would even go to trial. The arraignment was set for later that afternoon, and I was being charged with first-degree murder. I pleaded not guilty but was given a bail of $500,000, despite the fact that it was self-defense. Since there was no way I could put up the 10 percent that was required to walk out of there, I had to suffer.

It's amazing that when bad things happen, they all happen at once. Looking back on my life, I would have never guessed that I would be facing a life-term prison sentence.

I'm just going to let every woman know my story, my struggle, my heartache, and my pain. Hopefully I can reach every young girl out there living the fast life, loving the drug dealers. They all need to know that everything that looks good to you isn't always good for you. I need to let them know what happened to me, with hopes that it never happens to them.

CHAPTER 1

GISELLE: Like Mother, Like Daughter

1996

I sat there on the edge of the bed, watching my mother put on her makeup and praying that today would finally be the day that she would allow me to do the same. My mother was drop-dead gorgeous. She had long, jet black, silky hair that the Dominicans blew out for her once a week. She had skin the color of an Indian, but her eyes were hazel so she stood out immediately. Her body was definitely the most shapely I'd seen, with her butt being so round, it was almost perfect. Her abs were tight, and her 36D breasts were perky even after breastfeeding me. I always wanted to feel grown up, so the makeup was just a way to boost my confidence. Whenever I would ask, she would tell me I wasn't old enough yet, maybe one more year. Well, this was my 12th birthday and the way I saw it, I was almost a teenager and had waited long enough. I decided to give it a try since the worst thing that she could say was no.

"Mom, could you make my face up for my birthday, please?" I begged.

"Giselle, you know how I feel about that. I don't need you growing up too fast. Your face is beautiful without all of this nonsense," she said as she rubbed her hand across my chin.

I pouted as I jumped off the bed and began to make my way to the door.

"Giselle!" Mom called when she realized that she no longer had an audience.

"Yes?" I replied with sadness in my voice.

"Girl, your dad is going to kill me for this. Get over here so I can put this make up on you. Don't get too excited, because you're only getting a little blush and lip gloss."

I smiled, as I didn't care what she was putting on me. I wanted to be just like her, and at this point I felt that I was getting closer to mirroring her excellence. This is the way things went with me and my mother during most of my childhood. She was easily won over by my pouting and if it weren't for my daddy, I would have been wearing makeup a long time ago.

Daddy walked in just as I was glancing in the mirror at the masterpiece my mom had created.

"Alita, what the hell are you doing, putting that shit on her face? I told you I didn't want her wearing that! These perverts won't be out here drooling over her. You're going to fuck around and have me in prison!" he yelled before coming over to pull me off the vanity stool.

"Terrance, it's just a little makeup," my mother replied, trying to smooth over the situation.

"I don't care! Giselle, go wash your face off so we can go," he yelled.

I could hear them arguing about me through the walls. They were always at odds when it came to me. They both wanted me to have the best of everything, but since they both had different views of what the best was, it caused conflict. I did as I was told and made my way downstairs, where they were waiting for me. They were taking me out to a dinner for my birthday gift, and I was excited because I knew that my dad had something over the top planned, as usual.

I loved seafood, so Red Lobster was my restaurant of choice. My dad wasn't too keen on it, but he dealt with it since it was my birthday. Dinner went off without a hitch, and before we had dessert, my dad stood up and pulled a box from his pocket.

"Baby Girl, you're growing up now and each year I try to get you something that a princess should have. I know that I always go overboard, and one day I'll get it right; but for now, I'm going to fall in line with the way that I've been doing in the past. I hope you like it," he said before passing me the box across the table.

I opened the long, slim box to reveal a diamond necklace. I was so excited that I almost jumped across the table. The necklace was beautiful. I was used to him buying me some sort of jewelry, so it didn't seem overboard to me at all.

As I hugged him he whispered, "Sorry, I forgot something." He pulled another box out of his jacket pocket and gave it to me.

"Daddy!" I yelled as I quickly opened the box to see the matching tennis bracelet. I couldn't believe it.

My mother was sitting on the side, shaking her head because she knew that he would probably do something to outdo what he did the year before.

"And one more thing." He pulled out one more, smaller box.

I knew that I had been good in school, but not this good. Inside this box was a small diamond ring that was similar to a ring he'd gotten my mother for their anniversary.

"Terrance, you shouldn't have. Now what does she have to

look forward to?" my mother quizzed with her arms folded across her chest.

"She has a lot to look forward to. I want her to grow up wanting the best so that no broke-ass nigga could afford her!" he replied.

"Thank you so much, Daddy!" I said as I got up and hugged him once more.

We sat and ate birthday cake before we headed home. I refused to remove my jewelry that night; I wanted to sleep in it and though my mom yelled at me, I didn't care.

My mom hated to be spoiled, so she didn't want me to grow up that way. My dad was a king in the drug game. He started selling drugs at the age of seventeen, and by the time he was twenty-five, he was at the top of a major empire in South Philadelphia. He then stretched his empire statewide, then across to New Jersey, and finally into Delaware.

My dad was perfect, far above the average nigga. Big T was the kind of man I wanted to marry. My mom was lucky. She scooped him up when she was only fifteen, and even though he fooled around on her, he never disrespected home. She was the queen, and everybody knew not to fuck with her or there would be hell to pay.

My daddy was her one and only. She never really cared for drug dealers before meeting him, but there was just something about him that she couldn't resist. He wined and dined her until she finally came around, and it wasn't long before she was pregnant with me. Terrance was happy to have a daughter, and he promised that I would always have the best of everything, which he'd made sure of thus far. Since he was the king, I was automatically the princess, and I wore the title well.

When I was eight, I found out that I wasn't my dad's only child. At the time I didn't understand it, but later I figured it out. Akil was the name of the son that Daddy had when he was eighteen, before he met my mom. He met Akil's mother at a club and that one-night stand produced Akil. Janice was his mother's name and from what I was told, she was fine back then. She was mixed with Puerto Rican and had long hair, caramel skin and pretty brown eyes. Terrance never made her his girl; he just made sure she had everything she needed to take care of his son the way he wanted. He said that because of her ways, she wasn't wifey material, and I figured that he meant her drug habits because she died of an overdose when Akil was thirteen. That's when Akil came to live with us. My mom, being the real woman she was, took him in as her own.

"Why is it that you'd rather spend more time with your daughter than me?" my mother yelled at my father as I sat at the bottom of the steps listening. My father and I had just come home from a Sixers game and as I sat there eating my leftover popcorn, they were upstairs going toe-to-toe.

"That's not true, Alita! I promised her that I would take her to a basketball game and when the tickets popped up, I did what I said I would."

"You could have easily taken me to the game, Terrance!"

"You don't even like basketball!" he yelled.

"I just want us to spend some more time together. Every time you get a free day, you spend it with her!" she yelled in frustration.

"You act like she's not my daughter. What the hell is the big deal with me spending time with her!"

"She's your daughter, that's the point. Not your wife!"

"I'm not going to stand here and keep arguing with you about the time I choose to spend with my daughter. It's ridiculous that you would even be jealous of that. You act like I'm out fucking another woman or something!"

"You might as well be!" she screamed.

With that, Daddy came storming out of the room and down the steps. I sat there as he walked past me and out the door. My mother came to the top of the steps a few minutes later and stared at me before speaking.

"Get up here and take your bath. You have school tomorrow!" she yelled before turning around and going into her bedroom. I never understood why she was always so upset when my dad did something for me. I later found out that her anger had nothing to do with me at all; it was the fact that she knew he was having an affair, and she was pissed that his only time away from his mistress still wasn't spent with her.

Though my mother knew he would never leave her, she still worried from time to time. She never wanted to wake up without him and I could understand that, being that I loved my dad with all of my heart and couldn't imagine my life without him in it. We both had unconditional love for him, and we would fight to keep it for many years to come.

CHAPTER 2

Meet James: Son of a Hustler

1996

Niggas don't know my struggle, but that's why I'm here to let you know. I had dreams growing up, but not the average dreams of young boys. I dreamed the average dream of niggas growing up in the ghetto. I grew up in Philadelphia, Pennsylvania, the place that they call the City of Brotherly Love. I can honestly say that the nickname means nothing to me since the truth doesn't even closely resemble love. Niggas care more about getting to the top than watching out for someone else. They'll be your best friend and stab you in the back as soon as your eyes are closed.

I had learned early on that I had to look out for me, and that was it. I couldn't waste time trying to help another nigga, and as fucked up as that may sound, it was the truth and the mentality of most of the niggas I knew. I wasn't always like this, and I'm sure that the way that I turned out didn't sit well with a lot of people. When people get older and reflect on their lives, most people find things that they would have done differently if they could turn back the hands of time. Well, there was one thing that I would change, and it wasn't the lifestyle. It was the way that everything ended. I should have been smarter with the choices I made, and handled the distractions with ease. Things would have turned out drastically different had I not let my feelings get in the way of what I had originally set out to do.

The way that I grew up slightly directed the decisions that I made. Every day was a struggle for me. Many nights I had to fight just to eat. I had a big family—three brothers and two sisters—so you can imagine how that was, trying to live off the small amount of food stamps my mother received from the government. My mother, Marie, was one of the strongest women I knew and if I had met another woman as strong as her, it would have changed my opinion of black women. As I watched my mother work under the table washing clothes, babysitting, and cleaning houses, I had hoped that I might find a woman with her spirit. I always believed that there was one woman out there that would be that match for me, a woman that was never afraid to break a sweat if I needed her to get down and dirty to make ends meet. What amazed me most about my mother was the fact that as she struggled to take care of all six of us, she never complained, and I could definitely respect her for that. It ain't nothing worse than a woman who lies down and gets pregnant, only to blame the child for fucking up her life. Although her children didn't turn out the way that she might have wanted, she was proud that she was able to do it all on her own without the help of any of our sorry-ass fathers!

My father, if that's what you want to call him, was never around. Big Mike was the nigga who impregnated my mother and hung her ass out to dry. I despised that nigga for backing out on his responsibilities. While we were fighting over Oodles of Noodles, this nigga had a full stomach every day and night. I was his only bastard child.

All six of my mother's children had different fathers. My mother got pregnant when she was sixteen, and she was pregnant almost every year after that until she decided enough was enough and had her tubes tied. I think the absence of her own father made her yearn for attention from men, and each man she came in contact with took full advantage of the opportunity she gave them. My mother never knew her father, and because of that she always tried to keep some sort of father figure in the house for us. As we got older, it got old. The revolving door with men coming in and out only pissed us off. I never lost any respect for my mother, but I always wished she had more self-worth to get herself out of the pattern of "love me and leave me."

Now Big Mike, my father, was the man back in the day; he was big-time slangin' on the corners. Cocaine was the big moneymaker during the early to middle eighties, along with marijuana and the resurface of heroin. He chose to sell crack cocaine because of its fast turnover and the fact that the customers kept coming back to try and get the same rush they got the very first time they used it. Fresh gear, cars, bitches—he had it all, until he thought he was invincible.

The first time I met my father I was thirteen. My mother came home and informed me that he wanted to meet me. I wasn't really all that interested in meeting him, since I hadn't seen his ass in all of my thirteen years. At least, that was what I thought before seeing him. There was a bar that he hung out in called Scooters, off Lancaster Avenue. This bar was so packed on weekend nights that you had to pay a five-dollar fee just to get in the door. My mother drove me down to the bar where he sat in the back, drinking a Heineken. I was nervous as we walked through this bar in the middle of the afternoon. I had never been in a bar before, and after the initial shock, I was a little amused by the atmosphere. There was a row of booths down the right side of the bar. He was seated at the last booth, talking on his cell phone. He quickly ended his call as we approached.

"What's up, little nigga?" He reached out his hand for me to shake it.

I stood there, stunned, for a minute because I recognized who he was. My mother gave me a little shove and I reached out my hand to shake his. My mother stared at me, watching my facial expressions. I remembered seeing him in the neighborhood but never knew who he was. I did know that he was both respected and feared. You could cut the tension with a knife when he would drive through the neighborhood. You could practically see niggas shaking in their boots. He had never said one word to me before that day, and the intense feeling I got from standing there in front of him proved that I needed to be just like him one day.

"Thanks for bringing him by. I'll drop him off to you at your house in a few hours." He spoke, glancing at my mother's body as he did so, since even after bearing six children, she was still a brick house.

"No problem. James, I'll see you in a little while and you behave yourself, OK?" She bent down to kiss me on the cheek. I watched her leave, excited that I was the son of Big Mike and I was now going to get to know him. People would respect me, knowing that I was his seed.

"Sit down and get comfortable. Loosen up, too. You're standing there looking like a stiff tree." He waved his hand, motioning me to sit down. I was speechless and anxious as I sat opposite him in the booth. He ordered himself another beer and a Coke for me before he began to speak.

"So, we finally meet! How does it feel to be the son of a hustler?" he asked before lighting his cigarette.

"It feels good!" I said honestly.

"I know that I haven't been in your life, and you probably hate me for that, but I'm going to make things different from now on. If you ever need anything, you can call me and I'll make sure you get it. I'm going to be spending a lot of time with you, showing you the way to survive out here because niggas are ruthless and if you get caught out there slipping, your ass is grass. Niggas just need an inch and they'll take a yard to make their move. I learned my lesson a long time ago that you can't trust anyone. Not even your parents! So keep your enemies and friends real close, and keep your eyes open, even when you're asleep."

I never understood what he meant by that until I was old enough to be betrayed. It was then that I lost the trust that I had for everyone.

When I was fifteen, I came home from school to find out that Big Mike had been killed in a shootout with the police. *Damn,* I thought, *at least he went out like a soldier!* I knew from that day on that I was going to be a king one day, and that became my plan.

From what I was told, Big Mike's mother and father were both killed and their house was burned down with them in it. Rumors were that my father had killed them both after they stole money from him. I always wondered how a man could murder his parents. Big Mike would take that secret to the grave, but his cold heart led me to believe that he really was the person that killed them. Although it bothered me at first, the deeper I got into the life, the more I understood. I only got to spend a couple years with Big Mike before he was killed, but those years set the tone for my future. The time I spent with him taught me a valuable lesson about life: money was respect, and I was going to get respect by any means necessary. I demanded respect, and any form of disrespect would be handled accordingly.

All my life I dreamed about being the boss. I wanted to be the nigga laying down the rules, driving the expensive cars, wearing tailor-made shit, and have bitches eating out of my hands. I used my head and devised the perfect plan. First, it required a takeover. There were two bosses that I needed to take care of, and with the help of my main man, Mark, I was going to be on top. Nothing could stop me, or so I thought.

My mind was straight when I devised my plan, but then came the distractions. Women—they'll get you every time! Being in jail so long made me miss the women, and once I got a taste, I couldn't stop. Pussy was like eating steak and shrimp for the first time. The shit was good, and I couldn't stop going back for more.

"Who the hell ate my sandwich that was in the fridge?" I asked, yelling because my corned beef special was suddenly missing in action. I walked into the living room where my brother Timmy was watching reruns of *Martin*. Standing in front of the screen to block his view, I yelled, "Nigga, I know you heard me! Who ate my sandwich?"

"I didn't eat it. You better ask Sheena or one of them," Timmy yelled back, annoyed. Timmy was the youngest of my three brothers, and he was the one who was into the books. Growing up, Timmy rarely got into any trouble and had plans of becoming a criminal attorney after college. He was currently in his eleventh-grade year of high school, and already laying out his life plan. I wasn't interested in school. I couldn't imagine spending all of that time in school to end up working and still struggling. I needed my money fast. Fuck that white-collar shit!

"Your fat ass probably ate it. I better not find out who ate my shit, or I'm going to kick a bone out someone's ass!" I yelled in frustration.

"Whatever. Move out my way. I'm trying to watch TV!"

I left the living room, furious that someone was always touching my shit. Growing up in a house full of people, things were bound to go missing. I was the oldest one of my mother's children that still lived at home. I only stayed because none of their lazy asses would get a job to contribute to the bills. I stayed in the basement while the four of them shared two bedrooms.

I decided to go down to my room to give my girl, Trina, a call. I hadn't talked to her all day and I knew that if I didn't give her a shout out soon, she would be stingy with the booty. As the phone rang, I went over the lie that I was about to tell.

"Hello," she said softly in that sexy-ass voice that made me weak at the knees. Trina was sixteen, two years younger than me, but you would never guess that by just looking at her. Her body was banging—fat ass, small waist, and big-ass breasts that I loved to suck on every time I had a chance. I met her when I was in the eleventh grade. I never paid too much attention to the chicks who were in lower grades than me, but there was something about her that consumed my attention when she walked into a room. I remember the first time I spoke to her; she acted as if she wasn't interested in me. I knew that she was only showing off for her friends because she was all on my tip when I did a one-eighty and ignored her ass. I wasn't into playing games, even at a young age, and if games were what she wanted to play, she could do that shit alone.

We had been messing around for the last few years; not exclusively on my part, because I took a dip in a few other pools a few nights a week. I had been deep-sea diving up in one of my jump-offs earlier that afternoon, which led me to the lie that I was about to tell. Trina was the most insecure person I knew so even when I was telling the truth, she thought that I was lying.

"Hey, what's up? I called you earlier and you didn't answer your phone."

"You didn't call me, James. Stop lying. I've been home all day!"

"I did call. I was knocked out most of the day after I came home from the gym. So, what are you doing now?"

"Nothing. Lying down, watching TV."

"Are you coming over tonight?"

"I don't know if my mom's working or not. If she goes to work, I'll be there my regular time."

"Cool. Just hit me up in an hour. I'm about to go get a shower."

"OK. I love you."

"Ditto! Talk to you soon," I said before hanging up. Ditto was my way of telling her that I cared about her, because I wasn't sure if I loved her or not. I'd never loved any female other than my mother, and I wasn't about to tell her I loved her even if I did. There were easier ways to get the drawers, and I figured that out a long time ago. After I showered, I lay down and waited for her phone call. I was surprised when a knock at the back door turned out to be her. I was pissed that she came over without calling, like I had told her to do. I could have been in there ass-naked with another chick! It was a good thing I was alone, though, but I laughed to myself because I knew that she only came without calling to see if she could catch me slipping.

"Why didn't you call me like I told you to? I could have went out or something!"

"You could have been in here fucking around, too. I just wanted to make sure you weren't."

"Whatever, Trina. Come in!" I said, motioning her to come inside the door. "So, did you think about me today?"

"I think about you every day."

I walked over to the bed and spread out across it, motioning her to come over.

"James, I'm not trying to have sex tonight. Can we just chill?"

"Why? We ain't had sex all week, and now that you're here, you want to skip it?"

"James, please. I'm just not in the mood."

"I wish you would have told me that before you came over here, because you coulda kept your not-in-the-mood ass at home!" I yelled.

"What? Is that all you want from me?"

"Is that all I want? It ain't like I get it all the time or something."

"I'm just tired today."

"Well, I'm tired, too, tired of playing these childish-ass games with you. Every time I want to have sex, you don't. I have to wait weeks at a time, and then have you on my heels every day, asking if I'm fucking someone else. You wouldn't be so insecure if you were doing what you were supposed to do!"

"Are you fucking somebody else?"

"Don't even go there, Trina. I'm trying to have sex with you, my girl, but that always seems to be an impossible mission or some shit!"

"I know you were with Tia today. She told me."

"You keep believing everything you hear from these lying-ass hoes. I told you what I was doing today, so if you want to feed into that shit, then you go ahead."

"Whatever, James. I'm going home!" she said, walking toward the door.

"Well, go 'head, and don't be calling me when you need your hair and nails done, either!"

"Fuck you, James!" she said before walking out.

She'd be back in a few hours like she always was, apologizing for being so damn stupid. Every time we got into an argument, she would come back running when she realized that she wouldn't be able to keep her expensive style up to par without me. It was cool because I knew what I was doing behind her back and she had every right to be suspicious; but if she didn't have hard proof, then I didn't want to hear it. Without even thinking twice, I gave Tia a call to find out what the hell her problem was. She picked up on the first ring.

"Hello!"

"What the hell is wrong with you? Why did you tell Trina I was over there today?"

"Because you told me that you were going to stop fucking with her. I'm tired of playing second to that bitch!"

"I told you that I would stop fucking with her eventually. You can't even be patient."

"James, we've been messing around for a year now. How patient do you want me to be?"

"I don't need you stirring up no shit with her. If she knew that I was leaving her for you, she would never let me go!"

"She wouldn't have a choice if you didn't want to be with her. I am not going to keep hiding my relationship with you."

"You're not hiding it. You keep running your mouth to every person that will listen. You know the situation, and you damn sure don't hesitate to take the money I be throwing at you. You're all over me when I got cash and shit!"

"James, it's not about the money. I want to be your girl. I'm tired of being the jump-off!"

"Well, I'm tired of you running your mouth, so good-bye!" I slammed the phone down on the receiver.

Tia continued to call me, and I continued to ignore her ass. These chicks were so ungrateful. As much as I did for Tia, it was never enough. She wanted to be my girl, as if that would make things any different. I was still going to cheat. She should have been glad that she wasn't Trina, having to deal with chicks like herself, because she couldn't handle that shit. Tia was good as hell in the sack, there was no denying that; but she wasn't the type of chick that could be my girl. Men only wanted their girl to be a freak in the bed, but Tia had a problem keeping that freak shit under wraps. She was a freak inside, outside, day, and night. No matter when or where she was, her freakiness was sure to show.

The longer I sat there, the hornier I got. I just said fuck it and called Tia back. After all of her screaming and hollering, I went over to her apartment and fulfilled my sexual need. I didn't stay long after I hit it, because I had to hook up with my brother Rik anyway!

"Nigga, open the door. It's cold out here!" I yelled while banging on Rik's door. Here I was, standing outside in the dead of winter, and this nigga was probably in there with his dick up in some warm pussy. After about five minutes of knocking, his girl Lacy opened the door half-ass naked and obviously upset that I had interrupted them.

"Damn, J, why are you knocking on the door like that?" she asked, placing her left hand on her hip.

"Because it's cold as hell out here. Move!" I said, pushing past her. I walked into the living room where Rik was sitting on the sofa, watching TV. The room was a wreck and filled with the aroma of sex. I stood there smiling because I knew that I had pissed him off, but I didn't care. We had business to take care of.

"What the fuck are you smiling at?" he asked with seriousness on his face.

"Nothing at all. So, are we going to do this or what?"

"Yeah, let me get dressed," he said before going into the bedroom.

I stood there glancing at Lacy's body, and that shit was turning me on. She had long legs that were shined with lotion, making them glisten in the light. Before Rik and Lacy got serious, I thought about getting with her, but I decided to let Rik have her to himself. I met Lacy at one of the summer basketball games they held in North Philly up Sixteenth Street. It was thick with hustlers and wannabes. It was hard to sort them apart since the wannabees had mastered faking it. She was with a group of her girls when I approached her, and she was all over me. We were once close to getting it on, but her mother came home and busted the groove. I never told Rik about it since after I gave up on getting some, he slid right in. Interestingly enough, he was able to hit it within days when I had been trying for weeks.

As she stood there with her legs crossed, sitting on the sofa, I stared at every inch of her body. She returned the stare, saying nothing while I licked my lips, wishing there was some part of her on them. She smiled when she noticed my member beginning to rise in my jeans just from the thought of tasting her. As I heard the shower running from the master bedroom, I thought about going over to her and feasting on her down below. Instead, my soldier went limp when the sound of the running water ceased.

After Rik re-entered the living room fully dressed, he kissed Lacy goodbye and we were on our way. We entered his Lexus that was parked in the garage. He blasted *Ready to Die* by Notorious B.I.G. as I sat in the passenger seat, bobbing my head to the music while I thought about Lacy. I needed a dime like that, a down-ass chick that would always have my back no matter what. Lacy was the type of chick that even if she was pissed at you, she would ride you even harder than when she wasn't mad at you. Although I cared about Trina, I was tired of the bullshit. All of the arguing was wearing me down, and she knew it.

Pulling up in front of the spot where we usually discussed our plans, Rik turned off the car and lit a cigarette. I stood outside the car, waiting for him to finish.

"Nigga, hurry up! How long does it take to smoke a cigarette?" I asked.

"I'm finished, and I told you about rushing me. You're lucky you're my little brother, or I would have kicked your ass a long time ago for that shit!" he said, laughing.

"Whatever!"

We entered my boy Mark's apartment and found him sitting at the table, counting stacks of money. Mark had been my boy since grade school. There was never a time that he didn't have my back, and vice versa. For the last two years we had been robbing niggas. We hadn't been caught yet, and I loved the funds that I was getting from it. In the streets we would see the same dudes we robbed, and they would be telling people about how they would kill the people who had robbed them. I laughed because they weren't even smart enough to catch on to our game. We had planned to make a few more hits and be done with it. Deep down, I knew that I wouldn't be able to just walk away, but it was wishful thinking. I loved the money, and I wanted to use it to build my own drug empire like Big Mike.

Rik left the apartment after we divided the money up between the three of us. Mark and I sat there and talked while watching *The Godfather* on DVD. Mark's place was like a second home to me. I had brought many chicks there to get laid when I didn't want Trina popping up on me in mid-stroke.

"Man, Lacy was looking good as hell today when I picked up Rik."

"Yo, Rik would kick your ass if he knew you were looking at his girl like that!"

"I'm just looking, shit! You know I'm a dog. I can't help it," I said, laughing.

"You better not fuck around with none of my girls."

"Man, I wouldn't do that to you. I wouldn't do that to him, either. It's cool to look at the menu as long as I don't order, you know what I mean!" I said, laughing at how serious Mark reacted to my joke.

"Whatever!" he said before getting up to grab a beer.

"Bring me one, too!" I yelled before retrieving my ringing cell phone from the holder to answer it. "Hello!" I yelled into the receiver.

"J, they got Rik!" Lacy yelled.

CHAPTER 3

Mimi: First Time for Everything

1996

I couldn't understand what all the hype was about sex. There I was, lying on my back in a Holiday Inn resort, far from home, losing my virginity to Tony. That was some painful shit! I had always seen sex glamorized by the movies, videos, music, and TV shows, but at that moment I couldn't imagine how sex could be enjoyable to any woman. Watching it on TV shows could have never prepared me for this. I had even watched a few pornos, and the way that the women moaned couldn't have been anything but a front. I had never imagined losing my virginity this way. I had always imagined that I would be in love and possibly married. I might have loved Tony a little, but we sure weren't close to getting married. I knew that I could never get my virginity back, so I hoped that I wouldn't regret giving it to him.

My mother always warned me about sex, saying that it could end my life by either getting me pregnant or giving me a disease. She always blamed having me for destroying her life. Tonya Gordon was sixteen years old when she became pregnant with me. My father was her first boyfriend. Joe was twenty-two years old when she met him while watching a basketball game at the park. He approached her, and she said she instantly fell in love. The feeling wasn't mutual, though, because all Joe wanted was sex. He dealt with her long enough to convince her to lose her virginity and when she did, he left her and told everyone in the neighborhood about it. Three months later she found out that she was carrying me. Unfortunately, Joe was long gone out of her life and I had been fatherless ever since.

My mother tried to raise me by herself, but she blamed me for everything that went wrong in her life. Tonya hated her life with a child, and ultimately it was too much for her to deal with. She dropped me off at my grandmother's house when I was ten, and I haven't seen or heard from her since. I never received a birthday card, a Christmas card, or even a call to say, "Hello, I'm alive!" I hated her for that. How the hell could a mother just leave her child behind? There was no way in hell I could go through all of the pain of childbirth and then walk out of my child's life.

My grandmother Rose tried her best to be both of the parents that I lost, but there was no way that was possible. I needed them both, especially my father. I searched for the love of a man. I yearned for the attention from a man that I was never able to receive from my father. For that reason, there was nothing that anyone could tell me to make me leave Tony or not to give him the pleasure of taking my virginity.

Neisha and Leah were my two best friends, and we were always together. You could never find us apart except for the time we spent at home. Neisha and I had been friends since the day I moved in with my grandmother. I met Leah in school and we had been tight as vise grips ever since. I couldn't ask for better friends. They had been there for me in some of the worst times.

The three of us usually went out to Fairmount Park to smoke weed on Friday nights. There was a side off of Thirty-third Street where there were a few benches and a play set. The side of the street was lighted and it was only about two blocks from the Benjamin Franklin Parkway. It gave us a rush, wondering if the cops would drive by and catch us. We never did get caught, but the feeling of sneaking around was still intense.

I had known of Tony for years. Tony was fine and there was no denying that. He was a mix of Puerto Rican and black, and with his sexy-ass body like the model Tyson, he was hard to resist. It was well known that Tony was taken, but he also slept around with a lot of chicks and I just wanted a chance to get close to him, like everyone else. The chicks flocked to him like pigeons to a piece of bread in the street, so there was a line as long as ten city blocks to get near him. Tony sold drugs in the neighborhood, so I assumed that was how he could afford all of the ice he wore and the phat-ass cars he drove. From time to time, I would catch a glimpse of Tony in the park, so I made it my business to get out there every Friday. I knew where he would be most days, so I tried to be there to get him to notice me. Unfortunately, I was unsuccessful for two years.

The first time Tony finally spoke to me, I thought I was going to lose it, but I held it together. After getting high off the weed we bought from the little Jamaican variety store that sold weed out the back, Neisha, Leah, and I went back up to the block where Tony and his crew hung out. The Kensington part of the city was where you could find all of the Puerto Ricans. I knew that there was a little strip club off Allegheny, where Tony hung out most nights. My girls and I would hang outside until he would emerge, and I would put on a show every time. As Tony came out this one night, he noticed me on the corner. I stopped in my tracks when he called out to me.

"Shorty in the blue! Come here!" he yelled, motioning with his hand for me to come closer.

I walked over with my "get him, girl" strut and once I reached the spot where he was standing, I tried to act as though talking to guys of his stature was something that I did on a regular basis.

"What's up?" I asked in a sexy tone.

"What's your name, ma?"

"Mimi!"

"Mimi, huh? Well, Miss Mimi, how come you are always everywhere I am? Are you following me or something?"

"No!" I said in a defensive tone since I was embarrassed that he had noticed.

"I think you are, and I think you want me. Is that it? Do you want me, Miss Mimi?"

"I've never looked at you like that," I said, playing it cool.

"Really? I find that shit hard to believe since you're always getting dressed up to hang out wherever I am. Shit, you know my schedule better than I do," he said, laughing.

"I mean, you look good and all, but I ain't stalking you or nothing."

"I look good, huh?"

"Yeah."

"I knew you were looking at me," he said, laughing. "Well, it was nice meeting you, Mimi. I'm sure I'll be seeing you around," he said, and then he grabbed my hand and kissed the back of it.

"It was nice meeting you, too," I said, almost falling out from shock. I couldn't believe that Tony had kissed my hand. I was excited that he knew my name and that I had gotten a chance to talk to him. Leah and Neisha couldn't believe it either. It was about two weeks later before Tony spoke to me again, and I was still hanging around where he was, as usual. We had managed to get into the bar and get a couple of drinks. Leah and I were both sixteen, and Neisha was seventeen. Neisha knew the bartender, so he hooked us up with a couple of glasses of wine, nothing big. Tony came from the back of the bar and tapped me on my shoulder. I turned around and smiled when I noticed that it was him.

"What's up, Tony?" I spoke with a smile.

"I see you're still following me."

"If I was following you, would that be a problem?" I said, gathering up a little courage.

"If you want to be with me, that's all you have to say. You don't have to keep sticking your ass out at me whenever you see me. I'll take the ass if you want to give it to me."

"Who said I wanted to be with you?"

"Look, Mimi, let's stop bullshitting. I know you want me and I actually think you're cute. I can see me with you and I'm willing to give you a chance, if you're ready to stop playing these childish games."

"I do want a chance," I responded quickly, afraid of losing the opportunity that was being presented to me.

"You could have told me that a long time ago."

"Well, I'm telling you now, so where do we go from here?" I asked, placing one hand on my hip.

"Well, here's my number, so call me. What school do you go to? I might come scoop you up."

"Mastbaum," I replied.

"Oh okay, what you taking up in there?"

"I'm taking fashion design."

"Well, I can tell you are paying attention, since your outfits are put together pretty well. Anyway, make sure you call me, OK?" he said, kissing the back of my hand once more.

"OK, I will."

That night I could barely sleep because I was so excited. I kept seeing his face and his smile. I wanted him and I was surely glad that he wanted me. The next day I went to school and, to my surprise, when I came out of the building with Leah and Neisha, Tony was in front, waiting for me to come out. I never expected that he would really come and pick me up. I didn't know much about guys like Tony, but I did know that they talked a lot of game. I tried not to seem overly excited when I walked over to his car. Leah looked at me with a frown when I told them that he was there to see me. I wasn't sure what the look was about, but I brushed it off.

"I'll call and give you all of the details later!"

"I can't believe that you are going to leave with him! I told you what he's going to do to you!" Leah spat.

"How would you know? Did you experience it firsthand?" I quizzed, annoyed by her attitude.

"Does it really matter? I'm just trying to look out for you, and you should be smart enough to take heed to my warnings!"

"Look, Leah, I don't know what's up with you today, but I'm going with Tony and that's that!" I turned my back and put on a smile as I switched over to Tony's car.

I didn't understand Leah's position. I thought that she would have been happy for me since I'd been chasing Tony for so long. I would definitely address the situation later, but for now I was more interested in getting to my man. Once I reached the car, he reached out his arms and wrapped them around my waist. I took a deep breath to inhale the scent of his Cool Water cologne.

"I can't believe that you really came!" I said, blushing after noticing all of the jealous looks that I was getting, including the ones coming from the direction of Leah.

"I told you that I was probably going to come."

"Well, I guess I should have believed you."

"I guess you should have, but I wanted to surprise you anyway, and that's why I took it upon myself to go shopping and grab you some new clothes and shoes. I figured that you were about a size six. So I'm going to drop you off at home so that you can change, and then I'll pick you up and take you out to dinner."

"I can't believe you, Tony. All of this is for me?" I screamed, glancing at all of the bags in the backseat of his car.

"There's more where that came from, baby. Hop in and I'll drop you off at home."

"OK." I walked around to the passenger side door and hopped in. I sat there, nervous and unsure of what to say. Tony's look was mesmerizing and I was in a trance as I watched his every move.

"What's up, ma?" he asked, noticing that I was staring at him. "Why you staring at me? What's on your mind?"

"Nothing much. I just can't believe that it's really true. I never thought that a guy like you would be interested in me."

"Why would you think that? I mean, you're fine as hell! I noticed you a long time ago, but I'm a busy dude, and once I had the opportunity to holla at you, I did. "

"So are you sure that I am what you need?"

"I guess I'll have to find that out. I don't foresee you letting me down. You look like a girl that doesn't give up easily, and although I don't know much about you, I do know that you made it your business to be everywhere I was to get my attention. Since you succeeded at that, I think you'll make sure that you keep me happy, if you know what I mean. "

"Well, you know that I'm a virgin, Tony, and I don't want to be rushed into sex."

"I wouldn't rush you. That's something special, and believe me, I can wait for you to be ready even though I would love to tear that ass up!" he said, laughing.

"So does that mean you'll cheat on me?" I quizzed.

"Look, I told you I'll wait for you, and that's all that should be important. You should be glad to have a nigga like me on your arm. Most chicks would fight you for that spot, even your friends. For now, I'm leaving that space for you. I can't wait forever, but I will give you some time."

I didn't know what to think about his comments. Would he cheat on me if I didn't give it up? I knew that I had been trying to get with Tony for a while, and now that I had the chance, I wasn't going to let it slip away because of something as simple as sex.

Once we pulled up in front of my door I had to figure out how I was going to sneak all of the bags in the house without my grandmother noticing them. Tony told me that he would return to pick me up in two hours for a special date. He kissed me on the forehead, and I walked to the porch and sat the bags down. I peeked in and noticed that my grandmom was on the couch asleep. I quickly ran upstairs with the bags and hid them under the bed. Then I went back downstairs to greet my grandmom.

"How did you get home from school so early?" she quizzed.

"I got a ride home with my friend's mom," I lied.

"Do you have any homework?"

"Yes. I'm going to do it now. Is it OK if I go out with Neisha and Leah after I'm done?"

"I don't care, as long as you have your ass back in here by ten!"

"OK!"

I ran upstairs, excited. I locked my bedroom door so that I could rummage through the clothes and shoes that Tony had bought me. I tried on every outfit and each one fit perfectly. I wondered how he could have picked out clothes that were just my size without even knowing me that well. The outfit that I decided on consisted of a pair of low-rise Seven jeans, a pink bebe shirt, and pink and silver sandals. My accessories were a Tiffany necklace, bracelet, and earrings, and a pink Coach bag. I was dressed to impress, looking damn good, I must say. I wore my hair in a long wrap, which wasn't a weave. I was also the result of a mixed-race relationship. My mother was half Puerto Rican, so my hair was naturally long and silky.

Skipping out on my homework, I lied to my grandmom and told her that I had completed all of it. Rushing out the door, I went around the corner to the payphone and called Tony.

"Speak!" he said, answering the phone.

"Hi, Tony, this is Mimi."

"What's up? I didn't recognize the number. I almost didn't answer the phone. Where are you?"

"I'm at the payphone on Fifth Street. Are we still going out?"

"Yeah. Are you ready now, because I'm just chillin' at the barbershop, talking shit with my boys. I can come scoop you now, if you want."

"Yeah, I'll wait here for you," I said excitedly.

"OK, cool," he said before hanging up.

I hung up and sat on the steps of the Chinese store. About ten minutes later Tony pulled up, looking sexy as hell. I got in the car, and before pulling off, Tony told me how good I looked in the new outfit that he had bought me. First Tony took me to the nail salon to get a manicure, pedicure, and eyebrow wax. He sat patiently and waited until I was done. After leaving there, we went to dinner at Red Lobster.

"So, how does it feel to be my girl?"

"Great. I would have never expected you to do all of this for me. Can I ask you a question, Tony?"

"Sure, you can ask me anything."

"What happened to your girlfriend, Felicia? I know that you were with her for a long time."

"We broke up, but we are still friends."

"So are you sure that I won't have to go through any drama with her?"

"I'm positive."

"Well, in that case, I want to thank you for everything that you've done. I've never had anyone do such nice things for me."

"I'm just getting started. There's a whole lot more where that came from. So tell me a little more about you, something that I don't know."

"It's not much more to know. I love fashion and I've always wanted to get into that. That's my major at school."

"That's good. What about your mom? I know that you live with your grandmom. Where's your parents?"

"Well, I've never had a dad. Not a biological one, anyway. My father has been M.I.A. since day one. He got my mom pregnant really young and then skipped out on her as soon as he found out that she was carrying his child. All I know about him is that his name is Joe, no last name or anything. My mother's name is Tonya. I haven't seen or heard from her since I was ten. She dropped me off with my grandmom and bounced. So in a nutshell, that's my life!"

"That's crazy, not to know either of your parents. My life is crazy, too. I knew my parents, but both of them are dead; dead to me, anyway. They disowned me when I started selling drugs, so I moved on. I care about them just as much as they care about me, and that's not much at all."

"Wow, that's crazy, Tony."

"I know, but I'm a man. I'm always going to make it."

"That's a real good attitude. Never let anything or anyone get you down."

"I know, and that's why I like you because although you're young, I can tell you're smart. That's hard to find nowadays, for sure."

We sat and talked until our food came, and after we ate Tony drove me to his apartment. He surprised me by giving me a key. His apartment was nice, with wall-to-wall carpet and high ceilings with windows the length of the walls. His furniture was brown leather, and his tables were cream-colored stone. He had a huge television that stood almost my height from the floor. It was clean, and not a thing was out of place. It almost seemed as if he didn't even live there. I felt really comfortable in it. He told me that I was always welcome, and I appreciated the gesture. We watched TV for a while and then Tony dropped me off at home. He ended the night with a kiss, a wonderful kiss that I was sure to dream about for many nights to follow.

Every day with Tony was a new adventure, and I loved every minute of it. I never had to worry about anything with Tony. He loved me and he showed it every day. I continued to sneak around with Tony as much as I could. My grandmom and I had been fighting a lot because of it; but the way I saw it, Tony was willing to take care of me and if I had to leave, I could always go stay with him. I knew that I shouldn't have been sneaking around, but I was in love and I wished that she would understand. She was the closest thing to a mother that I had, and I hated arguing with her as much as I had been. Somehow my grandmom heard that I was sneaking out with Tony, and she was furious when she learned of the fact that he was 21 and sold drugs for a living. I still continued to lie, even after she caught me out with him. I began missing school. My grandmother got a phone call from the school stating that I hadn't been present in a week. I came home, as usual, to find her standing in the doorway, waiting on me to arrive.

"Hey, Grandmom."

"How was school today?" she quizzed, placing one hand on her hip.

"It was crazy. I have a lot of homework, too."

"Homework? How the hell would you know if you had homework? The school called today and it's interesting that you haven't been there all week. Where the hell have you been, Mimi?"

"I did go to school. I was just late and you don't get marked in when you're late," I lied.

"I'm in the mood to fuck you up right now, so you better stop lying! Have you been with that nigga after I told you not to see him anymore?" she yelled.

"No, Grandmom, I haven't seen Tony."

"Still lying? Keep sneaking around with him and I'll have his ass thrown in jail."

"Grandmom, it's not that serious."

"You're fucking up in school and it's not serious? Bad enough the nigga is too old for you, but he won't even push you to take your ass to school. I'm going to drive you to school from now on and pick you up, so tell Mr. Tony the shit with you and him is over. I mean it!"

"Grandmom, please!" I begged.

"I've said all that I am going to say about it, Mimi. I let you get away with this far too long already," she spat before walking into the living room and sitting down.

I turned around, furious, and stomped up to my room. After slamming the door, I lay down on the bed and cried. I needed to see Tony, and no one was going to stop me. She could drive me to school all she wanted, but she must have forgotten that she worked the night shift at the hospital. I could see him each night that she worked and she would never even know. I called Tony and told him about my argument with her, and he told me not to fret, and that everything would be OK.

My plan to meet Tony at night was an even better plan than sneaking around in the daytime, because Grandmom was working. She would have no way of knowing what was going down with me and Tony. Our nighttime sneaking around became more exciting each time we met. It had been two months and Tony still hadn't pressured me into having intercourse. He had showed me the proper way to satisfy him with oral sex, and I was learning how to master the technique each day.

Summer was rolling around and Tony wanted to take me off to Miami. I wasn't sure how I would get away with going, but I didn't care. I was ready to go and I was ready to be with Tony completely. I came up with a story of going to Leah's house for the weekend. My grandmom didn't know Leah very well, but she did know Neisha. Neisha told her mom the same story, and since Neisha was actually at Leah's I hoped I could get away with my story.

I was excited when we landed in Miami. It was still hard for me to believe I was there since I lied about coming. We drove to the Holiday Inn resort where we would be staying, and I rushed up to the room after Tony checked us in.

"This room is so nice, Tony! I can't believe we're here!"

"Well, baby, believe it!"

"I'm so excited. I'm going to take a shower now so I can change," I said, starting to get undressed.

"Damn, babe, my dick is getting hard just looking at you. Your ass is getting fatter, too! I like that," he said, licking his lips.

"Cut it out, Tony!" I said, embarrassed. "You know I'm sensitive about my body!"

"Come here!" He motioned with his hand.

"What's up?" I asked, walking over to him in my bra and panties.

He wrapped his arms around my small waist and kissed me. Damn, I loved this man! As he moved closer to me, I felt his hardness through his jeans. Although Tony and I had never had intercourse, we had oral sex on many occasions, and I knew that was where this show of affection would lead. Tony unhooked my bra and slid it off me. He began licking and sucking in a slow motion, making me yearn for more. He laid me on the bed, and after removing my panties, he French kissed my kitty cat, hitting my spot within seconds of contact. After getting me to the point of orgasmic ecstasy, Tony rose from the bed, let down his pants, and rubbed his erection, signaling me to go to work. Tony had taught me well how to please a man with oral sex, and I could always tell that I was doing the job well by the expressions on Tony's face. I paused for a second to let Tony know that I was ready to be his completely.

"Tony, I'm ready."

"Ready for what, baby? Don't stop," he said, instructing me to continue what I had started.

"To give myself to you, Tony. I'm ready to lose my virginity."

"What?"

"I'm ready, baby."

He kneeled down to kiss me, and it felt so good. I was scared of what would happen next, since I knew that there was no turning back, but I wanted to satisfy him in any way that I could. I tried to relax as he made sure his path was lubricated enough for entry, but I tensed up as soon as I felt the tip of his pole.

"Relax, baby. It will hurt more if you don't," he whispered in my ear.

I continued to tense up since I didn't know what to expect. I was certain from the rumors I heard that it would hurt. I had listened to Neisha's and Leah's accounts, so I knew the first time would be far from a slice of cake. As Tony pushed himself inside my tunnel, I felt a tear well up in my eye. I couldn't let on to Tony that I was in so much pain since he seemed to be enjoying himself more with each slow stroke. Tony tried to push my legs open, but the pain was worse and I begged him to leave them in a downward position.

"I can stop if you want me to."

"No, Tony, keep going."

Although it was only about twenty minutes, it seemed like hours. I could barely walk when we were through. The throbbing down below continued long after we showered and were on our way out of the hotel room. But I was glad that I could satisfy Tony in a new form, and once the pain subsided, I would be ready to do everything he wanted me to do.

We went shopping, to the beach, and we even went to the clubs with the help of the fake ID that Tony had gotten me. I decided to give my grandmother a call. Once she answered, I was afraid to speak since I didn't want to sound nervous or let on that I was lying about my whereabouts.

"Hello!"

Silence.

"Hello!" she yelled once more.

"Hi, Grandmom," I said in a low tone.

"Mimi, where the hell are you? I've been looking all over the damn city for you. I called your girlfriend's house to check on you, and they tell me you were never there in the first place."

"I'm OK, Grandmom," I said, reassuring her.

"I can hear that. But where are you?"

"I'll be home tomorrow."

"Tomorrow? You better bring your ass home now, or your

shit is going to be outside on the porch waiting on you!" she yelled.

"Grandmom, I can't possibly make it home tonight, but I'll definitely be there tomorrow."

"Where the hell are you that you can't make it home tonight? Are you with Tony?"

"No, Grandmom. I promise I'll be there tomorrow."

"Mimi!"

Click. I hung up to keep from telling more lies. I knew that my grandmother wouldn't put me out on the street, but I didn't want to keep lying to her either. I went into the living room of the suite and found Tony sitting there watching a basketball game.

"What's up? What did she say?"

"She said if I don't come how now, my stuff will be waiting for me out on the porch."

"Do you really think that she'll put you out?"

"I don't think so, but we've been at it so much lately that I wouldn't put it past her."

"Well, you know if she puts you out, you can always come stay at my spot."

"Really, Tony?" I asked, because I wanted to be sure that I heard him correctly.

"Yeah, so you don't even have to stress about that. I'll take care of you."

I would remember those words. Although I never expected my grandmom to put me out, at least if she did, I knew that I had a little security with Tony.

Once we reached the Philadelphia International Airport, I wanted to run back to the plane and get back to Miami. It was like leaving a dream and walking into a nightmare, because I didn't know what would be waiting on me when I arrived. We caught the shuttle to the parking lot where Tony left the car, and as I sat down, Tony noticed the despair on my face.

"Are you OK?"

"I'm just scared, Tony. My grandmom is the only family I have, and I'm afraid of losing her."

"You won't lose her."

"But that's what I'm afraid of. She hates the fact that I care about you. I'm not going to let you go, but I wish there was some way that she could understand how much you mean to me."

"She'll never understand, Mimi, and that's something that you have to come to grips with. I'm not trying to let you go either, but if your relationship with your grandmom is that important to you, I'm willing to take a step back so you two can work at it."

"I can't be without you, Tony. I'm just scared. I don't know what to do."

"Well don't think too much about it right now. Let's get over one hump at a time."

"OK," I agreed as we made the drive to my house. Tony dropped me off at the corner since I had lied to my grandmom and told her that I wasn't with him. I kissed him goodbye and slowly made my way up to the porch. I didn't see any of my belongings outside, so I felt a little better about approaching the door. I used the key to get in and found my grandmother in the kitchen washing dishes. I crept into the kitchen and took a seat waiting for her to start yelling, and she started within seconds.

"So you finally decided to show up, huh?"

"I told you that I would be home today."

"Well, you're lucky that your mother talked me into letting you stay, because you were so close to being out on the street!"

“My mother? I don’t have a mother. She lost that title when she dropped me off!” I replied.

“She’ll always be your mother, whether you choose to call her that or not. She’s trying to get herself together, and she wants to see you do well in life.”

“Please! She doesn’t give a damn about me!”

“I know you’re not grown, and I’m the only one that’ll use that language in this house. You need to call her and thank her because she’s the reason you still have a bed to sleep in. You need to remember that I didn’t give birth to you, so I don’t have to take care of you!”

“I will remember that! Now can I be excused?”

“Go ahead. Run up to your room and call that nigga like you always do! You better let him know how lucky he is, too, since his ass should be in jail!”

I bit my tongue to end the conversation as I made my way up to my bedroom. I didn’t even know that my grandmom still communicated with my mother. I hadn’t talked to her since the day she dropped me off, and that was seven years ago. In my eyes she didn’t exist, and it was sad that my grandmom still believed that she was coming back for me. I was damn near grown, and she hadn’t gotten herself together yet. If she hadn’t by now, she never would!

I tried to get along with my grandmom for the remaining weeks of the summer. Tony and I continued spending time together. There were times that he even brought Neisha, along with a couple of his friends, for company. Leah had been hard to catch up with, so she’d been missing out on all of the fun. I really enjoyed my summer, but it was soon time for senior year, and that’s when the drama began . . .

CHAPTER 4

Giselle: Things Fall Apart

2000

Boom . . .

I jumped up out of my bed, trying to figure out what the hell was going on. A tall guy with a muscular build and a ski mask covering his face quickly grabbed me. I was crying hysterically, and as I kicked and screamed he yelled for me to calm down. I didn't know what was going on, but I wasn't going down without a fight. As we neared the top of the steps, I put my arms out and tried to grab onto the wall so he couldn't take me downstairs. I didn't know what was down there waiting for me, and I was definitely in no rush to find out.

"Get the fuck off the wall!" he yelled while trying to move my hands. "Bitch, get the fuck off the wall!" he yelled before hitting me on the side of me head.

I cried as I began to call for my mother, who seemed to be absent until I reached the bottom of the steps and saw her and Akil tied up with their backs to each other. *Shit!* I thought. *What the hell is going on here? And where the hell is Daddy?*

"Get the fuck down there!" he yelled before letting me go and pushing me down on the floor, next to Akil and my mother.

"Are you guys okay?" I quizzed.

"No talking, sit down and shut the fuck up!" the shorter one with the deep voice yelled. The two of them stood there engrossed in a conversation for a few minutes before saying another word to us. I was becoming anxious, and I wanted to know what it was they were planning on doing to us.

"What do you want from us?" I asked the men.

"We'll ask the questions around here. All you need to do is sit there with your pretty little mouth shut!"

"What is it that you want?" I cried, disobeying his command.

"Didn't you hear what the fuck I said? Say another word and I'll blow your ass away!" the shorter one yelled.

My head was pounding from the blow he had placed to it before we came down the steps. The shorter one, who was obviously in charge, walked over to my mother and pulled her head back by her hair, forcing her to look him in the eye.

"Where is the fucking safe?" he asked in a deep, threatening tone.

"I don't know!" Tears rolled down her cheeks.

"I'm going to ask you one more time, and then I'm going to blow your fucking head off! Now, where is the fucking safe?"

Sobs racked my mother's body, and she was unable to speak.

He held the gun to her head and fired. Blood sprayed all over my brother and me. I screamed even louder because I thought for sure that I was next. Instead, the two guys backed away and left the house. I couldn't move.

"Giselle, untie me!" Akil yelled at me. "Giselle, snap out of it, untie me!" he yelled again.

I sat there frozen while Akil screamed at me. It wasn't until I heard a loud knocking at the door that I came back to reality. I got up to untie Akil before opening the door, and as soon as he was free, my mother fell to the ground. I bent down to try and pick her head up off the floor as Akil ran to open the door and let the paramedics in. *How the hell did they get here?* I wondered, because I knew that I hadn't budged until they knocked on the door. They pushed me out of the way and immediately began working on my mother. I knew that she was gone while I sat there in Akil's arms, crying. I couldn't wrap my mind around what happened, and I was deaf to the sounds around me as the police arrived to try and question me.

Daddy came running into the house after they had already taken my mom out in a body bag. He looked the worst I'd ever seen him, and I didn't know what to say. He came over to me and wrapped his arms around me. I finally felt safe with him and was able to speak.

"Daddy, they just shot her for nothing! Daddy, why did they have to kill her? Why?" I cried as the tears from my eyes landed on his shirt. "Daddy, I couldn't save her, it's all my fault!" I continued to cry as he tried to console me.

This was the first time I'd ever seen my dad cry. I knew he loved my mother more than he could ever love anyone, and though I felt guilty, I knew it would never amount to the guilt he felt. I knew things would never be the same after that day, and I was right.

I was stressed for months following my mother's death. I still hadn't been able to close my eyes without seeing her body slump over and hit the ground. I was devastated, and at fifteen, I was being forced to grow up and be a woman without my mother.

Akil was running wild, and I knew that it would eventually land him in a bad place. My dad snapped and tried every avenue to get the two men who did this, and the longer he tried, the more it killed him that he was still empty-handed. He had a few murders under his belt, since he wanted to kill everyone who'd ever disrespected him, with the thought that they could possibly be the culprits. I begged him to give it up because killing people would never bring her back. I had to get myself together and be there for them both. I had to walk in her footsteps and be the stand-up bitch that she was.

I cooked for them, I cleaned for them, and anything else that I could do to help us all get through it, I did. It was a struggle at first, but once I realized that she would have never wanted us all to sit around depressed, I stepped up to the plate. Daddy always told me how proud of me he was, since I had been able to overcome my grief and take care of them.

It wasn't long before Akil landed himself in prison, just as I had predicted. After Akil was incarcerated, I only had to look after my dad and though we were always close, this brought us even closer together. Eventually I was able to talk my dad into stopping his killing spree and settle down. He still wasn't himself without my mother, but he was as close as I would ever get to the dad that I had before all of this.

We moved into another neighborhood in the Northeast, and he hired men to drive around the house at all times to make sure no one would ever be able to break in and do the same thing. He had someone follow me everywhere I went for at least a year after we moved. I couldn't blame him, and it made me feel secure; though the longer it went on, the more annoyed I became. I was growing up, and I knew I would never be able to get a boyfriend with his hounds sniffing behind me all the time. I eventually would master the technique of eluding them, but it would be years before I did.

CHAPTER 5

James: Trouble Is Brewing

1996

"Who? What are you talking about?"
"The cops. They arrested him!"
"For what?"
"For the drugs and money he had here."
"Why the hell did he have that shit at the spot?" I yelled.
"I don't know. I told him not to bring that shit here! What am I going to do?" Lacy cried.
"I'll be over there soon. Chill out, OK?"
"OK," she said before hanging up.
"Yo, Mark, drop me off at Rik's. The cops just got his ass."
"What? Got him for what?"
"That nigga had the drugs and shit at his spot!"
"What? Well, let's go over there and see what the hell is going on."
On the drive to Lacy's apartment, I was nervous. I wondered what the hell made the cops come to his spot, and I wondered if I would be next. I figured that one of the niggas

we had robbed must have found out that it was us and dimed us out. I wasn't trying to go to jail, and although I knew Rik wouldn't snitch, I had to find the nigga that had. After reaching the apartment, Lacy explained everything that had went down, and I was even more furious. She said that Rik had received a phone call from this nigga named Lex, who we hit last week.

Lex was a hustler from West Philly, "down the bottom" as they called the area. Lex and Rik had been cool once, back when Rik was trying to sell drugs in high school. Lex believed, to this day, that Rik had stolen some of his product and made money off of it. When he approached Rik about it at the time, things got ugly and in turn, they went their separate ways. Back then, Lex wasn't as deep into the game as he was now. If the same thing happened now, Lex would probably make sure that Rik was six feet under.

During the phone conversation that Rik and Lex had, Lacy told me that Lex asked Rik to meet him so that they could discuss the return of the money and drugs that we had stolen from him. Rik wasn't about to do that. He decided to meet Lex, but his plans were far from returning anything. Rik was on his way out the door with an empty duffle bag and two loaded guns tucked in the small of his back. He thought that he would fool Lex, but Lex had plans of his own. The joke was on Rik. Upon opening the door, the cops had him surrounded. Lex made it a point to call Lacy and let her know that he was behind everything and that he still wanted his money. Now that I knew who snitched, I knew what I had to do, but I had to fall back for a minute until the heat died down. I assured Mark that it was cool for him to leave, and I agreed to stay at the spot with Lacy.

Rik called the next morning and explained that he wanted me to contact his lawyer and pay him the money he had stashed. I agreed and followed through with his orders. Rik's lawyer notified me that he would do some time, but he was unsure of how long it would be. I was pissed, but Rik told me not to fuck with Lex until he got out. He wanted the pleasure of killing Lex himself. One thing about Rik was that he kept his word, and if he promised that he would murder Lex, I knew that he would.

Rik didn't live the same life that I did, and even though we were brothers, our values were different. Rik's dad wasn't a hustler like mine. His dad was a straight-up, nine-to-five dude who struggled to make ends meet. I never knew why Rik hated his dad so much, because out of all of our fathers, his was the one who hung around the longest. Rik dropped out of school at sixteen and never had any intention on going back. His excuse for dropping out was that it didn't fit his style. Although I never planned on continuing my education past high school, I figured that I might as well get a high school diploma. It made no sense in this day and age to be stupid.

After Rik dropped out of school, hustling became his main idea for life. Rik loved the luxury, and I loved the power. I wanted to be on top like my father, but Rik just wanted get dough. We both ended up doing the same thing, but for different reasons. Yeah, I loved money, but I loved control more. He had never been able to make it big, especially after he and Lex fell out. Lex made it his business to block any new avenue Rik tried to take to get dough. Rik resented him for that and he always knew that the only way for him to succeed was to get rid of Lex, and now that Lex had sold him out, Rik had no other choice.

Sitting in Rik's apartment was boring me. I had been there for the last four days, and I was horny as hell. I was tired of going to the bathroom every night and stroking myself until I let loose. I needed to leave, but I had promised Rik that I would stay there with Lacy for at least two weeks. I hadn't talked to Trina, and I was glad because I didn't feel like hearing her yell.

I sat on the sofa watching a porn flick, since there was nothing else to watch, along with the fact that I couldn't keep sex off my mind. I had my hands in my pants, thinking about sticking Tia when Lacy walked in the door.

"What are you doing?" she quizzed, frowning at me.

"Minding my business. Why, is there a problem?"

"You couldn't find anything else to watch?"

"Nope. You might as well watch it with me."

"Whatever, J. I'm about to take a shower. Enjoy yourself!" she said before walking into the bedroom and closing the door.

I sat there thinking about her naked body with water running all over it. I unzipped my jeans, pulled my member through my boxers, and began to masturbate as thoughts of Lacy consumed me and the view of the porn excited me. It wasn't long before I heard the door to the bedroom open. Instead of Lacy yelling at me for what I was doing, she walked over to me naked and stood in front of me. I was stunned because after all of the times I had dreamed of this moment, I wasn't sure if I should move forward.

"Thinking about me?" she asked in a sexy tone.

"What are you doing?" I asked, trying to avoid the question, because I didn't know what state of mind she was in. I knew that I was as horny as a cat in heat, but I couldn't allow myself to fall victim to any game she was trying to play.

"You know you want me, J, and I want you. I'm tired of playing," she said before getting on her knees and taking my member in her hands. "I want to make you feel good. Is that OK?" she asked before licking the tip of my pole.

"Ooooh shit!" was all I could say as she wrapped her lips around the head of my shaft and stroked my length at the same time. I laid my head back and enjoyed the fellatio that I was receiving. Lacy continued going up and down on me as I closed my eyes and moaned in delight.

"You like it?" she asked, looking up before deep throating me, introducing my member to her tonsils. "Tell me you like it, J!"

"I love it, baby. Don't stop!" I said, trying not to explode prematurely.

Lacy continued the motion until I couldn't take it anymore. I exploded and she took it all in, causing me to shake a little. I picked her up off the floor and laid her down on the sofa with one leg up on the back of the chair. I buried my face deep in her nest and she used her hips to grind against my tongue. Her juices were filling my mouth with a wonderful taste as I massaged her clit with my tongue. She moaned as she caressed the back of my head, assuring me that I was doing the job well. Once my soldier was at attention again, I raised up and quickly drilled her wet opening with slow strokes. She continued to call my name as I worked the position that we were in. I knew that what we were doing was wrong, but the lust had won.

"Keep going, J. Don't stop!" she whispered before sucking on my ear.

I turned her over and entered her doggy style. She moaned even louder as this position intensified the atmosphere. I stroked harder and harder as she yelled my name, boosting my ego. The feeling was unlike any I felt before, and maybe it was because it was wrong, but I didn't care. All I cared about now was one more nut, and it wasn't long before that happened. I pulled my shaft from her inside her and exploded all over her back.

"Damn, that was good!"

"It was great, J, but you have to keep this between us," she insisted.

"Definitely!" I said before taking a seat on the sofa.

"Cool. I'm going to go get that shower now!" she said, smiling before bending down to kiss me.

I sat there for a minute, mad at myself because of what I had just done. I should've said no, but I had thought with the wrong head for sure. Damn! I couldn't let Rik find out, or Mark either. I knew that since Lacy and I had gone through with it, it would be hard not to do it again. I still had a week and a half to stay there with her, and I figured that the deed was already done. The regret I was feeling didn't take long to disappear, because later that night we did it again, and at least two times a day for the next week.

Once I went home, I ended my relationships with both Trina and Tia. Lacy and I became close and although the relationship was forbidden, I couldn't stay away. I knew Rik would be in jail for months before he would even go to trial. That was enough time for us to continue our forbidden relationship. I began to stay with Lacy almost every night, and continued to have sex with her in almost every inch of that apartment. Rik would check in periodically when he was allowed to make phone calls, and Lacy and I both went to visit him once a week. The visits were hard because Rik would sit there and tell Lacy how much he cared about her and she would do the same, while I sat there ready to vomit. Deep down I cared about her, too, and I wanted her to be mine all the time, not just inside the walls of the apartment.

"Hey, let's go out to the movies or something," I suggested on our ride home from visiting Rik.

"J, you know we can't do that."

"Why not, Lacy? It's not like Rik's coming home anytime soon."

"So what? If someone sees us, he'll find out what's been going on."

"No, he won't, Lacy. He knows we spend time together."

"Yeah, but he doesn't know what kind of time!"

"Look, it's just a movie."

"Let's just go home and watch a movie. Then I'll treat you real good, J, the way you like it."

Knowing that I'd take sex over damn near anything, I agreed to her proposition. This was basically the way things went with us, and things didn't change until Rik received a sentence of five years. Although I wished he didn't have to stay in prison, I was glad that Lacy could be mine. We went out for the first time after we got the phone call about Rik. After dinner we came home and had the best sexual experience yet. After about an hour of sex we were interrupted by a knock at the door. I threw on my boxers and went to open the door as Lacy lay naked on the floor.

"Who is it?"

"It's Mark, man."

"Oh, what's up?" I asked, opening the door.

"We need to talk," he said sternly, noticing Lacy's naked body.

"Cool. Let me throw on something."

"All right, I'll wait in the car."

I threw on my clothes and went outside to Mark's car to see what was up. After sitting down in the passenger seat, I noticed the angry expression on Mark's face.

"What's up, man?"

"What the hell are you doing, J? You're fucking Lacy?"

"Man, it ain't even like that."

"You said that you wouldn't do that. How could you do that to your blood, man?"

"I don't know, but it's done now and I can't take it back. I do care about her."

"That's messed up, J."

"I know it's fucked up, but what am I supposed to do about it now?"

"I guess nothing. Shit, it's done now. It's real fucked up and you better hope that he never finds out about it."

"You won't tell him, will you?"

"I wouldn't do that, J. I just can't believe you did that to him."

"Neither can I," I said honestly, because even after all of the months that Lacy and I had been sneaking around, I still felt bad about what we were doing.

"Well, I came here to talk to you about what we were going to do, now that Rik got time."

"We can continue to work. We got to keep the money flowing. You know that."

"Yeah, I know."

"Well, hit me up tomorrow and we'll meet to make plans."

"No problem. I'll talk to you tomorrow, then," he said before giving me dap.

I exited his car and re-entered the apartment to finish what I had started with Lacy. I did feel bad that I was betraying my brother, but just not bad enough to stop. The feeling that Lacy gave me was enough to almost erase Rik from my mind.

Over the next six months I did just that, and Lacy did too. We were together and enjoying life. I had heard through the grapevine that Rik knew about us. I wasn't surprised, because niggas find out everything in jail. I was anxious about talking to him because I wanted to get it over with. I was ready to lay everything out on the table. I hoped to feel better after getting it off of my chest. I knew that he would be contacting me soon. When we did finally speak, I never expected the conversation to go the way it did.

"So how does it feel to be fucking my girl while I'm stuck in here?"

"She's not your girl anymore, Rik."

"She'll always be my girl. You're just borrowing her, man."

"You think so?"

"I know so. She told me about everything, J. I'm mad as hell that you, as my blood, would betray me like that."

"She told you?" I quizzed, stunned.

"Yeah, and she also told me that she's done with you. She aborted your baby last week, too."

"What?"

"You heard me right. I hope you enjoyed that shit while it lasted, because it's over now," he yelled.

"Who said that, you? Don't make me laugh, man. What the hell can you do from behind bars?"

"I can do more than you think, J."

"Really?"

"Really. You should be glad I let you breathe."

"Fuck you, Rik. You're going to act like this over a bitch?"

"She was my girl, J. Off limits and you didn't care. It's not about a bitch. It's about the principle. You're my fucking brother, and you're foul for that shit."

"I know I was wrong, but so was she."

"Yeah, and she's going to pay too!"

"What the hell is that supposed to mean?"

"You'll see!" he yelled before hanging up.

I was so furious. That bitch played me, and I was waiting for her to walk through the door so I could kick her ass. This whole time she was fucking me every night, telling me she loved me, and then she told Rik everything. And she had an abortion without me knowing! I got dressed and sat for hours waiting for her to come home. When she didn't show up, I decided to go look for her. But when I opened the door to leave, the cops were there waiting for me, just as they had waited for Rik the day he was arrested.

"What the hell is this?" I asked, shocked by the scenery.

"You're under arrest for robbery," one officer said, motioning me to come down the stairs.

"What?"

"You have the right to remain silent. You have the right to an attorney. Anything you say can and will be held against you in a court of law . . ." the officer recited to me as he handcuffed me.

After they placed me in the car, I wondered what damn robbery they were arresting me for. Once I was in the interrogation room they told me that I was being charged with multiple robberies. I sat there, stunned, as the cop named each one. I wondered how they could have found out about all of the robberies. Soon, I found out that my brother Rik had snitched and would get an early release for his testimony in my trial. I never thought that he would do some shit like that, but he fooled me. Now I knew what he meant when he said that I would pay. This nigga was going to get out of jail while my ass went in. I guess I should have considered the consequences of messing with Lacy before I did, but it was way too late for that.

I was only sentenced to three years, and Rik was released shortly after I was sentenced. He wouldn't be able to enjoy his freedom very long, though, because about six months after his release he was murdered by Lex. I got revenge without even trying, and I wasn't even sad about his death. I had two and a half more years to serve, courtesy of him. My mother was the one hurt by his death. She never knew that he was the reason I was in jail, and I would never tell her. I figured it was bad enough without any more information. I stabbed him and he stabbed back, one brother versus another, but I was the one left standing!

I never talked to Lacy after I was arrested. Every attempt that I had made to contact her was unsuccessful. Mark told me that she had moved and he wasn't sure where. I knew that I had at least ten grand in the apartment, and once Mark couldn't find it, I knew that she had taken my money and run with it. The result of my lust was hard to bear. Lacy made me think about women differently. They couldn't be trusted, and I vowed that once I was released, a woman would never play me again. Once in a lifetime was enough!

CHAPTER 6

Mimi: Should've Seen It Coming

1997

That summer Leah seemed to change. She didn't hang around us as much, and she didn't call much, either. Many times I went to her house or called her phone and couldn't get her to even come out. Neisha assumed that she was having some type of reaction to the new friends she had after she and her parents moved. In our senior year, Leah transferred to Ben Franklin High, all the way in Center City. I knew it would be a little harder for her to come around, but she had totally been M.I.A. I remember calling her on her birthday to see if we would be going out. It had become a ritual for the three of us to get together on birthdays and go clubbing, for as long as we'd been friends. I dialed her number, but I assumed that she would duck my call since she had been doing that for weeks. I was surprised when she actually picked up.

"Hello!"

"Hey, Leah, what's up? Happy Birthday!"

"Thanks," she said blandly.

"So, are we going out tonight?"

"No. I don't even feel like it tonight. Maybe this weekend."

"We always go out on birthdays. What's up?"

"I just don't feel like it."

"Is it because of your new friends? If so, just say that."

"What are you talking about, Mimi?"

"Ever since you started at that school, you act like we don't exist anymore. I don't understand it."

"Well maybe it's because there's nothing to understand. I just don't feel like hanging out, that's all!"

"Whatever!"

"Look, I have to go. I'll talk to you later," she said quickly before hanging up.

Later that night I went past her house, only to see her getting into a car full of girls. They appeared to be going out partying, judging by their attire. I was angry because she lied to me and she didn't have to. When I first met Leah, we clicked and we were so tight that I felt nothing could break our bond. Neisha never really liked her, but on the strength of my word, she was civil toward Leah. I was upset by Leah's continued rejection. I had been her friend for the last six years, and I thought our friendship was stronger than anything.

I later found out that Leah had even begun spreading rumors about me. I didn't know where all the hatred was all coming from. Neisha was the bearer of the rumor information, and each rumor was worse than the previous one. Most of them were damaging to Tony and my relationship. I had only been with Tony, but leave it up to Leah and I had been with every dude in Frankford. After hearing about the numerous lies she told, I decided to confront her once and for all. I had to know what I did that was so bad to force her to do a total one eighty. I walked down to her house upset, and when I reached her door I counted to ten before knocking.

"Mimi, what's up?" Leah asked, surprised.

"Can you come outside so I can talk to you for a minute?"

"Sure. What's up?" she quizzed before stepping onto the porch and closing the door.

"I thought we were cool, Leah, and now I keep hearing that you are spreading mad rumors about me. Every time I'm in the hair salon I have to hear a bunch of shit that you've said about me. I mean, what's the deal, Leah? What's going on?"

"I haven't said anything about you, and you're not that important to me that you would be the subject of all of my conversations, anyway!"

"What the hell is that supposed to mean?"

"It means what I said! I don't know why you don't get the point. We are not friends anymore!"

"So, now that you got new friends and a new school, you want to give me your ass to kiss? Fine, Leah, you are not that important to me either!" I said, raising my voice.

"Good. Now we have mutual feelings! You think that you are the shit because you got Tony spending money on you, but all of that is going to crumble soon. Believe that!" she said, turning her back to me and beginning to walk to her front door.

"What do you mean by that?"

"Exactly what I said. That nigga doesn't love you! You're just a trophy. He wanted a virgin and he got one. Now that you gave that shit up, there's nothing left!" she spat.

"Where is all of this coming from, Leah, and how is it that you know so much about my man?"

"It doesn't even matter. You'll find out soon enough!" she said, reaching her door.

"I'm not finished talking!"

"Well, I am!" She opened her door, walked inside, and slammed the door shut, making the wood porch shake a little bit.

I stood there for a minute, stunned, because I didn't even understand what had just happened. Here I was, being dissed by someone I once considered my best friend, and I didn't even do anything wrong. I called Tony to vent my anger. His words of wisdom were not to stress it, and for one time in my life I took someone's advice and dropped it. He easily brushed her accusations about him off his shoulders. He told me that I should have known before dealing with him that chicks would be jealous and try to steal my spot. I did know that, but I would have never guessed my best friend would turn on me once I got with him. Before I got with Tony, Leah was there, pushing me to go stand post wherever he would be. I decided to give up on our friendship. I was no longer going to kiss her ass just to stay friends.

I began to spend the night over Tony's a lot, even when he wasn't there. Since my grandmom did still work nights, I was able to stay there without her knowing. I would have the phone calls to the house transferred to the cell phone that Tony bought me to catch her check-in calls. She never knew that I was out since I would have to leave for school before she would get home, anyway. I felt like an adult, spending so much quality time with Tony.

Tony's birthday rolled around and since he was turning twenty-one, he was having a private party at A Brave New World. The party was jam-packed, and niggas were everywhere. Neisha and I were enjoying ourselves at the bar. Far under the legal drinking age, we were ordering Thug Passions and taking them down like pros. Tony looked like he just stepped out of a *GQ* magazine ad, dressed in Armani and ordering bottles of Cristal. He smoked weed with his boys in the back of the club and watched my every move on the dance floor as I tore it up. I was on my way to the bar to get another drink when I noticed Leah and her new friend Chanel, talking to Tony and his friends. I quickly changed my direction and once she noticed me coming, she and Chanel quickly moved out of the way.

"Tony, what the fuck is she doing in here?"

"I invited her!" he spat, obviously drunk and high from the weed he was smoking.

"Why the hell would you invite her here? She's not my friend. I can't believe that you would do some nut shit like that, Tony."

"Look, it's my fucking party and I invited her because I wanted to. I'm not going to sit here and argue with you on my damn birthday, Mimi!"

"Well fuck it then, I'm leaving. I hope you have fun with that bitch!" I screamed.

"Bitch, who are you calling a bitch? Don't forget who I am," she yelled, pointing in my direction.

"Am I supposed to be scared? Fuck you, Leah, and that bitch you're with!"

"If you want to see me, Mimi, you can, anytime! I'll gladly give you that ass-whooping you're asking for!"

"Look, both of y'all are going to cut this shit out at my party!" Tony said, standing in between the two of us.

"I will see you, bitch, and you better not forget that shit!" I yelled before grabbing Neisha and storming out of the club.

What the hell was his problem? I was so damn mad, and that bitch Leah trying to stunt on me in front of everyone was definitely not going to be forgotten. I didn't care where or when I saw her next, but I knew for sure that when I did, it was going to be on. I didn't take that type of disrespect lightly, and she was going to eat her words one way or another. I took my ass home that night. I didn't even want to see Tony's face right then. I hopped in a cab and was fuming the entire ride. When I got home I took a shower and went to bed.

When I woke up in the morning I was still mad, but I wanted to call Tony before I went to school. I called his house and his cell and he didn't answer. I got dressed and instead of going to school I went to Tony's apartment. His car was parked in front so I knew that he was home. I used my key to go in and noticed a pile of clothing on the floor. Looking through the pile, I noticed a female's clothing. I walked in the direction of the bedroom with tears forming in my eyes. Standing at the bedroom door, I became furious. Tony and Leah were lying together, naked and asleep in the bed. I dropped my purse, ran over to the bed, and began punching Leah. Waking up, she tried to fight back, but it was too late. Tony woke up and tried to pull me off her.

"You little bitch! I knew I shouldn't have trusted you," I screamed. "Get the fuck off me, Tony!" I struggled. "I hate you, Leah! Tony, let me go! I'm going to kill that bitch!" I screamed, struggling against Tony's strength to get loose.

Leah gathered her clothing with her bloody lip and nose and ran out of the room tripping all over the place. I could hear her fumbling with her clothes to get dressed. I fought with Tony to get loose. I wanted to kill them both. After hearing the front door open and close, he let me go. I turned around with tears streaming down my face and hatred evident in my eyes.

"What the hell is wrong with you, Tony? How could you do this to me?" I cried in frustration.

"Look, that bitch doesn't mean nothing to me. That was just some pussy!"

"What? How long has this been going on behind my back? Obviously I don't mean anything to you either. I can't believe this shit!"

"I'm sorry, Mimi, but you were tripping at the club last

night and she was there to talk to! I swear that it's never happened before last night."

"Bullshit, Tony. You've probably been fucking her all along. That's why the bitch stopped talking to me and started spreading rumors and shit. She wanted you! I kept questioning you and you kept brushing that shit off like I was a damn fool. I guess I was a fool, since I believed that shit!"

"Mimi, I don't want her. I want you. I told you about those hoes from the beginning. All they're good for is sex. You knew they'd be throwing the ass at me all the time. Leah's been trying to get with me for a while, even before I started dealing with you. A man is going to be a man, and that's some real shit for you!"

"Fuck you, Tony! And if that were really true, why wouldn't she have said something to me about it before?" I yelled, throwing him his key and walking toward the door.

"I don't know why she didn't say anything to you. Mimi, come on now, it's not that serious!"

I didn't say another word. I just left the apartment in tears. I called Neisha and told her what had happened and she was in shock. I was still in shock myself. How could I let myself get played like that? I should have seen it coming. I called Leah's cell phone and filled her answering machine with obscenities. After venting, I turned off my cell phone and once I got home I turned off the volume on my house phone. I told my grandmom that I didn't feel well and that I didn't want to see anyone. I lay on the bed and cried. I loved Tony. I trusted him, and I truly believed that he was being honest with me. Being that naïve had left me brokenhearted. The next morning when I woke up, I checked my voicemail and Tony had not called. I guess he really didn't care about me. I knew in my heart that it was time for me to move on.

I went to school the next day, which seemed like the longest day ever. I was so stressed. I barely paid attention in class and I daydreamed the entire day. I decided to walk home from school that day to try to clear my mind before I got home. On my way home I stopped at the corner store to get a spring water and I saw Tony on the corner. I tried to quickly turn my back, hoping that he wouldn't notice me. Unfortunately, he did.

"Mimi!" he yelled from the car.

Trying to ignore him, I kept walking.

"Mimi! I know you hear me!" he yelled, getting out of the car and walking across the street in my direction.

"What the fuck do you want, Tony?" I yelled

"Look, I just want to talk. Don't make a scene out here."

"I don't want to talk, Tony. You hurt me! And you don't have the right to tell me not to make a scene. You lost that right when you fucked that whore!"

"Look, baby, I'm sorry. I don't care about that chick. I told you that I love you! I was high and I was drunk, and I promise you that it will never happen again."

"That was my friend, Tony! How could you do that?"

"I don't know, ma, but just give me another chance. I know that I fucked up, but I'll make it all better for sure."

"Was that the only time, Tony?"

"Yeah. I never even looked at that girl before! That liquor had me trippin'!"

"Don't try to blame everything on alcohol. You're a grown-ass man and you didn't have to have sex with her. Is it because she's more experienced than me? Or is she prettier than me?"

"It didn't have anything to do with that or you, for that matter. I told you that I was drunk and I'm sorry! It will never happen again. I mean that!" he said, pulling me close to him to hug me.

In a way I wanted to just walk away and leave him on the corner looking stupid, but I couldn't. I loved Tony and I knew that I had to be with him. There was no way that I would let any bitch take my man. That just was not an option! I told Tony that I would give him another chance because I had worked to hard too get him and keep him by satisfying him. I guess Leah thought that she would be able to steal him away by getting close to him, but she was wrong. I was going to make sure that she remembered that since she made it a point to rub the fact that I would soon be without him, in my face. He hugged and kissed me, then held my hand while we walked to the car so that he could drive me home. Pulling up in front of my house, he kissed me and told me that he would be back later to pick me up. I got out of the passenger seat, shut the door, and waved good-bye. I spotted Neisha down the street. I called to her and motioned for her to come down to my house.

"What's up, chick? I just saw that nigga Tony drive by. Y'all made up?"

"Yeah. I couldn't stay mad at him. That nigga does too much for me. Fuck that bitch, Leah. I'll see her ass again for sure."

"I still can't believe that she was that damn slimy. She deserves an ass-whooping for that!"

"She's going to get one, too. What were you about to do?"

"About to go in and get dressed for my date!"

"A date? With who?" I quizzed.

"Some dude named Mark." She smiled.

"Where the hell did you meet him at?"

"He's my cousin's friend. We've been kicking it for the last two weeks. He's taking me out to dinner tonight."

"Oh, that's what's up! I hope you have fun. Call me tomorrow and let me know what happened."

"I will," she said as she hugged me and turned to walk to her house.

I went up and showered and laid down to wait for Tony's

call. I dozed off and when I woke up it was eight and Tony still hadn't called. I dialed his cell phone.

"Yo!"

"Yo, where are you, Tony? I thought you were coming to get me."

"I am. I had some business to handle, but I'll be there in like a half hour."

"OK!" I said, now happy again.

I got up and got dressed and waited downstairs for Tony to arrive. He beeped the horn about ten minutes later. I ran outside, looking like a model on the runway. I was dressed in black Prada slacks, a black and silver corset with a blazer, and black Jimmy Choo shoes, hot off the press. My hair was curly and my M·A·C makeup was applied perfectly. When I got in the car Tony looked me up and down, licking his lips, and I knew that it was because I looked good enough to eat.

"Damn, you look good!"

"Thanks. Where are we going?"

"Where do you want to go?"

"I don't know. I really just want to be with you. We can just go to your place, if you want."

"That's cool," he said, driving off.

We stopped at Blockbuster to rent some movies and then we stopped and grabbed some Chinese food before going to his apartment. We spent most of the night watching movies until we took a couple shots of Absolut that Tony had stashed. The liquor had me barely standing up straight, but I knew that I wanted him. I knew that I needed him inside me, and I took it upon myself to initiate it. I unzipped his pants and he smiled when he realized where I was headed. I eased down to my knees as I pulled his length through his boxers and wrapped my full lips around it. Tony leaned his head back and used his right hand to guide himself in and out of my mouth. I struggled to get every inch of him inside my mouth, and he struggled to hold himself together. I sped up the pace as I felt him nearing an orgasm, and he quickly pulled himself away.

"Damn, baby, I'm not ready to bust yet!" he said as he pulled me up to kiss me. He pulled off my shirt and began to suck on my nipples. I moaned in anticipation, waiting to feel him inside me. After grinding on his pole, which caused my wetness to rub off on his length, I begged him to get inside me and he agreed. I straddled him slowly and eased him in and out of me, moaning in delight. I continued to ride his stick as he pushed one finger inside my asshole, causing an instant orgasm. I slowed down to enjoy the feeling as my body trembled. Tony smiled before our lips met, and I stuck my tongue into his mouth to massage his with mine. He screamed I love you before exploding inside me.

I was exhausted and I assumed that Tony was too since he almost fell asleep with me still sitting on top of him. We both did a quick clean up before going to sleep for the night. I closed my eyes with thoughts of our lovemaking flashing through my mind.

The following morning I got up and realized that I wouldn't make it to school. Tony woke up and after we both got dressed, we went to breakfast at IHOP on Aramingo Avenue. After breakfast Tony dropped me off at home. My grandmother was asleep, so after taking off my clothes, I got in the bed and went back to sleep. I was happy that my man and I were back together. Even though we were only broken up for a day, it seemed like an eternity, and I didn't want to revisit that again. I wanted to be happy and I had to trust Tony. I couldn't waste my life away worrying about these scandalous-ass chicks in the streets.

For the next six months, everything with Tony and me was going better than I could have imagined. We had our little arguments here and there about the late nights out and the chicks calling his phone, among other things, but overall I had learned to deal with it. I tried to ignore the many run-ins with Felicia as well, but since she seemed determined to get Tony back, I knew that I had to fight to keep him.

It was a Friday evening and Tony had just left the apartment. I was almost asleep when I heard the phone ring. Tony was out making his midnight runs, so I figured it might have been him letting me know that he would be getting in late, as he usually did on Fridays. I knew his routine, so I didn't get upset when I got the phone calls anymore. I would always shrug it off and go to bed alone. The phone rang three times before I answered it since it took me a few seconds to get to it.

"Hello?" I said in a groggy tone as I leaned over the edge of the bed.

"Is Tony home?" a female voice asked.

"Who the hell is this?"

"Don't act like you don't know my voice. Where is Tony?"

"Felicia, I don't know why you continue to waste your time calling him. He doesn't want you!" I yelled, now wide-awake.

"Bitch, please. He's playing the shit out of you and you're just too blind to see it!"

"He's not playing me. He's playing you. I'm the one lying up in his apartment!"

"Well I'm sorry to bust that bubble you're living in," she said, laughing, "but I'm the one that's lying up in his house! He bought a house and that's where I stay!"

"Whatever! Hoes will say anything!"

"Hoes? Bitch, if you weren't a little girl, I'd come over there and fuck you up, but I'm a grown-ass woman and you're not worth the time and effort. He's not your man, bitch. You're the jump-off, get it?"

"Fuck you! You must have me mistaken. You need to look

in the mirror because that jump-off you're talking about is you!" I screamed.

"Don't make me laugh! If he stops by, tell him his woman is waiting on him!" *Click.*

I stared at the phone. I wasn't even going to waste my time calling Tony about what she said. I knew that it was just her attempt to get him back. It wasn't going to be that easy. I learned my lesson from the situation with Leah to never give up that easily. Tony was definitely worth fighting for, and if it was a duel that she wanted, that was what she would get. The next morning when Tony came home I greeted him naked as if the conversation with Felicia had never happened. I satisfied my man and pushed the thoughts of her far into the back of my mind.

Soon it was the day before my birthday and Tony had planned a big party for me at Chrome Beach on Columbus Boulevard. Tony took me shopping and bought me an outfit from Prada, head to toe. It was a pink-and-white ruffled mini and tank that boosted my breasts, making them look two cup sizes bigger. On the day of the party Tony got me a massage, pedicure, manicure, and eyebrow wax at the spa on South Street. I felt so good after leaving there. Then I went to the hairdresser and she curled my hair really curly, the way Tony liked it. It was my eighteenth birthday and I was extremely excited. My grandmother and I had recently patched things up a little since she realized this thing with Tony and me wasn't a phase. Her feelings for Tony remained the same but since I was turning eighteen and graduating from high school, soon there wasn't much more that she could do to tear us apart.

Once I was home I showered and put on my new attire. Before my grandmom left for work she knocked on my bedroom door.

"I'm leaving for work now. Be careful at this party!"

"I will, Grandmom."

"Be careful with Tony, too. You know how I feel about him."

"I know, Grandmom. You don't have to keep reminding me."

"I do have to keep reminding you, because I'm the closet thing to a mother that you have, and I care about your welfare. I don't want to see you get hurt, that's all."

"OK, Grandmom. You're going to be late for work if you stay here and keep preaching to me." I smiled.

"I'll see you tomorrow morning," she said before coming close to give me a hug.

After my grandmom left, I quickly removed my robe that concealed the scanty outfit that was underneath. I looked at myself in the mirror once more before calling Tony to pick me up. He was in awe when I walked down to the car, strutting like Tyra Banks on her last Victoria's Secret show. I wanted to kiss him, but I didn't want to smudge my lipstick. I opted to hold on to my kisses for later, when I would be ready to kiss him all over.

Once we reached the party and noticed the line turning the corner, I became overjoyed. I didn't know that it would be this jam-packed. I was sure that the line would have to be shut down soon since the inside was almost filled to capacity.

I drank Absolut with cranberry juice and danced all night. I was eighteen, and I finally felt like a grown woman. My man was looking good and he knew it. He paid me much attention, and I surely appreciated it. I felt like a queen as he devoted all of his time to me to let everyone know that I was his and vice versa. The DJ played most of the songs I requested before one o'clock. I tried repeatedly to get Tony to dance, but each time he would play the shy role. Although I could honestly say I never saw Tony dance before, I hoped he would at least give me one spin for my birthday.

The party was over at two, but Tony told me that the night was far from over. He took me to a Holiday Inn over in Cherry Hill, New Jersey. He had rose petals all over the bed and champagne was on ice. Smooth R&B was playing on the stereo, and the lights were dimmed perfectly.

"Tony, I can't believe you. All of this for me?" I asked, shocked.

"My girl deserves the best of everything," Tony said, pulling me close and hugging me.

"I love you so much, Tony, and I can't imagine living without you."

"I never thought that I would love a chick, especially a young chick like you, but you got me open," he said, smiling.

"I never knew what love was until I met you. I could have never imagined that back when I was chasing you and sticking my ass out like you say"—I laughed—"that we would be here, feeling the way that we feel about each other. I don't ever want to wake up from this dream."

With that Tony kissed me, slowly and sensuously massaging my tongue with his in small strokes. Each time his tongue went into my mouth, I sucked it as if it was an ice-cold, cherry Popsicle. This kiss was much different that any other kisses before it. I instantly felt my panties getting wet.

Tony slowly undressed me and laid me down on the rose petal-covered bed. He kissed me from head to toe, making sure that each part of my body received the same amount of affection and attention. I loved him even more at that moment because he had never showed me so much attention. Usually he would rush to get me to give him oral sex and a quick screw so he could go to bed or go back out to work, but not this time. He undressed and before entering me, he whispered "I love you" in my ear. The repetition of those words continued to induce me to have multiple orgasms. Before that day I wasn't sure about Tony's love for me, but now I was absolutely certain that it was true.

The next morning, we ordered room service for breakfast and after showering and getting dressed, Tony drove me home. He was on my mind for the rest of the day. I couldn't wait to tell Neisha that I had made love. Making love was much more enjoyable than having sex, since Tony took his time satisfying me. He continued to kiss every part of my body, and with every orgasm he held on to me tightly so that the length of the orgasm would stretch out for a few more seconds.

Following my birthday, I enjoyed my time with Tony more because I was able to spend even more time with him. He continued to love me and make love to me every night, intensifying my feelings for him. For the first time, I was starting to plan what I would do after my high school graduation. I knew that I loved fashion and I planned on possibly opening my own business one day. I figured that it might never really happen, but I wasn't going to give up on it either.

It was a Wednesday when I realized that I hadn't had a period in two months. I went to the free clinic, accompanied by Neisha, to take a pregnancy test. It was positive. What the hell was I going to do now? The second the doctor read the results, I recalled what my mother had said about sex. It would end your life, either by getting you pregnant or giving you a disease! I couldn't let this end my life. I was too young for this. I didn't want to end up like my mother, blaming my child for my own downfalls.

I cried the entire ride to Tony's house. When I got there he was sitting on the couch, watching TV and talking on the phone. He hung up when he noticed the sad look on my face, accompanied by the dried tears.

"What's wrong, baby? Why are you looking so sad?"

"Tony, I'm pregnant!" I started to cry again.

"Pregnant! Damn, that's crazy!"

"What am I going to do, Tony? I can't have a baby right now. I'm too young!"

"Don't worry about it. I'll pay for the abortion!"

"Abortion! I can't have an abortion. I could never kill a baby!" I yelled, shocked that he would even suggest an abortion as a problem solver.

"Well, what the hell are you going to do, Mimi? I'm not ready to have a kid right now!"

"I can give it up for adoption."

"Bullshit! You'll have that baby and won't want to give it up."

"Tony, an abortion is murder."

"Well, you won't be the first person to get an abortion, and you damn sure won't be the last."

"Please, just give me a couple days to think about it."

"Well, I'm going to tell you like this. You have that baby and it's over between us. I told you I don't want no kids!"

"What? How could you say that?"

"Because I'm your man! You should care about my feelings," he yelled.

"I do, Tony! You know I don't want to lose you."

"Well ,then, you need to get rid of that baby."

"Can we just sleep on it tonight and talk about it in the morning?"

"That's fine, but you know where I stand."

That night was horrible. I barely slept. Tony slept so far away from me that he was damn near off the bed. He was so angry. I knew that I didn't want a baby, and I definitely didn't want to lose Tony. I had to make a choice that night. After tossing and turning for hours, I chose Tony. I didn't want a repeat of what had happened to my mother. I told him the next morning and he was relieved. We made an appointment, and after the counseling session the following week, I was no longer with child. The baby that Tony and I created was nothing but a memory.

I saw a change in Tony during my six-week, no-sex recovery period. He barely talked to me and was hardly ever home. I didn't understand it because I had the abortion like he wanted me to. I sat up many nights, waiting for him to come home. Most times I fell asleep on the couch, awaiting the arrival that would never happen. Tired and furious, I called Tony on his cell after sitting up until two o'clock, when he promised me that he would be home by ten.

"Speak!" he yelled into the receiver.

"Tony, where the hell are you? You promised me that you would be home by ten. It's two o'clock!" I yelled in frustration.

"I'm out working, trying to get money to buy all of that expensive shit that you like!"

"I thought we were going to spend the night together."

"I'll be there when I can!"

"When you can? What the hell is that important that you can't pull yourself away from it to spend one night with your girl?"

"Work. And why the hell do we have to keep having this conversation?"

"Because I want to!" I yelled.

"Well, I want you to stop calling me with this bullshit every night, but that doesn't stop you!"

"What?"

"You heard me, Mimi. I'm tired of you calling me stressing about this bullshit! I don't need this shit! "

"All I am asking is for you to spend some time with me. We haven't even had sex, Tony. You used to want it every night. Now it's like you don't even care. Are you fucking somebody else?"

"Is that what you want to hear?"

"I want the truth!"

"Well maybe I am! Good-bye, Mimi!" he said before hanging up.

I tried to hold back the flood of tears that I could feel building up. I didn't want to sit there and feel sorry for myself, like I usually did when Tony and I had an argument. Instead I decided to go to sleep because I knew that in the morning he would be home, kissing me and apologizing for what he said. When I woke up the next morning I was surprised to find that he hadn't come home. I dialed his cell and only got the voicemail. I didn't have time to wait and see what time he would stroll in since he wasn't there to drive me to school. I had to take the bus, and I was already late.

After school I went back to Tony's apartment, and after trying to use my key, I realized that it didn't work. I guess he had the locks changed. I knocked on the door, and about five seconds later a female answered. She was tall and light-skinned with long, black hair. She appeared to be about twenty or twenty-one.

"Hello! You must be Mimi! We finally meet face to face," she said with a smile.

"Yes, I am. Who are you and where is Tony?" I asked, annoyed.

"He's not home. He told me that you would be by to pick up your things," she said, reaching behind the door to pass me two suitcases obviously filled with the random things I had left there over our two-and-a-half-year relationship.

"What are you talking about? And who the hell are you?"

"I'm Felicia, the chick that you've been disrespecting for so long. I always thought that when I saw you I would want to rip you to shreds, but I actually feel sorry for you. I'm Tony's fiancée now, and he wanted me to make sure I told you face to face so you could leave him alone."

"What? Fiancée? So now you are getting married? Where the hell is Tony so we can get to the bottom of this? I don't even know why he continues to play this game with you. We are going to be together. We almost had a child together."

"Yeah, almost is the key word there, and he told me about that. He also said that it was a mistake. I'm sorry that you're hurt, but you'll find someone to be with. Tony's a man. They all cheat, so get used to it, honey!"

"Get used to it? Where the fuck do you come off telling me what I should do? Move out of my way so I can call Tony and speak to him about this," I said, pushing past her.

"Go ahead and call, but I already told you what he said."

"Well, we'll see about that!" I was confident because I couldn't wrap my mind around the fact that Tony would be a coward and send a woman to do his dirty work. I had just spoken to him last night and even though we argued, it wasn't that bad of an argument that he would break up with me. And how the hell could he be engaged when he continued to come home to me most nights? I didn't know much about Felicia, but from the run-ins that we'd had, I knew that she would have rubbed that in my face a long time ago if it were really true. I dialed Tony's cell number and he answered it after the second ring.

"What's up?" Tony yelled into the receiver over the loud music that was playing in the background.

"Tony, what's going on?" I yelled.

"I'm sure Felicia made everything pretty clear."

"What? You are seriously breaking up with me?" I sat down on the chair to catch my fall.

"This relationship has run its course, Mimi."

"I don't get it. I had the abortion like you asked me to. What did I do wrong?"

"I damn near had to force you to get that shit, even after I told you how much I didn't want a child. That was a test for me, and you failed that shit! When I said I didn't want a child, you should have agreed to get rid of it, no questions asked."

"But, Tony, I did. I was scared, and you're going to hold that against me?"

"Mimi, it's over. Felicia's been down with me from day one and that's who I'm sticking with!"

"All of this out of nowhere? I just don't understand this!" I cried.

"Well, there's nothing else that I can say. I've told you how it's going to be. I have to get back, but take care of yourself."

"Take care? After all that we've been through, that's all you have to say to me? Fuck you, Tony!"

Click. He cancelled the call and I sat there, staring at the phone since I hadn't had the opportunity to say all that I wanted to say to him. Felicia stood there with her hand on her hip, waiting for me to leave. I was beyond hurt and extremely embarrassed. I made the decision not to embarrass myself any further. I grabbed the bags that she had packed, and without making a scene I exited the apartment.

All I could do was cry. What the hell had happened? Was this just a bad dream that I would wake up from? Felicia waved good-bye as she closed the door and left me standing in the hallway with two suitcases full of clothing. I stood there in shock for about five minutes before gathering my bags and calling a cab. I cried uncontrollably the entire ride home. I couldn't even bring myself to call Neisha and tell her what had happened. I was so embarrassed. I had saved myself for Tony and look what I got! Maybe it was best that I got the abortion, because I would be stuck with a baby and no baby's daddy, becoming another statistic like many young girls.

I was so depressed, and I began to give up on myself. I was barely eating or sleeping. I didn't talk to my grandmom much, and although she continued to try to figure out why I blocked everyone out while I tried to clear my mind, I told her that I was just having a bad year and things would get better. Neisha stood by me the entire time, and I was so happy to have a friend like her. I knew that I had to get my life together. I couldn't let Tony ruin my life, so I had to move on. Every day was easier than the one before, and eventually I would get over Tony.

CHAPTER 7

Giselle: At First Sight

2000

"Giselle! Come down here. There's somebody I want you to meet," Daddy yelled through the house.

I hurried downstairs and was almost knocked off of my feet when I saw this fine-ass man standing in front of me. I tried to wipe the big grin off my face before my father noticed. I was only fifteen, and I couldn't even look at boys or my dad would flip.

"Giselle, this is Shawn, one of my new partners. You'll be seeing a lot of him, so I wanted to make sure that you knew who he was."

"Hello!" he said, extending his hand so that I could shake it.

I shook his hand and smiled.

"Hi!"

"You can go back upstairs and study now," my dad said after noticing the look on my face. "I'll see you later."

"OK. Nice meeting you, Shawn!"

"You too!"

I couldn't wait to get up to my room and call Gina. I ran up to my room and dialed her number.

"Hello!" she answered.

"Gina, girl, let me tell you. My dad just called me downstairs to meet his new partner. He is so fine! I almost fell down when I saw him. He looks like he has money, too. He touched my hand, girl. I'm not going to wash it for a week!" I said, lying back onto the pillow.

"For real? What's his name?"

"Shawn! I never saw him around the neighborhood before, so he must be new around here."

"So, is he working for your dad?"

"No, he's his partner. He looks older. I know he wouldn't mess with someone my age."

"Your dad would kill him, anyway. You know he ain't having that!"

"I can dream about it, though!" We both started laughing.

"Are you still coming over tonight?" Gina asked.

"Yeah, my dad is going to drop me off later."

"All right, well, call me when you are on your way."

"OK."

I sat in my room and studied until I fell asleep. About three hours later my phone rang. It woke me up out of my sleep.

"Hello!" I said, still half asleep.

"Hey, Baby Girl. I can't run you to your friend's house, so I asked Shawn to take you. He should be there shortly to pick you up, so get your bags together."

I was so excited. Since it was against the rules to wear anything sexy, a velour sweat suit was the cutest thing that I had to put on. I quickly got dressed and waited downstairs for Shawn. After a few minutes he beeped the horn, and I ran outside.

"So what's up, Shorty? How old are you?" he asked, looking me up and down.

"I'm fifteen. Why?"

"You look older than that!" he said, shocked.

"Well, that's a good thing!" I exclaimed.

"Why is that?"

"It got you to notice!" I said, trying to sound mature.

"Not really. I just asked. You ain't even my type, little girl!"

"I'm not a little girl. I'm just young. I ain't no virgin, either!"

"I didn't ask you all that! You think that's cute to tell me that? You think that will make me want you?"

"It works for other guys!"

"For little boys, maybe. I'm a grown-ass man. Don't get it twisted. I was trying to spark up a conversation when I asked about your age, because I didn't want to ride in silence. But since you obviously got a little crush on me, I won't ask you any more questions. We'll just leave it at that!"

"That's fine!" I said, annoyed.

He was being rude, but that still didn't stop me from wanting him. He dropped me off at Gina's. I introduced them and then he left after we were in the house.

"Girl, he is fine! Did y'all talk on the way over?"

"Yeah, a little. He said that I look older than I really am. I told him that it was a good thing since it got him to look at me."

"What, you said that? You are so bold. What did he say?"

"Nothing much. We left it at that. But I'll see him again to finish the conversation. Maybe I could lose my virginity to him!"

"Girl, I forgot that you were still a virgin. Anyway, let's go watch a movie."

We went up to her bedroom and watched movies until we fell asleep.

During the following weeks I saw a lot more of Shawn, and he really meant what he said, because he was totally ignoring me. I was bored too, because Gina had a new man that I'd never met. She said she had to keep things a secret because he was older than her. She told me that she met him one day when she was leaving my house. She also said he was good in bed. I was jealous because I couldn't find a man. I was cute, with long hair, light brown eyes, a Coke-bottle shaped body, and breasts to die for! I guess I was *too* good looking, because I was scaring the men away.

It was a Friday morning when I headed down to Gina's house. By this time she had moved out of the Richard Allen projects and lived a couple of blocks down from me. Her mother worked nights, so I always had to wake her up for school. As I was about to turn the corner, I noticed her on her steps kissing none other than Shawn! I was enraged. This was why she wouldn't tell me who her new man was. She knew I would flip. What kind of friend would go after the man that I had been chasing? I was so upset that tears began to flow down my cheeks. I turned around and walked in the direction of school. I walked alone that day. I needed time to think, as well as time to cool off because at that point I wanted to hurt her. I wanted to make her feel the pain that I was feeling. She stole Shawn from right up under me without me even knowing.

After first period I ran into Gina in the hallway at school. I couldn't believe that she would smile in my face after she just got finished fucking Shawn.

"What's up, G? What happened to you this morning? I waited for you to come past."

"I came a few minutes early, caught you kissing Shawn. I

guess you fucked all night, huh? I hope it was good for you to do that to me."

"G, it's not like that. I didn't go after Shawn. He came after me."

"But you knew I liked him, Gina. That should have been enough for you to tell him no! All that time you were telling me about this new guy, how his sex was good, and how he spent money on you, and it was him. You knew I liked him, and instead of being honest, you rubbed that shit all in my face!"

"I didn't mean to. You knew I thought he was cute. He surprised me by coming at me. I wasn't expecting that at all!"

"But you welcomed it with open arms!"

"Look, G, how come you can't just be happy for me? I got someone that takes care of me, that can give me the finer things in life. You already have money and nice clothes. I don't!"

"So? That's no excuse. I'm glad that I know who my real friends are. You are definitely not one of them! Now do me a favor and forget my number. As a matter of fact, forget you ever knew me!"

I walked away and went to my next class, and that was the end of our friendship. I knew that a man should never come between friends, but there were certain things that you just didn't do, and stealing someone's crush was one of them. I never got over that. It hurt me a lot to see her walking around school with tailor-made shit on that he bought. He was supposed to be buying those things for me. I was the sexy one, and look what he chose. Gina was so plain before dealing with Shawn. Her mother never had money to buy her nice things, and there were plenty of times that I took the money that my father gave me and spent it on her. I couldn't have her hanging around me wearing shit from Rainbow! That's what real friends did—look out for her friend in times of need. Friends didn't steal each other's men! And although Shawn wasn't mine as of yet, he was going to be eventually, and that was the most important thing.

I told my friend Toya about it and she was just as pissed as I was. She told me from the beginning not to trust Gina, and me being me and not wanting to listen, I did my own thing. From the first day Toya laid eyes on Gina, she said that there was just something about her that she didn't trust. I guess I was blind because I didn't see it. Never in a million years would I have expected this betrayal from Gina. I moved on, and although I saw her almost every day, either at school or around the way, it was as if we never knew each other.

CHAPTER 8

Mimi: No One Can Compare

1998

My life was shaping up. I was focused on going back to school. I was almost at the end of my senior year, but I had screwed things up so badly that I knew I wouldn't be able to graduate on time. Neisha and Mark were still going strong, but I opted to be man-less to get my grades back on track. I couldn't have a man mess me up again. I never heard from Tony after that day, which was good. I had closed that chapter of my life and moved on.

At the end of the school year Neisha's mom was planning a big barbecue for Neisha's good grades. All of our friends from school were invited. The oversized backyard was full of people, all of Neisha's family and friends. There was one guy that I didn't recognize. He stared at me the entire time. I pulled Neisha in the house and asked her who he was, because I had never seen him around the neighborhood.

"Yo, who is the dude in the black Dickies?" I quizzed.

"Oh, that's my cousin James. Why?"

"I've never seen him around before, that's all."

"He just got out of jail a couple weeks ago. Him and Mark are best friends."

"Oh. How old is he?"

"He's twenty. What's up with all of the questions?"

"He's been staring at me since I got here. I just wondered who he was."

"He probably likes you! I'll hook you up, if you want me to."

"No, girl! I don't want any man. I was just asking. Now, let's get back to the cookout."

"OK, girl," she said with a sly smirk on her face.

James. I said the name over in my head. He was cute indeed. He was tall, about six feet, and he wore black shorts and a white T-shirt. His hair was freshly cut, and his sneakers were brand new, but he didn't look like he had much money, I guess because he just gotten out of jail. And for that reason I tried to put him out of my mind. I was just getting myself together, and I didn't need any drama to steer me wrong. I enjoyed the rest of the cookout, and around nine, I made my way down the street to go to home.

I reflected on the way that my life had changed in the last few years, and it was scary. Three years ago I was a shy virgin that had never been touched by a man. Now I was fiending for that same touch, the touch that had landed me in an abortion clinic. Although sex got me in a lot of trouble and caused me much pain, I missed it. I missed loving a man and a man loving me mind, body, and soul. I know that most people would say that I was a fool for even thinking that Tony loved me, but I truly believed that at one time he did. Tony did so much for me, and I felt that there was no way a man would do all of that for someone they didn't love or care for, even if only a little bit. I remembered the times that Tony made me laugh, and the times he smiled at me and made my body weak. Tony would always be my first love, regardless of the way things turned out. I had forgiven him for the pain that he caused me. I realized that if I continued to be mad at him, he would rule my life and I couldn't have anyone rule my life besides me.

I tossed and turned that night, thinking about the mysterious man named James. As much as I tried to deny it, I wanted to know more about him. Being lonely was now very different for me. I was with Tony for two and a half years, so I was used to having a man. I decided that I wouldn't throw myself at him. I would wait and see if he would come to me. I knew that I was fine. My mixed race made me shine above the other neighborhood girls, for sure. And I also looked much older for my age. My body was definitely that of a grown woman—hourglass shape with big breasts, a small waist, and nice, round hips. I also had full lips and long, silky hair. What man could pass up a chance to be with me?

The next morning, I decided to go to South Street. I didn't have much money, but it was something to do. I got dressed in a Baby Phat mini skirt and tank with a pair of wedged sandals to match. I caught the 47 bus all the way down. After browsing the many stores that lined the busy street, I didn't see much that I wanted to buy. I went into a small designer boutique and tried on a few things. As I was looking in the mirror, I noticed a tall, dark-skinned guy staring at me. I looked at myself in the mirror a little while longer before going into the fitting booth to change. When I came out, the dark-skinned stranger was gone. I found the saleswoman to give her the clothing I had tried on.

"Oh, they fit you perfectly. Let me bag those up for you!" she said, smiling.

"Oh, I'm not buying them. I just wanted to return them to the rack," I informed her.

"The clothes are already paid for. The gentleman, who

was here earlier, paid for them. Here's his business card. He left it for you."

"What? He paid for them?" I asked, startled. "This is like two thousand dollars worth of clothing!"

"Well, honey, be glad that you have someone to buy you such nice things."

I didn't know what else to say, so I grabbed the bags of clothing and made my way out of the store. I read the name on the business card. The dark-skinned stranger's name was Maurice. Who would be crazy enough to spend that kind of money on a chick that they didn't even know? That was something that automatically got my attention. I had to find out more about the stranger named Maurice. I was definitely going to do that! I laughed as I walked to the bus stop to go back home. Excited about my new gear, I barely paid attention to where I was going. Eventually I made it to the right bus stop where I waited for fifteen minutes for the bus to arrive.

As soon as I reached home, I pulled the clothes from the bags, neatly placing each outfit in my drawer. I pulled the business card from my purse and looked at it for about five minutes before gathering up the nerve to call. Lucky me! The answering machine! Now I could leave a message and wait for him to call me back. By then I wouldn't be as afraid to talk. I spoke after the beep.

"Hello, Mr. Maurice. My name is Mimi. We haven't actually met, but you did drop over two thousand dollars on me today, which is a different kind of introduction, if I must say so myself. Anyway, I was calling to find out what's up, so whenever it's convenient for you, give me a call at 215-555-1212. Holla!" I hung up the phone with a huge smile on my face.

About a week passed before I heard from Maurice, and it caught me off guard when I did. I was home, watching the movie *Boomerang* with Eddie Murphy, almost dozing off when the phone rang and ended any chances I had of falling asleep. I groggily answered the phone, not expecting the surprise that I was soon to receive.

"Hello!" I whispered.

"Can I speak to Mimi?" a deep-toned, male voice asked, sending chills up and down my spine.

"Speaking. Who's this?" I asked, now fully awake.

"Maurice. What's up, sexy?"

"Nothing. Just surprised to hear from you, that's all."

"Why is that? You think that I would spend that kind of money on you and never call?"

"I don't know. I never had that experience before, so I really wouldn't know what to expect."

"Well, expect to be seeing a lot of me. Matter of fact, what are you doing now? I can come scoop you. I'm not really into talking on the phone. I'd rather see you face to face. You can't see emotion over the phone."

"I'm not doing anything, actually. I'll just have to get dressed real quick."

"Well, throw on something that I bought you. I want to see how well my money was spent!" he said, laughing.

"OK!" I gave him my address and quickly jumped in the shower to freshen up. I got dressed in a pair of tight-fitting Cavalli jeans, knee boots, and a beaded tank top. I fluffed my hair, applied some lip gloss, and waited for him to arrive. When I heard the sound of a beeping horn, I rushed downstairs and kissed my grandmother good night. I went outside and was shocked by the black Lexus that was double-parked in front of my door. Maurice was standing outside of the driver's side door, waiting for me with a smile on his face.

"Damn, you look good!" he said, reaching out to hug me.

I didn't even know this man, but his touch felt so damn good.

"Thanks!" I said, smiling.

"Well, hop in!" he instructed.

I got in, unsure of the destination, but excited at the same time. We made small talk in the car, neither of us giving much information to the other. I watched him lick his lips as he talked, and I was so turned on by that. We pulled up into the driveway of a big house off Roosevelt Boulevard. I instantly began to question our destination.

"Whose house is this?" I asked quickly.

"Mine. What's wrong? I just want to run in and grab something real quick. Is that cool?"

"Yeah, that's cool!" I said, getting out of the car.

We walked into the large house and it was nicely decorated. Everything appeared to be new, like the chairs had never even been sat on.

"You can sit down, or you can look around, if you want. I'm just going to run upstairs and change real quick."

"I'll look around. Your furniture is so nice that I'm afraid to sit on it," I said, laughing.

"Cool!" he said before running upstairs.

I walked around, glancing in every room. I was surprised that everything was so nice. Guys weren't usually this neat; not the ones I knew, anyway. I went upstairs and looked into the bedrooms. The master bedroom had its own bathroom. I could hear the shower running. I went into the room and sat on the bed, waiting patiently for him to emerge. I was in awe when he walked out in a towel, water still dripping from his muscular body. I could have never foreseen the beauty that lay beneath his clothing. I wanted to jump all over him and lick every drop of water from his body, but I held my composure as I sat there on the edge of the bed with my legs crossed.

"I decided to take a quick shower. My bad for having you waiting."

"It's cool. I like your house. It's really nice."

Standing in front of me naked, he continued to dry off. "Thanks," he said.

"Well, I'll go downstairs and let you finish getting dressed." I was uncomfortable seeing his naked body in front of me.

"You can stay here," he said, smiling.

I wanted him. It was definitely having an effect on me seeing him that way. I couldn't allow myself to give in, though. I had just met him, but damn he was fine! I sat back down, trying to look in the opposite direction. He noticed me trying to avoid the view. Suddenly he walked over, kneeled down, and kissed me. I couldn't stop him because it felt so good. He laid me down on the king-sized bed and began to undress me. I didn't resist. He kissed me softly up my legs before laying me back, spreading my legs, and guiding his tongue into my tunnel. I gave in and allowed him to take over. I closed my eyes, enjoying the pleasure of the slow and steady circles he was making on my clit with his tongue.

He began to caress my clit with his fingers before sliding three fingers in me, one by one. The strength of his fingers was unlike anything that I had ever experienced before. I grabbed onto the pillows at the head of the bed as I exploded all over his fingers. He stood up and sucked my juices off his fingers while I lay there still paralyzed from the orgasm. He stood in front of the bed, stroking his manhood to keep it at attention, and then pulled out a condom from his bedside table. Putting it on, he then entered me slowly, but with much force at the same time. I was in heaven and I didn't want to leave. Maurice knew how to work every position like a professional. Tony was good, but Maurice was better for sure. After our explosions, we lay there for a minute talking.

"So, you want to go grab something to eat? I'm hungry as hell!" Maurice said, rubbing his stomach.

"That's cool, because I'm hungry, too," I said, laughing.

We both got up and began getting dressed. In a way I was embarrassed by my behavior. This was the first time I had ever slept with a guy on the first night. This was much different, and I didn't want Maurice to think that I was a ho who did this on a regular basis. I had to set the record straight so I could feel better about the events that just took place.

We walked out to the car, got inside, and began our drive to Friday's to eat.

"Maurice, I don't want you to think that I'm some type of ho because of what just happened."

"Why would I think that?" he asked, smiling. "I would be a ho too, if that was the case!"

"Well, it's OK for men to be hoes!" I said, laughing.

"I like you a lot, even though I just met you," Maurice said. "There's something about you that makes a nigga weak. I ain't ever experienced that before today. That's why I dropped them two stacks on you earlier!"

"I'm glad. I recently got out of a bad relationship. I got hurt real badly and I'm not trying to get hurt like that again."

"I'm not trying to hurt you. I just want to make you feel good, and haven't I done that so far?" He smiled.

"Yes, you have!" I said, giggling.

"So, how old are you?"

"I'm eighteen."

"I'm twenty-five. I hope that doesn't scare you away!" he laughed.

"Nope. My first boyfriend was twenty-one!" I said, reassuring him.

We pulled up into the Friday's parking lot. He kissed me once before exiting the car. We went in and ate. After dinner he asked me to spend the night and I agreed.

Summer was almost over and Maurice and I were still

going strong. I was falling in love with him and he knew it. Maurice taught me how to drive that summer, and he made sure that I perfected it and passed my driver's test the first time. He also bought me my first car. It was a white Honda Accord.

When school began everything felt much different. I was older than damn near everyone there since I had to repeat the twelfth grade. I hated feeling out of place because all of my friends had graduated. I walked the halls alone, portraying the look of someone that didn't give a damn. I was now getting a lot of evil looks. I knew that the girls were just jealous because Maurice treated me so well. Those girls never had a man like I had, and they were full of envy.

I felt that I deserved a man like Maurice for everything that I went through with Tony. This was a definite comeback, and for every chick that dissed me when Tony left me, they could kiss my Cavalli jeans-covered ass! Soon the rumors about chicks that Maurice was supposed to be screwing started. I knew that it would happen sooner or later. I really didn't care because he made sure that I had any and everything that I wanted. After first period on a Friday, I was in the bathroom at school when a group of girls led by one of my rivals, Octavia, came into the bathroom.

Octavia never liked me since the first day of school. We had many run-ins where we came close to blows. For whatever reason, she always had something to say about me, and I knew once I had the chance I would beat that bitch down for everything that she had ever said. Octavia was once the girlfriend of Tony. He left her after she got pregnant, almost like he did me, except I was smart enough to get an abortion. She, on the other hand, was stuck to take care of a four-year-old all on her own.

Once the news spread that Tony and I were no longer together, she made every attempt to rub it in my face. She even went so far as to put letters in my locker about how stupid I was for falling for Tony. I stood in the bathroom stall quietly listening to their conversation.

"I see Mimi has a new car now!" Lisa said.

"Who cares? I should flatten that bitch's tires. She messes with Maurice now. He probably bought her that shit. I could have been with Maurice, but he's not my type," Octavia said, looking at herself in the mirror.

"How could you have been with him?" one girl quizzed.

"Girl, please. Every nigga in the hood wants me. Maurice tried to come at me on many occasions. He still does to this day. I let him eat me out before, but that's about it. I might get at him, though, to steal that bitch's shine. She thinks she has some type of prize. She better think again!" Octavia said, laughing before exiting the bathroom.

I was furious. I left the bathroom and called Neisha on my cell. I told her what I had overheard and she told me that she would meet me after school to have my back if I wanted to settle things with Octavia once and for all.

I was steaming mad all day in school. I waited for Octavia to come out of the building after school. Without saying a word, I rammed into her, causing her to fall to the ground. I began punching her in the face and slamming her head against the ground. The crowd began to form and Neisha stood guard, having my back and making sure none of her girlfriends tried to jump in. I continued ramming her head into the cement, not giving her the chance to hit me once. Soon the cops were pulling me away, but I continued to kick her as I was lifted away.

She cursed and screamed obscenities as her friends tried to console her. I laughed as they put me into the back of the police car. I was taken to the police station where I was fingerprinted and photographed like a criminal. The crazy part about it was that I felt so good, because I finally got to give her the ass whopping that had been building up for so long. I had to call Maurice to come pick me up. He was upset, of course, that I was locked up, but he said that he hated Octavia and he was glad that I did what I did. He laughed all the way home as I told him how I repeatedly banged her head into the ground. Once we reached his house I sat down on the sofa and took off my shoes.

"Let me rub your feet for you. I know they have to be killing you. That's why you should carry a spare pair of sneakers in case you have to knock somebody out!" he said, laughing.

"I'll make sure I keep that in mind," I said, relaxing as he removed my stockings and began rubbing my aching feet.

"I love you, baby. I just want you to know that," he said.

"I love you, too!"

Within a few seconds his hands began to slowly move up my legs. Once he reached my thighs, he grabbed for my panties and pulled them down around my ankles before removing them completely. He worked his magic with his fingers on my clit while removing his clothing at the same time. I moaned as his fingers went in and out of me.

Before feasting down below he stood in front of me, signaling me to taste his manhood, and I was happy to do so. I sucked while he forced his length farther back near my throat. I had mastered the deep-throating technique and was able to get all but maybe one inch of Maurice inside my mouth. He exploded once and I continued sucking on him to bring his member back to attention. Within seconds he was back up and ready to go, and he quickly bent me over the arm of the sofa and entered me from behind, going deep inside me as I raised one leg and placed it on the seat of the sofa. We went at it for at least an hour before retiring to the bedroom and falling asleep. I lay there smiling, reflecting on the high points of our relationship and how much I was in love with him. I was extremely happy with Maurice. Nothing could break us apart, or so I thought . . .

CHAPTER 9

Giselle: Baby Girl

2003

It was nine A.M. when I woke up, very anxious about the day's events. It was my eighteenth birthday, and I knew that it would be the best birthday ever. I jumped out of bed and ran over to the window to look outside, hoping that there would be a car waiting, but there wasn't! My dad told me he would get me the Toyota Avalon that I wanted. I could have asked for a more expensive car, but I was cool with that. I rushed out of my bedroom to my dad's room and he wasn't even home. Damn it! I was having a party tonight and I wanted to shine on all these neighborhood bitches!

I heard my dad's car pull up in the driveway. I rushed to the door, and when I opened it I was let down again. It wasn't Daddy. It was Shawn.

"Oh, it's you!" I was disappointed

"Not happy to see me?" Shawn asked, smiling.

"Why should I be? You ain't never did nothing for me!" I said, walking back into the house.

"Oh, so now I ain't never did nothing for you?"

"Not what I wanted you to do!"

"I told you that you are too young in the mind for me. You ain't ready for a nigga like me!"

I sucked my teeth. "You don't know what I'm ready for!"

"You think you're ready, but you're not. You're too busy trying to be cute. I see you walking around half-ass naked, trying to get attention. You are too young in the mind!"

"Where is Daddy?" I interrupted.

"He's at the club. He told me to come pick you up!"

"For what?"

"It's your birthday, right? It's probably for your gift!"

"Well, let me go get dressed."

"Try to hurry up. You know T hates to be held up!"

"I'll try!"

I went upstairs, upset by the comments Shawn had made. I knew he wanted me, but he was probably just scared of Terrance. I was just in need of a man, and Shawn was perfect. He was sexy as hell, and paid! I needed a piece of that.

I took off my clothes and got in the shower. After a few minutes Shawn knocked on the door, saying that he needed to use the bathroom. We had four other bathrooms in the house, so why he needed to use this one was beyond me.

"Fine. Just don't flush the toilet!" I yelled through the glass of the shower.

"All right!"

He came in trying not to look in the direction of the shower. The door was glass so you could see right through it. As he stood over the toilet I peeked over and was instantly horny, seeing how large he was even in his limp stage.

"I know you're looking at me!" Shawn said quickly.

"And? The problem is?" I quizzed.

"Ain't none! They are your eyes and you can look where you want to."

"I'm trying to get some of that, but you are being stingy!"

"Maybe one day! We ain't got time for that right now, anyway!"

"Yeah, all right! Why don't you have a seat and watch, then?"

"I can do that!" he said, sitting down.

I was glad because I knew that I would get to him sooner or later. Now that he had agreed to sit and watch me shower, I decided to put on a major show. I took the soap and rubbed it over my body in sexy motions, trying to make him horny. After letting the water rinse the soap from my body, I propped my leg up on the shower seat and began to masturbate. I immediately saw him squirm. He then released his hardness from his pants and began to do the same, and I was loving it. We both continued to please ourselves while watching each other until we climaxed. He got up and cleaned himself off, looked at me, and laughed before exiting the bathroom. I washed off once more and then I got out of the shower and dried off. I went into my room and decided to wear an extra-mini denim skirt with a pink bebe shirt and sandals. I fixed my hair in a loose ponytail and rushed to get downstairs. I walked down the steps slowly and sexily. Shawn wasn't impressed at all.

"See what I'm talking about!" he said, pointing at the lack of clothing I was wearing.

"What?" I quizzed.

"Your clothes! Always half-naked. You could never be my girl!"

"I just want to have sex with you!" I said softly.

"Yeah, all right. Let's go before T suspects something!"

"Well, we ain't do nothing anyway!" I said with sarcasm.

"Let's go!" he said quickly, walking to the door.

After entering the car Shawn turned on the radio and tried to ignore my presence. I knew that he was thinking about what happened earlier, probably thinking that I'd tell all my friends or Daddy. I know he didn't care if Gina found out. He always cheated on her, but she was so caught up in the money that she was blind to his ways. She was a trophy for him, the ghetto girl that he had helped along, and nothing more.

Gina betrayed me. Her head became so blown up when he started spending money on her. I always had money and dressed nice, but Gina wasn't used to the nicer things in life. She lost many friends because of her attitude change. She was cute, but before the money she was nothing but a ghetto-ass, project chick!

Gina was the same age as me and graduated from the same high school. The guys in the school never tried to talk to her because of Shawn's reputation. He was the man! I wanted him and I planned on being with him soon. I didn't care that Gina was once my friend. She wasn't my friend now, and she would never be again. That's what was important to me.

I looked over at Shawn as he licked his sexy-ass lips. I couldn't go the whole drive in silence. I had to make some conversation.

"So, how are things between you and Gina?"

"Why are you worried about her?"

"I just asked. What's wrong with that?" I snapped.

"A lot, because you weren't worried about her earlier when you wanted some dick!"

"Neither were you, Shawn. I don't know why you are playing hard to get!"

"Because it wouldn't work!"

"You'll never know unless you try."

"Well, I know your ways, and that shit don't work for me!"

"But Gina does? She's just like me! She wants to be me!" I raised my voice.

"No, you want to be her! You want me and you can't handle the fact that she got me. That's why y'all aren't friends now!"

"Whatever!"

Angry, I sat silent the rest of the drive. I couldn't believe that he thought I wanted to be her. That bitch had nothing on me. I looked ten times better. Every dude wanted me, even Shawn. He could play games all he wanted, but I knew the truth.

As soon as we got to the club I rushed out and slammed the car door. I heard Shawn giggling behind me but I didn't find shit funny! I opened the door to the club and saw my dad and his other partner, Mark, watching basketball on the plasma TV.

"Damn, what took so long?" my dad quizzed.

"It was my fault, Daddy. You know I have to be perfect when I come outside."

"You almost messed up your gift!"

"But you promised!" I whined.

"Well, don't be upset, but I decided to get you something different."

"Why?" I asked, already upset.

"Just go see it. It's out back!" he said, tossing me the keys.

I walked toward the back of the club and Shawn was standing at the door.

"I don't want to hear about that shit from earlier!"

"You won't! Now can I get by?" I said, annoyed.

"Sure you can," he said, smiling, and then he moved away from the door.

I opened the door and had to look twice to make sure I wasn't dreaming. There sat a convertible BMW. Daddy had outdone himself this time. Everyone was sure to hate me now! I was so excited that I forgot to go back into the club to thank my dad for the car. I just got right in and drove off. I needed to shop for an outfit anyway, so I started toward South Street.

I had no idea what I wanted to wear, but I knew that I didn't have all day to shop. I still had to get my hair and nails done. I chose to go into this small boutique that had everything that most people couldn't afford. I entered the store and was immediately approached by the salesperson. I told her the type of event that I was shopping for. I guess she could tell my style by the way I was dressed, because the outfit she picked out for me was perfect. It was me all the way up and down. I went to the back dressing room and tried it on, and it even fit to perfection. After I changed back into my clothes, I took the new outfit to the register and paid the $989. It was a lot of money, but with my new BMW and this new outfit, I was sure to shine that night.

On my way back to my car some ghetto-ass young boy tried to get my number. I quickly dismissed him and made my way to the car. I opened the trunk to put my bags in and my cell phone rang. "Money, Power, Respect" by The Lox was the ringtone that played continuously as I fumbled through my Gucci bag to locate it. Finally getting my hand on it, I answered.

"Hello!" I said, hoping to catch the call.

"What's up, ho? What car did you get?" the voice quizzed instantly.

"Girl, he got me a BMW!"

"What?" my friend Toya asked, screaming into the phone

"I still can't believe it myself. I'm down South Street now. I had to come scoop me up something to wear for tonight."

"You should have come and got me. I don't know what I'm going to wear."

"Is Shay and Juanita coming to the party?"

"They said that they were, but I'm coming. You know that is guaranteed. So, where are you on your way to now?"

"I'm going to the shop now to get my hair done. Why?"

"Well, come scoop me, 'cause I can get Lala to tighten my hair up for tonight."

"All right. I'll be there in like fifteen minutes."

"All right," she said before hanging up the phone.

Toya had been my best friend since we were four years old. Anytime I got into trouble, she was always right there with me. A lot of girls around the way didn't like her because she was known for speaking her mind, and if she had a problem with you she was sure to tell you about it, but I liked that about her. That's why we were so cool. We had a couple of bumps along the way, though. Toya was jealous when I started getting close to Gina. She never liked Gina, and they fought on many occasions when Gina first moved into the neighborhood. She never trusted Gina either, so she was quick to tell me "I told you so" when Gina and I were no longer friends. Toya and me almost came to blows over that because I was never in the mood for "I told you so". I loved her, though, and we were tight like sisters.

I put my bags in the trunk, and as I got ready to drive off, my cell phone rang again. I looked at the caller ID and noticed that it was my dad.

"Damn, you could have said thank you!" he yelled.

"Daddy, I'm sorry. I love it. Thank you so much! I just got so excited and I had to drive it at that moment."

"Well, I'm glad that you like it. I just wanted to tell you that I have to go out of town tonight so I'm not going to be at the party. Mark and Shawn will be there with extra security, just in case a nigga want to act stupid. Shawn said that he'd stay at the house tonight if you're scared to stay there alone."

"OK, Daddy. I wish you were going to be there," I said, lying because I was ecstatic that I could now enjoy myself without him watching my every move.

"Maybe next time. Just have fun, Baby Girl."

"OK," I replied before ending the call.

I knew that tonight was the night. Shawn was staying at my house with my dad gone, so he was sure to be mine by tomorrow. Gina could kiss his ass good-bye! I rolled up on Toya's block and she was sitting on the steps waiting for me.

"Girl! This shit is the bomb! We are going to be riding in style!" she said, looking at every angle of my new BMW.

"I know. I can't wait until tonight."

"So, who do you plan on going home with? I know that you're done with Tyrone's sorry ass!" she said, laughing.

"Girl, I'm done with young guys, period. I got my eyes on someone with much more experience!"

"Who?"

"I can't tell you until it's final. You know how you be running your mouth!"

"Well, anyway, what are you wearing tonight?"

"I can't tell you. I want it to be a surprise."

"What's up with all the damn secrets?"

"You know you're my girl! It ain't no secret. You'll see later!"

"Yeah, all right," she said, annoyed. Toya hated when you withheld information from her. She had to know everything.

We pulled up in front of Lala's salon just as Gina was walking out. I figured I would run into her today because we always got our hair done on the same day. It had been a routine for both of us for years. I jumped out of the car quickly to make sure that she got a glimpse of me and my new BMW. She gave me a fake-ass smile as she passed. That bitch just didn't know that her man was about to be mine. She could finally get a taste of her own medicine! Man-stealing bitch!

We walked into the salon and spoke to everyone. Lala told me I was next. I was glad because I didn't feel like sitting for too long. We sat in the shop and talked about everything—who was screwing who, and who wasn't screwing anymore.

The salon was one place where you could find out what was going on in the neighborhood. Lala curled my hair and then she re-curled Toya's. We were on our way. I dropped Toya off and made my way to the nail salon to get a manicure, pedicure, and eyebrow wax. Once I was done there I rushed home to get ready for my party.

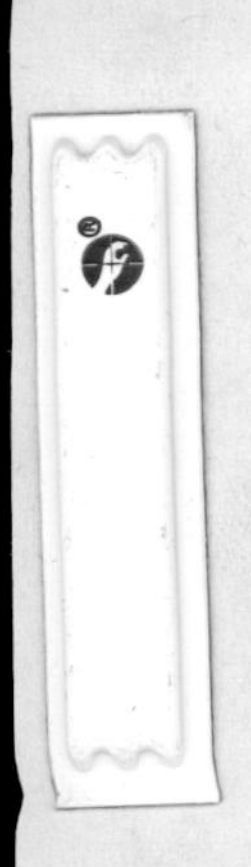

CHAPTER 10

Mimi: You Know You Want Me

1999

Neisha and I decided to go clubbing, since it was her cousin James' birthday and he was having a party at the Stinger on Broad Street. We were equipped with fake IDs to gain entrance to the club that was always packed. We hadn't been spending much time together, so it was a nice thing for us to do since both of us had men that we spent most of our time with. I had missed spending time with Neisha because in all actuality, she was the only friend that I had since the fallout with Leah. Although it didn't really bother me not to have an abundance of friends, I did miss hanging out with the girls.

I got dressed for the club in a Prada mini-dress. It was all black, and I wore jeans under it, turning it into a shirt. Maurice wasn't too fond of the skimpy clothing I had grown to prefer, so I had to be creative in order to wear all of the clothes that Tony once loved to see me in. I also wore a pair of black-and-white, studded boots that Maurice bought me from South Street. My hair was in a wrap with the front ends flipped, and I applied my makeup to perfection. Maurice really didn't want me to go out, but after our earlier sexual episode, he said it was OK.

I picked Neisha up from Mark's house and we were on our way. When we reached the party, the line was long, as usual. We showed our invitation, paid the ten-dollar donation, and went inside. It was packed on each level, and the music was jumping. Neisha and I walked around until she spotted James engaged in a conversation with a group of guys. We made our way over to him.

"What's up, J? Happy birthday!" Neisha said, hugging him.

"Thanks. Who's your friend?"

"J, this is Mimi. Mimi, this is J, my cousin."

"You look good, Shorty. You a model or something?" He smiled.

"I wish!" I giggled. "Thanks for the compliment!" I said.

"Well, I hope you enjoy yourself, and I hope I'll get to dance with you later."

"Sure. It's your birthday, so why not?" I said, throwing up my hands.

"Cool. I'll catch you out there later."

"Cool."

Neisha and I made our way through the crowd to the bar. She giggled the whole way.

"He likes you, girl," she said, laughing.

"How do you know that?"

"I know my cousin, and I can tell by the way you were looking at him that you like him, too"

"Girl, please. I was just being friendly. I love my man."

"Whatever. I love mine, too, but I'd still let another nigga hit it if the money was right!" she laughed.

We ordered two Thug Passions, and after gulping them

down we went out to the dance floor and began dancing. After about ten minutes I felt a strong pair of hands around my waist. I turned around and noticed that it was James. Damn, he was fine! I danced with him like a professional had choreographed my steps. James was all over me, too. I could even feel his friend down below begin to bulge. After the dance, we went to the bar. He ordered me a drink and we talked.

"So, what's up? You got a man?"

"Yeah."

"For real? Who's your man? I'm sure I can take you from him!" he said with confidence.

"My man's name is Maurice."

"Oh, yeah, I know that cat. That's no problem, though. He's small weight. I'm trying to make you mine. I need a dime like you on my arm."

"Well, I'm happy with my man."

"What does that have to do with anything? I can make you much happier, for sure!"

"That's good that you have that much confidence, but I'm happy with my man," I reiterated.

"That's cool for now, but I'm not giving up because I know you want me. Just know that I'm here when that nigga falls short," he said before kissing me on the cheek and rising from the barstool.

I found it amusing that he was so confident. The truth was that I did want him from the first time I saw him, but I was in love with Maurice and I couldn't risk that. Maurice did everything right, so I didn't expect him to fall short any time soon. Although James' offer sounded as good as smooth R&B to my ears, thoughts of Maurice in the back of my head definitely added a sour note to the R&B song. We partied until two A.M. and after the party was over Neisha and I, along with James and his friends, went to IHOP to eat.

James stared at me the entire time we were there. I tried to avoid looking at him because the way he smiled and licked his lips was just so damn sexy! I ordered pancakes and sausage and you would have thought it was the best meal that I'd ever tasted because I was trying extremely hard to avoid any eye contact with James. Before leaving, he walked me to my car since Neisha had already left with Mark. I knew that she purposely left me alone with James to reel me in. She tried to fill me in on his past, and how he landed in the Camp Hill Correctional Facility for robbery. She also told me about his fallout with his brother, who was now deceased. There was something about his thug mannerisms that turned me on. He was focused on being with me, and the determination was definitely a plus. I could see myself with a man that set a goal and refused to give up until he attained it.

"Why don't you go home with me tonight?" he asked, moving close to me as I began to back away.

"No. Are you crazy? Maurice would kill me."

"What he doesn't know won't hurt him. I'm trying to give you a sample of what you could have all the time if you were my girl."

"I can't, I—"

He stopped me with a kiss, and I didn't resist him. I couldn't because it felt so good.

"Just go home with me tonight. If you're not satisfied, I'll leave you alone. I promise."

Although I knew it was wrong, I agreed to his proposal. I got in my car and began following him to his apartment. I called Maurice, and, luckily, he didn't pick up. I left him a message telling him that I was going to stay at Neisha's because I was too drunk to drive home alone. Once we drove up to James' apartment building I was so nervous that I couldn't even park straight.

"What the hell am I doing?" I asked myself out loud. James walked up to my car and opened the door to let me out.

"Come on, ma. Don't get scared now."

"I'm not scared!" I lied because I was definitely afraid of the act of betrayal that I was about to commit.

We entered the apartment building and made our way up the stairs. I was hoping that he couldn't see me shaking because I was nervous as hell. I wanted to just turn around and run back down the stairs, but my body wouldn't budge. After entering the apartment, James wasted no time leading me to the bedroom. He began kissing me unlike any kiss that I'd ever had in my life. My panties instantly became wet from his touch. He undressed me and leaned me against the wall. Getting on his knees, he began kissing me down below. I moaned loudly, as I was in heaven from the treatment that I was receiving. With my leg over his shoulder, I moaned continuously to let him know that I was satisfied. After what seemed like a half hour, he laid me on the bed and gave my body even more attention. I loved it! He undressed and without hesitation entered me. I came instantly before he could even reach the full depth of my walls. His stroke was slow and steady, more like making love. I came so many times that I lost count. He continued working it out until he exploded inside me. He lay on top of me, both of us sweaty.

"So did you enjoy that sample?" he asked.

"Yeah, it was great."

"Well, there's even more where that came from. You just gotta give me a chance to show you."

"James, it was great. But I can't leave Maurice, not right now. I'm sorry." I slid my body out from underneath his and got out of bed to begin to get dressed.

"So that's it?"

"I'm sorry, James, but I can't. I have to go." I finished getting dressed and ran out of the apartment to my car.

I felt so guilty that I cried the entire ride home. I got to my house and showered for an hour to wash away my sins. I cried myself to sleep that night because I didn't know how I could look Maurice in the eye after what I had done. I made a big mistake, but I had to move on. Hopefully Maurice would never have to find out.

I finally fell asleep, and when I woke up around ten-thirty I called Maurice.

"Hey, babe, what's up? You got tore up last night, huh?"

"Yeah. I was drinking those Thug Passions. You know how that is!"

"Yeah. So did you make it home?"

"Yeah, I'm home. I just got up. Where are you?"

"I'm out handling business. Why don't you meet me at my house, at like, twelve? I miss you."

"OK, I'll be there. I love you."

I hung up the phone. I still felt guilty, but I felt a little better now that I had talked to him. I got up and got dressed—nothing fancy, just a pair of jeans, a fitted shirt, and my Dior sneakers and sunglasses. I drove to Maurice's house and let myself in. I sat in the living room and watched music videos on MTV. My cell phone rang. I was a little hesitant to answer it since it was a number that I didn't recognize.

"Hello!"

"Hey. I can't leave you alone because you said that it was great!"

"How did you get this number?" I quizzed, annoyed that James was calling.

"Neisha gave it to me. Anyway, I want to see you again."

"That's not possible. I told you that last night."

"I'm not going to give up."

"Look, I have to go. Maurice is coming in the house," I said before hanging up.

"All right, I'll holla."

I hung up the phone just as Maurice walked in the door. I went and greeted him with a kiss and a hug.

"I missed you," I said, smiling.

"Oh, yeah? How much?"

"This much," I said, spreading my arms apart to show how much.

"I got you something."

"What is it?" I asked curiously.

"I'll show you later. Right now I need you to ride me real good. I was dreaming about you all night. I missed having you in my bed," he said, wrapping his arms around my waist.

He began kissing me, again making me feel guilty. My insides were still throbbing from last night's activities. I had to satisfy my man, though, because I had just given away the one thing that was supposed to be only for him.

I moved down from his lips and began loosening his belt. I noticed his excitement by the erection protruding from his boxers. I licked the pre-cum off of the head and moaned as I savored the taste. Maurice leaned his head back and sighed as I placed every inch of him inside my warm mouth. I played with my clit as I continued to stroke his manhood at the same time. Maurice, excited, pulled his erection from my mouth and slid underneath me as I squatted on the floor. I exploded instantly as his tongue made contact. I rocked back and forth, grinding his tongue against my clit before resuming the oral sex that I had initiated on him. We were now in the sixty-nine position. We satisfied each other, showing just how much we had missed one another. After he sucked most of the juices from me, I straddled him and rode him while he sucked each nipple equally. It didn't take long before we both exploded again.

Afterward, Maurice gave me a Tiffany necklace and bracelet that I had wanted for so long. I kissed him to thank him. We stayed in that day, talking and watching movies, but all day it was hard for me to concentrate on anything except for James. What had I gotten myself into?

CHAPTER 11

James: Eye On The Prize

1999

Mimi was fine, and there was no denying that. I knew that I would hit that from the first day that I saw her at Neisha's cookout. Sexy was an understatement when it came to describing her. Grading her looks on a scale of one to ten, she was an eleven, and the sex was even better. I knew that I wanted to wife her, but I wondered if she could be loyal or even trusted for that matter. Shorty had a man and still gave me the booty. What would stop her from giving it to the next man? I figured I would just have to put her ass in line, and I was definitely capable of that. That fat ass she carried behind her would be mine, and that was my decision. Fuck the nigga she was wit'!

The morning after Mimi came over, I called Mark to make some plans for the day, and the nigga was asleep. It was nine and his ass was snoring.

"Nigga, get up! It's money to be made," I yelled into the receiver.

"I was up, nigga," he said groggily. "What's the deal?"

"We got to meet at the spot to cook this meal, you know what I mean. A nigga is starving!" I said, speaking in codes.

"All right, man, I'll be there at ten."

"All right," I said and hung up the phone.

I was pissed that he wasn't ready. He was probably up fucking Neisha all night. He had to get that shit together ASAP. I went out to my car, got in, and blasted my radio. "I Got A Story To Tell" by Biggie Smalls was playing. I laughed because I, too, had just hit another nigga's girl, just like Biggie did in the song. I stopped at the corner breakfast store and ordered some breakfast. I still had time to waste since Mark was going to meet me at ten.

After eating I drove to the spot and waited for Mark to arrive. He arrived late, talking on his cellular phone. I smirked before he felt my wrath.

"Man, it's ten-thirty. Where the hell were you at? Time is money, man."

"Look, I'm here now. What the fuck is wrong with you today? You got your period or some shit!" he asked, ending his call.

"I'm just trying to get to work!"

"Well, let's get to work then."

We sat and cooked our product, distributed it to the runners, and were then done our work for the day. Mark picked up the money, so I was completely free. I went back to my spot and called a few people, doing some research on this distributor named Big T. I was finding out everything I could about him. Day by day I compiled enough information to ruin this nigga's life. I had to make it to the top by any means necessary. The City of Brotherly Love was too small for two kings. I found out that Big T didn't really deal with people too well on a friendship level. I could understand that because having too many friends could ruin you. But my angle was to get close to this dude and gain his trust, and when it was all said and done I would have everything of his, including his fine-ass wife!

The chick Mimi stayed on my mind. Although I had plenty of girls to hit on a regular basis, none were like her. I made sure that I was every place that she would be, with information courtesy of Neisha. Although I had been with many women, there were none that I could compare to Mimi. She was a perfect ten in my book, not on no love shit, but a ten with her figure and sex game. Any chick that could keep my attention days after I hit, that was definitely wifey material. I knew that she loved her man, but she already fucked it up with him by giving it up to me. Now that I had a taste, I wasn't going to give up, even if I had to go give that nigga Maurice a shout out myself. But Mimi still went clubbing on the weekends, and clubbing was cool for me too, so that's where I tried to see her.

It was always packed at Chrome on Columbus Boulevard on Sunday nights. I knew that Mimi would be there since Neisha told me that she would. I even knew what she would be wearing, so that it would be easier to spot her. Once Neisha and Mimi arrived, Neisha sent me a text message that simply said they were there. I put on my game face and began looking for them. Once I spotted them, I waited until Mimi was alone and I approached her.

"What's up, sexy?" I spoke in her ear.

"Nothing!"

"I know you miss me. I miss you. I want to smack that ass again!" I joked.

"People in hell want ice water too," she responded without any amusement.

"That's funny. But for real, you still holding on to that boy you were fucking with, or are you ready to get with a man?"

"I am with a man, and that's where I'm staying."

"You'll need me one day, baby, trust me. I'll make sure of that," I said before walking away.

I knew that she wanted me, but I guess she felt an obligation to her man. Soon he'd be out the way, though, and I would move right on in. I knew how to handle a chick like Mimi. She wanted to play hard to get, and that was OK. Eventually she'd be mine, whether she wanted to believe it or not.

I stayed at the club and got a few numbers before settling on a chick to take home The winner was this chick named Brenda. She reminded me of the LL Cool J song, "Big Ole Butt." This girl had the fattest ass I'd ever seen, and her small waist made it look even bigger. It was the type of ass that you could see from the front. I bought her enough drinks so that I was guaranteed to hit it. Even with all of the arguments from her girlfriends, she still stumbled her way out to my car. After closing the passenger side door, I gave Mark dap and hopped in my car to join her.

"You ready for a real ride, baby?" I asked with a devilish grin.

"I'm ready for whatever it is that you have to give me!"

"I hope you can fit all of me inside, because my stroke game is a beast!" I said, laughing.

"Oh, I can fit it anywhere you want to put it, baby!" She raised her skirt and pulled her panties to the side. Spreading her lips apart so that I could see her clit, she licked her index finger and began slowly stroking herself. She moaned loudly as I damn near crashed, getting excited from the scene that was playing out in front of me. Every so often she would take two fingers and put them deep inside, and then remove them to suck off her juices. I was so hard that I thought I was going to bust through the jeans I was wearing.

Once we pulled up to my spot I parked quickly, but before

I could get out she grabbed my arm and motioned for me to stay put. She unzipped my pants, pulled my length through the zipper, and began feasting on me. The warmth of her mouth wrapped around my shaft, along with the excitement of receiving head in this parking lot gave me a rush. I tried my hardest not to release too early, but I was fighting a war that I would not win because Brenda was like a professional when it came to giving head. She even swallowed every drop of cum, not letting any of it seep through her mouth.

I rushed to get out of the car to head upstairs and finish what we started. She quickly followed behind me as we ran to the door. As soon as we entered she began to remove her clothes. Her body looked even sexier naked. Her perky nipples stood at attention as I began to follow her lead and get undressed. I sat down on the chair as she got on top of me with her back facing me and rode me like there was no tomorrow. I reached my hand around and played with her clit with one hand while playing with her nipples at the same time. She contracted her walls around my shaft as I moved in and out of her. After she was satisfied with that position, she reached into her purse and pulled out some K-Y Jelly. I looked at her, stunned for a second because I had just felt how wet she was and knew that she didn't need any lubrication.

"What do you need that for?" I asked while stroking my shaft.

"So you can fit all of that into my ass!" she said, pointing in the direction of my length.

"Are you serious?" I asked, stunned. Although I had dreamed of giving a back shot, I had never found a woman who was willing to allow me to try it. I had heard so much about how tight it was and how it felt like you were fucking a virgin. I was excited that I was now going to experience it firsthand. Brenda walked over to me and poured some of the

K-Y Jelly onto my shaft as I stroked it. Then she bent over and poured some on her butt, letting it run between her cheeks. I walked over, and with a little force entered her hole and was shocked at how good it felt. It was as tight as a firmly gripped fist. I stroked in and out as she continued to moan until I exploded deep inside her. I pulled out and sat on the sofa, exhausted from the workout.

"So was it good to you, baby?" she asked, sitting down next to me.

"It was great. I'm definitely going to keep your number!" Brenda got up and began to get dressed as I sat there and watched. I was getting horny again just thinking about what had just happened. I put on my clothing and gave her a hug before going to the car and beginning the drive to her home. After driving her home, I called Mark to set up the schedule for the next day, and then I went home and took my ass to bed. I was beat. Good pussy will do that to you!

CHAPTER 12

Giselle: It's Party Time

2003

I knew that all eyes would be on me that night. As I looked in the mirror once more before I left, everything was perfect, as usual. You wouldn't catch me dead and looking a mess. My outfit consisted of a beaded Dolce & Gabbana jacket, denim booty shorts, and Manolo Blahnik knee boots.

I got in my car and made my way down to the club with the convertible top down, blasting "The Baddest Bitch" by Trina. That was my theme song. As I pulled up to the club, I could tell that it was packed because the line was wrapping around the corner. Mark was standing at the door with a couple of the club's security guards and bouncers.

"What's up, birthday girl? You look fine as always!" Mark nodded his head after looking me over.

"Thanks, Mark. Did my girls get here yet?"

"Yeah. They're up in VIP at your booth."

"Oh, OK. I'll see you later."

I walked through the club, saying hello to everyone while

making my way up to VIP. I spotted Shawn sitting at the bar, so I decided to make a pit stop and say hello.

"What's up, Shawn?" I asked, leaning in close to him.

"Nothing. What's up?" he replied, looking me up and down.

"I just wanted to say hello, that's all!"

"Oh, all right."

I turned around and began to walk away, hoping that he was watching my ass. He knew that I didn't come over there just to speak to him. I just wanted to make sure that he saw how good I looked. I turned around quickly before walking up the steps to the VIP lounge, and noticed that Shawn was still watching me. I switched my ass even harder.

Walking through VIP, I noticed my friends all sitting at the booth in the back. I walked over without them even noticing me.

"What the hell are y'all doing sitting down? This is a party!" I yelled, smiling.

"It took you long enough to get here. I like that outfit, girl!" Toya said after rising up out of the booth to hug me.

"Let's go out on the dance floor. I'm not about to sit up in here all night!" I directed as I began walking away from the booth.

They all followed my lead. Dancing was one thing that I loved. I knew that Shawn would never dance with me, since he wasn't even the dancing type. Instead of being shot down, I grabbed Tyrone, my ex, and went to work. Tyrone loved every minute of it. I had just broken it off with Tyrone two weeks ago, but I still had sex with him almost every other day. A girl still had to get hers, you know!

I was with Tyrone for two years, but I always knew that it wouldn't last forever. I met him at school. He was the same age as me and he didn't have any income except the money he begged his mother for every week. Going out to the movies with his broke ass every weekend was getting to be lame. I needed a dude with some real money, and I needed him quick. Tyrone did have a good shot, though. That's the only reason I was still having sex with his ass! Dancing freaky on the floor, I made sure that I was in Shawn's full view. Surprisingly, after seeing how freaky I was getting, Shawn came over and pulled me aside.

"Don't make me have to fuck one of these niggas up in here!" he said, yelling in my ear over the loud music.

"Why are you worried about me? You don't want me, so don't cock block the next nigga. You got a girl, remember!"

"Keep dancing like that and these niggas are going to think that they are getting some pussy!"

"Maybe they will!"

"Not tonight! You're going home after this party!"

"Shawn, you are not my father! My father's not here! If I want to go get some dick tonight, then that's what I'll do. I'm tired of chasing you around, Shawn. I need to get off just like you do!"

"By acting like a ho?"

"Whatever, Shawn! I've been with Tyrone for the last two years, and he's been hitting this almost every other day since day one. He's entitled to it if he wants it."

I turned my back and walked away. I didn't even want to hear another word from him at this point. I found Tyrone and continued working him on the dance floor, as I had been doing before I was so rudely interrupted. I didn't care if Shawn could see me or not!

After dancing to a few more songs, I went over to the bar to get me a drink. I was thirsty as hell after all of the dancing that I had done. Shawn came over and sat down next to me.

"Having a nice time, I see!" he said sarcastically.

"Why are you even talking to me, Shawn?"

"Look, I don't know what the hell your problem is tonight."

"You know what my problem is! I'm tired of playing these games with you, Shawn. Why don't you hurry up and get home to Gina, and let me do me! I'm sure that she would be very happy to see you."

"Why are you always bringing her up? This ain't got nothing to do with her. You say you want me, and I tell you to go home tonight partly because I'm going to be there, and you keep talking a bunch of other bullshit! Now if you think that going home with that broke-ass nigga and getting fucked is going to make me jealous or something, you're wrong! That will be on you!"

"Who said anything about making you jealous? I just want some dick!"

"You know what, Giselle? Do you!" he yelled angrily as he got up from the barstool and walked away.

At this point I was really confused on what Shawn was feeling. Sometimes it seemed as though he liked me, but then at other times he acted like he could never be with me. I wanted to be with Shawn since the first day I saw him three years ago. I could understand him not wanting me at fifteen, but now my age wasn't an excuse. And his girl was the same age as me, so that bullshit that he kicked back then about me being young meant nothing.

My brother once told me never to keep chasing a man because it made a woman seem desperate. If the nigga wanted you, he would chase you. I never listened to my brother, though, especially since he was always in trouble. He'd been in jail up Camp Hill for the past two years for a robbery. I thought that he could have gotten himself together, but he didn't want to. He loved the life that he was living. He wanted to be like my dad, and now he'd be in jail for the next three years!

I sipped my drink and thought hard before I decided that if, after tonight, nothing changed, I would stop chasing Shawn and move on with my life. It was almost two o'clock and they were playing the last song. My girls and I danced, and after the music stopped we said our good-byes. I looked around and noticed that Shawn had left, but Mark was still there. I walked over to where Mark was standing to ask him a question.

"Did Shawn leave yet?"

"Yeah, he left! He seemed like he was upset about something!"

"Oh, OK. Well I'm going home now. Thanks for everything," I said, beginning to walk away.

"All right. Be careful going home," Mark said before I left.

I left the club and made my way home. After getting in the house I realized how tired I was. I went upstairs and took a shower. After drying off, my doorbell began ringing. I put on a robe and went downstairs to answer it.

"Who is it?" I asked from behind the closed door.

"Who do you think?" Shawn asked sarcastically. I opened the door.

"What do you want?" I asked. "I told you that I didn't need you to stay here tonight."

"I was making sure you got home all right."

"Well, as you can see, I'm fine. Now you can go!" I said, beginning to close the door.

"I'm not leaving," he said, putting his hand in the door. "I told T that I would stay here with you tonight, and that's what I'm going to do." Then he pushed me out of the way and entered the house.

"Well, whatever. I'm going to my room. You know where the guest room is!" I began walking away in the direction of the stairs.

Suddenly I was startled when Shawn came up behind me

and wrapped his arms around me. He slowly kissed my ears and neck as I tilted my head back just enough for him to reach that spot that just made me weak. He untied my robe to expose my naked body underneath. After dropping my robe to the ground, he began to lower me down to the plush, carpeted floor. He stared into my eyes in silence and then leaned in to kiss me. His soft lips were even softer than I had expected.

After kissing and licking me from head to toe, I was exhausted from the many times I climaxed. But instead of taking off his clothes and continuing with the act that he had started, he picked me up off the floor, carried me to my bed, and laid me down. He stripped down to his boxers and slid under the covers behind me. After wrapping his arms around me, he fell asleep. I followed him into sleep shortly after that.

CHAPTER 13

Mimi: The Secret's Out

1999

The next two months were hard. I tried my best to duck James, but he somehow always found me no matter where I was. Maurice and I were still going strong and I was happy. I had moved past that dreadful mistake that I had made and I no longer felt guilty about it. Everything was going so well that I knew something had to go wrong. I could never have predicted the turn that my life was about to take. When things hit, they hit hard and that's what happened to me.

I began getting that sick feeling again, the one that I was getting every morning when I found out that I was pregnant with Tony's child. I was scared because I definitely wasn't ready for this now. I took a home pregnancy test and, sure enough, it was positive. Damn! I didn't want Maurice to do me like Tony did, so I had to make a choice. I could tell him and hope that he wouldn't dog me, or I could go get an abortion and never tell him about it. Then I began thinking that this might not be Maurice's baby. We always used a condom. *Shit! Shit! Shit!* This would definitely ruin my life. How the hell could I have been so stupid to get pregnant on a one-night stand? I never even thought to tell James to wear a condom because I was so caught up in the moment.

At this point I felt like my life was definitely coming to an end. I was so in love with Maurice and I could quickly lose everything all because of a mistake. I had to tell Maurice, since I wasn't about to get another abortion. Maybe it was his. Condoms did break! Maybe he wouldn't suspect me of cheating. I made my doctor's appointment for the following week. I would hold off on breaking the news to Maurice until then. But I decided to call Neisha and tell her the news.

"Hello!" she answered, yelling into the receiver.

"What's up? Girl, I got something so scandalous to tell you."

"For real? What's up? You know I love to hear some dirt!"

"You know that night after James' party I went home with him, right?"

"Yeah, he told me, even though you didn't!"

"Anyway, we had sex and now I'm pregnant!"

"What? Get the hell out of here! Do you know if it's his or Maurice's?"

"Maurice and I always use a condom. I am so mad at myself, Neisha. I love Maurice. I can't believe I did this."

"So what are you going to do?"

"I'm going to tell Maurice that it's his. What else am I going to do?"

"You can't do that, Mimi. You can't lie. If you are going to keep the baby, you have to tell both of them the truth. They are going to find out eventually, and you don't want to be on *Maury* ten years from now, trying to find out who's your baby's daddy!"

"I know. I'm going to the doctor on Wednesday, so I'll make my decision then."

"Well, OK. Just think about it before you do something crazy that could really ruin your life."

"I know. I'll call you later. I'm about to get dressed for school."

"OK."

Neisha was right. I couldn't lie. I didn't want to raise a child on a lie. A child needed a father, and the real father was even better.

I got dressed and went to school. After classes let out I was shocked to see James standing out in front of the building. Damn! What the hell was he doing here? I tried to act as if I didn't see him standing there, and he noticed my intent. He walked over to me and grabbed me by the arm.

"Get the fuck off of my arm like that!" I yelled, loosening my arm from his strong grip.

"So, what's this I hear, that you are pregnant with my baby?"

"What? Where the hell did you get that information? You better check your source because they are lying to you." I was going to kill Neisha. I loved her, but she had a big-ass mouth!

"My source is right. I see your ass is getting fat! Why weren't you going to tell me?"

"Tell you what? It's nothing to tell. I'm not pregnant!" I yelled.

"Whatever. You better not lie to that nigga and tell him that's his baby. Ain't no other nigga going to raise my baby. I'll make sure of that!"

"Whatever!" I said angrily, walking to my car.

After driving away I began crying. I didn't know what to do. My cell phone rang and startled me.

"Hello!"

"What's up? I came past your school today because I missed you. Seen you talking to that nigga James. What the hell was that about?"

"That's Neisha's cousin," I answered nervously. "He was telling me about a fight he had with Neisha and he asked me to talk to her for him."

"Oh, really? So if I ask him the same question will he tell me the same thing?"

"Yeah!" I lied, because I was sure that whatever he said it would far different from the lie that I just told.

"Well, where are you on your way to now?"

"I'm going to run home and see my grandmom and change my clothes."

"Well call me when you get done. I want to see you."

"OK! I love you."

He hung up. I cried the whole drive to my grandmom's house. My grandmom was sitting in the dining room reading the *Daily News*. I tried to conceal the sadness on my face with a smile, but she instantly noticed my despair.

"What's wrong, baby? You don't look so good."

"Grandmom, I don't know how to tell you this because I don't want you to be disappointed in me. I've been trying so hard to get my life back on track since Tony, and now I've screwed things up."

"How?"

"I'm pregnant!" I said as I began to cry.

"I had a feeling that you were, but I just wanted to wait and see if you would be honest with me. I'm not disappointed in you. I know that you've been trying. What is Maurice prepared to do?"

"I haven't told him yet."

"Well, you have to tell him."

"I'm just afraid that he won't want to be with me."

"Well, that shouldn't be the thing that makes you decide

what you want to do one way or the other. If you decide to have this baby, you have to know that ultimately this baby is yours. He might not always be around, so if you are going to have this baby, do it for you and only you."

I sat there quiet as I took all of it in. I was glad that my grandmom and I had been able to get close again. I let the relationship with Tony ruin everything. We had been getting back to normal, piece by piece. I would have never expected things to go so smoothly once I told my grandmom about the pregnancy. I just hoped that I would get the same reaction from Maurice, because I had settled on telling him that I was pregnant. I wasn't going to tell him about James, though, because I needed him to be with me. I had used him as a crutch since breaking up with Tony and just as if I had two broken legs, I needed him to keep standing.

I went upstairs and searched for something to wear. The few pounds that I had gained in the last two months were limiting my options. After I had changed I heard a knock at the door. I ran downstairs to answer it.

"Hey, baby, I was just about to—"

"You lying bitch!" he yelled, wrapping his hand around my neck. "After all the shit that I've done for you, and you go and get pregnant by another nigga? I should kill your ass right now!" Maurice yelled.

"What are you talking about?" I cried.

"Get the fuck off of her!" my grandmom yelled after hearing the commotion.

"It's OK, Grandmom."

"No, it's not OK. I'll be dammed if he's going to come here and hit you. I'll kill his ass first!"

"No, Grandmom, it's OK," I pleaded, trying to calm the situation. I began crying. "Maurice, please let's go somewhere and talk about this," I begged.

"Talk about what? That nigga James told me all about your

little one-night stand. I know that you haven't had a period, and I always use a rubber I can't believe you!"

"He's lying, baby. I'm not pregnant!"

"Mimi, don't lie to him. And who the hell is James?" Grandmom asked.

"Please, Maurice, let's go somewhere and talk!"

"Talk? The shit's hit the fan now, so you can kiss my black ass good-bye! This shit is over. You better hope that nigga treats you as good as I did!" he yelled, walking toward the door.

"Baby, please don't go. I love you! I'm not lying. I'm not pregnant, and I didn't cheat on you," I cried on my knees.

"Fuck you! You are just like the rest of these lying-ass hoes!"

He walked out and slammed the door. What the hell had just happened? My grandmother stood there with a disgusted look on her face. I knew that she didn't understand what was going on, and I knew that she definitely didn't know my reasons for lying to him. When I saw the look on his face I couldn't tell him that I was really pregnant. I knew that Maurice was smarter than that, and he would know that it couldn't possibly be his. I got up off the ground and didn't look my grandmother's way. Instead of speaking, she turned around and made her way back to the kitchen. I was embarrassed, and most of all pissed that I ruined the one good thing that I had going for myself.

I went upstairs and tried to hold it together so that I could ream Neisha out. I called Neisha to find out why she had ratted me out, and of course she didn't answer the phone. I screamed because I was so upset. What the hell was I supposed to do now without Maurice? I remembered what Tony had done to me, and that's exactly what I had done to Maurice. How could I have done that knowing how painful it was? I called James.

"Speak!"

"Why the hell are you trying to ruin my life? What did I ever do to you?"

"Look, I'm trying to make your life better. I told you that no other nigga was going to raise my baby. Did you think I was bullshittin'?"

"What am I supposed to do? The man I love just walked out on me all because of a stupid mistake. I wish I never met you!"

"That's not true, ma. I made you feel good that night, and something good came from it. I'm glad that you're having my seed. You have no other choice but to be my girl now."

"I do have a choice. Fuck you!" I yelled before hanging up.

I fell down to the floor crying. Was he right? Did I not have any other choice? Without a man there was no way that I could take care of a baby, nor could I get an abortion, because without Maurice I was broke as a joke!

I did some serious thinking over the next few weeks and nothing was panning out for me. Since my grandmom was pissed that I lied, she hadn't been much help in steering me in the right direction. Once the weekend rolled around I was excited since I needed time to relax. I came home from the school that Friday damn near running to the bed. My grandmother wasn't home, but I didn't think much of it since she sometimes went to her girlfriend's house. The following morning when I woke up and checked her room I noticed that her bed hadn't been slept in and I began to worry since my grandmom never stayed out overnight. I went downstairs and saw the light flashing on the answering machine. I pressed play, hoping that there was a message from her.

"Hey, Melissa, this is your mother. I'm here at Hahnemann Hospital in Center City with your grandmom. When you get this message, you need to get down here as soon as you can because the doctors aren't sure how long she's going to hold on. She's really sick, Melissa, so hurry!"

I stood there in shock for a second. I had just seen my grandmom the previous morning before I went to school and she definitely didn't look sick. I didn't know what the hell was going on, nor did I know how the hell Tonya found out before me. I knew that my grandmom and her still talked, but did she come by the house when I wasn't home? I wondered if she'd been around the entire time and my grandmom just never told me. I got dressed and drove down to the hospital. After passing patient information I was on my way up to the twelfth floor intensive care unit. I noticed my mom standing by Grandmom's bed side and I grew sick to my stomach. Here she was, playing the caring daughter when she never even cared about her own daughter. I walked into the room and she turned to look at me.

"I'm glad you made it," she said, reaching out to hug me.

"Well, what happened? And how did you get here?" I asked, walking past her and ignoring her call for affection.

"Your grandmother hadn't been taking her heart medications correctly. I tried to get money to her so that she could always keep a stock of medication, but sometimes she wouldn't let me know that she was out of it. She hated to beg me for money. She told me that you had been helping her out with buying the medicine, and I believed her. She had a severe heart attack yesterday, and the only thing keeping her alive is the ventilator and all of those fluids you see going into that IV."

"So what are you trying to tell me? My grandmom is going to die?" I asked as tears began to flow.

"I'm telling you that she's already gone, Melissa."

"No, she's not gone."

"Baby, I only kept her on the machine so that you could see her before she went. There is nothing else that they can do."

"You are not taking her off anything! You haven't even been around. I have, and I'm not going to let you kill her!" I yelled as I cried uncontrollably.

"Melissa, I'm her child and I am the one that has the authority to make that decision!" my mother yelled back.

"Is everything OK?" the nurse quizzed after hearing our voices from the desk.

"Everything's OK. She's just upset," Tonya informed the nurse.

"OK. Well. let me know if you need anything," the nurse said before leaving the room.

"I sure will," Tonya replied. "Look, Melissa, I'm not here to fight with you, and I know that you love your grandmom, but there is nothing that is going to bring her back to you now. You have to come to grips with that."

"I don't have to do anything! And if you wouldn't mind, I would like to have some time alone with my grandmom, please."

"I'll give you some time, Melissa, but it's not going to change anything."

"Please go!" I yelled as the river of tears continued to flow.

I walked over and stood next to the bed. I couldn't believe that I was about to lose the only family that I had. I grabbed onto one of her hands as tears dropped onto them and rolled off. She was swollen everywhere, which I assumed was because of the tremendous amount of fluids they were giving her. I didn't know what to say or do, but as I sat there I felt like I should apologize for not paying closer attention to her.

"Grandmom, I hope you can hear me. I am so sorry. I wish that I had known you needed money for your medicine. I need you, Grandmom. You know that you're all that I've got.

I wanted you to be here and see your great-grandbaby. I know that somehow you'll always be around, but I don't know how I am going to keep myself straight without you here to crack that whip. Why did this have to happen now?" I asked as I laid my head down on the bed next to her. "I love you, Grandmom!"

I sat up and looked at her once more before I kissed her good-bye. I knew that my mother was going to take her away from me and there was nothing else that I could do. I wasn't going to sit around and watch my mother end the life of the only person that meant more to me than myself. I walked out of the room and past Tonya without saying a word. I couldn't even bring myself to look her in the eye. I went out to the car and screamed. I beat on the steering wheel and dashboard to try to release my sadness. Nothing could bring her back. I needed to call someone before I lost it.

I called Maurice because I needed him, and I cried when he told me to go to hell and hung up on me.

I couldn't think of anyone else to call but James since I was still pissed at Neisha. I dialed his number, and after I told him what had happened, I was totally shocked when he offered to meet me at my house and lay with me. He came over, lay in the bed with me, and never said a word. With his arm wrapped around me, I cried for what seemed like hours until I fell asleep.

James was there for me that day and every bad day I had thereafter. He stayed at my house with me every night making sure that I was able to fall asleep. Even though I was upset by the way he forced himself into my life, at this point it didn't matter. He was there for me in my time of need.

The day of the funeral was really hard. James helped me get dressed and helped me fix my hair. I was so depressed. I sat in my room staring at the floor when Tonya walked into the room.

"Hey, Baby Girl! You look so grown up now. I didn't really get to talk to you the other day at the hospital."

"What are you here for?"

"It was my mother, Melissa. What do you mean?"

"Now she's your mother? Where have you been all of these years?"

"I've been living in New York, trying to get my life together. I'm doing well now. I've been talking to her almost every day."

"Well, hooray for that! Guess you forgot you had a child, huh?"

"Never. I love you, Melissa, and I think about you every day. I miss you."

"Well, sorry, but I didn't miss you! You left me. How could you just leave your child?"

"Melissa, I'm sorry. I know that I was wrong, but I was young and dumb. I'm older and wiser now, and I can admit to my mistakes. That's why I want you to come to New York with me."

"Never in a million years. My life is here. And the name is Mimi, so please stop calling me Melissa. I hate it, just like I hate you!"

"Well, I tried. I wanted to tell you that your grandmom left this house to me, and I'm selling it. So I guess you'll have to find somewhere else to live."

"What?" I asked angrily.

"She'll be fine. She's marrying me anyway. Come on, babe, let's go to pay respects to your grandmom, who was obviously a better woman than your mother!" James said, grabbing my hand and leading me out of the room.

"Well I'm glad you have someone to help you. I would hate to see you out on the streets!"

"You don't care about me, so stop acting like it. I hope that the rest of your life is as miserable as you made mine when you walked out on me!" I turned my back and walked toward the stairs where James was waiting. I walked out and I vowed never to talk to her again. I never even wanted to speak her name. This so-called mother of mine would be wiped completely out of my life.

Nothing had changed with her. Tonya was still all about Tonya, and no one else mattered. Not even her daughter.

CHAPTER 14

Shawn: Daddy's Little Girl

2003

I decided to hit Gina one more time before I let her go. I have to admit that during the last two years, she'd been the best of them all. I went to her crib early after skipping out on Giselle the morning after her birthday. I had recently put up the money to get Gina an apartment of her own, since it was hard to get with her at her mom's house. I used my key and found her asleep in the large, king-sized bed. I took off all of my clothes and slid in bed behind her. She woke up a little startled.

"Damn, Shawn, you scared me!"

"Oh, really?"

"Yeah. Where were you last night?"

"Home," I said, kissing her neck.

"Shawn, stop."

I continued to kiss her softly on her neck,

"Did you miss me?" I whispered in her ear.

"Of course I did, Shawn!" She smiled.

"Well, show me how much."

"Where have you been, Shawn? I'm not trying to go down on you after you've just been fucking somebody else."

"I haven't been fucking nobody else, Gina. Why the hell would you ask me that?"

"Because I know you, Shawn, and I know that you fuck around."

"Look, I'm with you now, so let's not talk about nobody else," I said while I began to caress her breast.

"Shawn."

"Come on, Gina, I know you want it," I said, moving my hands down into her shorts.

I continued to caress her down below, and it wasn't long before she gave up her fight. She began to go down on my erect member, wrapping her lips around it. I let out a loud sigh as she made contact with her tongue. I had trained Gina well over the course of this relationship. She had gone from practically a virgin to a vixen, and it was great. Not wasting any time, I bent her over with her hands holding firmly on to the headboard. She arched her back without hesitation as I entered her. Her large breasts swung back and forth as I pumped harder and harder, picking up speed.

I tore her back out like it was the last time I would ever get some ass in my life. She enjoyed it, too, just as much as I did, if not more. After the episode was over, I took a quick shower. Dropping Gina two Gs, I told her that it was over. I know that it was cold, but at least I gave her some dough. She'd find another nigga anyway, especially after being with me. She was a prize now. She cried, of course, but she'd get over it. I closed that chapter of my life and left the apartment.

After checking in with Mark, I drove back to Giselle's house. I had finally stopped fighting my temptation to be with her. Giselle had been in my mind since the day we went to rob her house. I couldn't kill her that day because there was something about her that weakened me a little. When she looked up at me with tears in her eyes, I felt bad about what I'd done. I wanted to tell her that I was sorry, but I couldn't. I couldn't deal with her back then because I would continuously get flashbacks of the night that I snatched her mother away from her. I knew that it would be hard to deal with her under T's nose, but I had to make up for what had happened to her, since she was never the intended target. Although I was cold when it came to men, I did have a soft spot when it came to women. I mean, what man didn't?

I still had to go through with my plan, and I prayed that dealing with Giselle wouldn't fuck things up. I thought that this angle would only get me closer to Big T. If I treated Daddy's little girl right, Daddy would fall right into the trap.

CHAPTER 15

Mimi: A New Life

2000

I moved in with James the following week. My mother didn't waste any time putting up the for-sale sign on the house, either. I didn't care because I was beginning a new life one that would only make me stronger in the long run. Things between James and I were turning out much better than I had originally expected. I was growing bigger every day and although I hated the new look, James never stopped telling me how beautiful I was. His compliments made it that much easier for me to overlook the fact that I was turning into a whale. I was almost five months pregnant when James surprised me with a special date. We hadn't been out that much since most days, I was too tired to do anything. He bought me a beautiful Chanel dress that was amazing on me with the glow that pregnancy had contributed. The black-and-white dress complemented my skin tone and was enough to turn heads. I was excited when James came home, and ready to go.

"Damn, you look great, baby. That dress is crazy!" He smiled before hugging me. I was falling in love with James over and over again. I never would have thought that it was possible after the turmoil our connection caused. I was unaware of how loving and affectionate he could be, since he had come into my life like a menace.

"Thanks. I'm so excited about going out tonight. It's been such a long time."

"I know, but this is going to be a night that you won't forget."

"Well, I'm ready to go when you are," I said, extending my hand for him to hold.

Once we reached the restaurant, we were escorted to the table that he had previously reserved. I smiled as he sat down in front of me and blew me a kiss. James looked remarkable in his all-white linen suit. His smile sparkled and made me melt inside.

"So what's so special about tonight?" I was still in a trance and mesmerized by his beauty.

"Look, I know that when we met I came off a little crazy, but I believe that I've made up for that. I really wanted to be with you because I saw something special in you. I wanted to get a hold of you and never let you go. Now that I have you, I intend to do that. So, basically I want you to agree to be mine forever. I want you to marry me," he said, pulling a small black ring box from his pants pocket. I still wasn't sure what was happening. I was dumbfounded as he opened the box that displayed a huge yellow solitaire diamond. I wanted to snatch it out of his hand, but I wanted to make sure that it was something that I really wanted to do. Did I really want to marry him? Was I capable of holding down the title of a wife? James waved his hands in front of my face, trying to get me out of the daydream that I was in.

"Baby, are you going to answer me so I can put it on your finger, or are you going to keep staring at it?"

"Yes, baby, I'll marry you," I said as a tear dropped out of my eye. I extended my hand so that he could place the ring on my finger. I stood up from the table to lean over and kiss him. I was on cloud nine as I stared at the beautiful jewel he'd given me.

"I want to get married before the baby is born. I think it's important for a baby to be born with married parents."

"I can't believe that you actually want to marry me."

"Believe it, because you're mine forever!"

It wasn't long before we were on our way to Las Vegas, to return as husband and wife. It was only a month after the engagement and it was still too good to be true. Once we landed back in Philly he took me to a house that I didn't recognize. I sat there in the car as he got out and walked around to the passenger door.

"Whose house is this?"

"It's my mom's. It's about time that you meet her, don't you think?"

"What? Why didn't you tell me, James? I look horrible."

"My mom won't care about that. Besides, you don't look horrible. You look gorgeous. Come on, let's go," he said, motioning me to get out. I stood up with butterflies in my stomach. I wished that he had told me that we were coming here so that I could have prepared myself. We walked up to the steps. I stood nervously as James used his key to open the door.

"Mom!" he yelled as we entered the small row home.

"I'm in the kitchen!" a voice yelled from the back of the house. He grabbed my hand and led me through the hallway into the kitchen.

"Oh. So, this must be Miss Mimi. We finally get to meet,"

she said, rising from her chair to hug me. I stuck my arms out to return the affection. She stood back and smiled as she began to rub my round stomach.

"Nice to finally meet you."

"Yeah, I've been fussing at him for months to bring you by. How was Vegas?"

"Besides the heat, it was wonderful."

"Well, let me see the ring," she said, grabbing at my hand. "You outdid yourself, James. This is beautiful!"

"I know," James said, smiling. "Well, Mom, we have to get home, but I just wanted you two to meet. I'll give her your number so she can call you sometime."

"OK, baby. Well thanks for coming. She sure is pretty, James. Good job, baby!" she said before hugging him. She walked over to give me another hug before we were on our way. I was pleased that I'd finally met his mom. I'd heard numerous stories about her, but I'd never thought about bugging him to meet her. I figured that he would take me when the time was right.

Things were getting better by the day with James, and in a way I was glad that I'd met him. He was changing my life for the better. My past was just a distant memory, and all of the heartache was long gone. I ran into Maurice around the way every now and then, but he didn't even speak to me, which was just fine with me. His new girlfriend, Octavia, made sure of that!

James and I made love that night and it was much different than any other time, because now we were husband and wife.

The day before my ninth month of pregnancy was to begin, I went into labor and it was the scariest and most painful thing that I ever experienced in my life. How women do this over and over again, I'll never know because this was my last time going through this for sure. Our daughter, Alyia Renee

Wilson, was born that night, and that changed my life forever. I was now a mother and no longer a little girl. I had to be an example for her and I vowed to do that from that day forward.

Alyia was the most beautiful thing I'd ever seen. She had jet black, curly hair and fair skin. I fell in love with her instantly. How could you be in love with someone that you just met? That's exactly how I felt as soon as the doctor placed her on my stomach. James was so supportive. He was there with me every step of the way. He even stayed in with me for a week, once I came home from the hospital. He allowed Mark to handle all of his affairs so he could take care of the two women in his life. James's mother, Ms. Marie, was at the house as well. She warmed up to me quickly and I warmed up to her, too.

My daughter had the best of everything. Her father made sure that she wore baby Dior every day, since he loved expensive things.

After my marriage to James and the birth of Alyia, Neisha and I patched up our differences. I now knew what and what not to tell her. Even though everything turned out good for me in the end, I knew that I could never tell her any important information that could have a detrimental effect on my life.

After Alyia was born, I was finally able to finish high school. It was hard, but I made it through. I had no job except for caring for Alyia, so James decided that I would be his personal tailor. Since he was beginning to make more money, he wanted to dress the part. I put my fashion designing talents to use, and my man was sharp every day, wearing custom-made shit.

One Saturday morning, as I was fitting him for a pair of jeans, James told me briefly about his master plan to be on top of the drug game.

"I got a plan, baby. I'm going to be on top, believe me."

"I believe you."

"I don't think you understand. It's real serious, and I need to be sure that you will stand by me all the way."

"You know I will. I just hope that this plan doesn't put me or your child in danger."

"Never that. You'll be fine. Trust me. We are going to be rich one day."

I did believe him. Why wouldn't I? He told me that his plan meant that he basically had to become a different person. He also told me that he would have to deal with a few chicks to get to the big man on top. He said that this new name and persona would just be an act, an act that I would have to deal with. I had no other choice because I was his wife, and I had to be the best wife that I could be.

In the following weeks I continued to live normally. My life had fallen into a routine. I woke up, played with the baby, and sewed for James. I waited for him to come home every night to have sex, and then I went to bed. How lame was that?

One Sunday night I waited and waited for James to come home. It was four A.M. and he still had not arrived. I was worried. Because of the life he lived, I never knew what to expect. I called his cell phone and only got the voicemail. I went downstairs and sat, and then I went back up to the room and sat. I was driving myself crazy. When he finally arrived, he had a look on his face like he had seen a ghost. Sweat was pouring from his face and his clothing was soaked.

"Baby, what's wrong? What happened?"

"I fucked up, I fucked up!" he yelled.

"What are you talking about? What happened?"

"I went to rob this house of this big drug distributor. That was plan A. The nigga wasn't there. His wife and kids were. I knew that the bitch knew where the money was, but she wouldn't tell me. She just wouldn't tell me. I didn't go there to kill nobody, baby. I just wanted to get the money for us. That's all."

"Kill somebody? James, what did you do?" I began crying.

"I killed her!"

"You killed who?"

"His wife. I killed her. It happened so fast. It wasn't supposed to happen like that. I fucked up!"

I didn't know what to say and I didn't really even know how to feel. I did feel sorry for that woman's children, and I did feel that what he did was wrong, but I had to stick by him, even though I knew that what he did could never be forgiven. I cried that whole night while holding him. He had never killed anyone before, but this event would change him for the worse. As if killing this man's wife wasn't enough, he had to go deeper to get what he really wanted—the title of king. He vowed to snatch the title from this man at any and all costs.

CHAPTER 16

Giselle: Where Do We Go From Here?

2003

I woke up the next morning and found only an empty space next to me with a note Shawn had left. The note read:

Hey, Shorty,

Sorry I had to run out so early this morning. I have some things to handle. T should be back in town tonight, but if there is anything you need later, call my cell and let me know. I'll holla!

I wasn't surprised that he left. He probably had to run to see Gina. I wasn't even going to worry about that because I received the best treatment to my body last night, including the best oral sex anyone had ever given me. I got up and took a shower quickly because for some reason, I was starving. I got dressed and walked to the breakfast store around the corner. I wasn't sure what I would do today since it was Sunday.

I could go shopping, but Toya probably wouldn't feel like going.

After going home and eating my breakfast, I picked up the phone to dial Shawn's number. I wasn't sure what to say. I didn't know where we would go from this point. Did last night mean that we would eventually be together? Or did he just satisfy me to shut me up? I put the receiver down quickly and decided not to call. Instead, I dialed Toya.

"Hello!"

"What's up, girl?"

"What the hell are you doing calling me this early? You know I sleep late on Sundays!"

"I just wanted to know what you were doing today. I was bored as hell. I can't stay in here all day."

"I don't know, but I'll call you later when I get up."

"OK!" I said, ending the call.

I wished that I could sleep late like that, but I was an early riser. I sat down and watched TV, thinking about the previous night's events. No one ever treated me like that. No one ever cared if I was satisfied too. I was so deep in thought that I didn't hear the doorbell ring. I did hear a loud knock, though. I got up to answer the door.

"Surprised to see you!" I said.

"Why is that? After last night I thought you'd be glad I came back," Shawn said, smiling.

"I'm glad, but why did you have to run out so early?"

"I told you in the note that I had some things to handle."

"Well, come in," I said, glad that he was there.

"Naw. I came to scoop you up to go out to lunch. We need to talk."

"OK, but can I change first?"

"For what? You look fine like that!"

"All right." If he felt that I looked good, I was cool with that.

We sat silently on the ride to the City Avenue Olive Garden. When we reached the restaurant and were seated, I quickly asked Shawn what it was that we needed to talk about.

"I ended it with Gina today," he said. "That's one thing that I handled this morning."

"Why did you do that?"

"Because I'm going to give it a try with you. Hopefully you can change some of your ways and things can work out."

"I'm me, Shawn! What's wrong with the way that I am?"

"You know what I mean. The clothes, the dudes, the attitude!"

"Well, what about you? What about all of those chicks that you be having sex with?"

"Look, you know the life that I live, and those hoes are nothing to me. Either you want to be my girl, or you don't."

"So what does that mean?"

"Exactly what I said. The choice is yours."

"Shawn, you know that I've wanted to be your girl since I was fifteen."

"Well then, it's settled. Tell them corny, broke-ass niggas to back down or their asses are going to end up in the morgue."

"Why do I need to say all that? If they know that I deal with you, then that will be enough said."

"Whatever! You heard what I said. Now since you're my girl, after we eat we are going back to my place so I can give you this mean stroke!"

We both laughed. I felt so close to Shawn, and I was excited about our future. I knew that those chickenheads he fucked on the side were no match for me, but the test would be in how long I could deal with them. I knew that Gina would be torn because her money train just went to a new station, but hell if I cared I got my man.

We talked over lunch and I learned so much about Shawn that I never knew. He told me about his life growing up. He grew up with his mother and five brothers and sisters. Their family never had much because his mother was raising all six children alone. They never had money or new clothes, and sometimes they didn't even have food to eat. She never received money from their fathers. Shawn's father was a big-time drug dealer back in the day, and Shawn always wanted to live like that one day.

His father had all the cars, women, and anything else a man could dream of. Although Shawn despised him for not taking care of his responsibilities, he loved the life that Big Mike lived. When Shawn was fifteen, Big Mike was killed in a shootout with the Camden County Police. Mike's family sued the city and actually won, but because Mike had so many children, by the time Shawn got his share, there wasn't much left.

By that time Shawn had already started selling weed. He then moved on to cocaine and heroin. He made a lot of money, but not enough because he still wanted to be the big man on top. Even though he was a partner with my dad, he wanted to run his own empire, like Big Mike.

Shawn also told me about his oldest brother being killed in a drive-by shooting. Shawn's mother worked from job to job, trying to make ends meet for the remaining children. She turned to God and was now doing fine. All of her children were grown and had moved out. She could now relax and live her own life after all of those hard years.

We finished lunch and made our way to Shawn's car. Hearing the way Shawn grew up made me look at him differently. I now understood why he was the way he was.

On the drive to Shawn's place I was excited. I'd never

been inside his house before. I'd only sat outside in the car while my dad went inside. I always dreamed about the day when Shawn would take me to his home for mad, passionate sex, and now my dream was about to come true.

We pulled up in the driveway, and to both of our surprise Gina was sitting on his front steps. I knew that I should prepare myself to fight, so I took off my earrings, placed them in my purse, and reached for a band to pull my hair back.

"What are you doing?" Shawn asked.

"Getting ready in case this bitch wants to fight."

"Ain't nobody fighting! Just sit here and let me handle this!"

"But—"

"I said sit here, Giselle, and I mean that shit!" Getting out of the car and slamming the door, Shawn began to walk in Gina's direction. "What the fuck are you doing here, Gina?" he yelled.

"Look, baby, we can work this out. It can't be over. Come on, let's go inside and talk," she begged, grabbing his arm as he approached her.

"You need to go home! I told you this morning we were through. I'm not going to say that shit again!"

"Are you showing off for that bitch in . . ." Noticing that it was me in the car, she continued on a different track. "You frontin' on me for that ho, Shawn? What the fuck is this about? You with her now?" Then she began to cry.

"It doesn't matter. I'm not with you, Gina."

"Why don't you get out of the car, bitch!" Gina yelled in my direction. "Stop hiding."

"Get the fuck out of here before I hurt you," Shawn yelled with frustration evident in his voice.

"I'll leave now, but this shit ain't over. Bitch, I know where you live. You better believe that you'll be seeing me soon!"

I gave her the middle finger as she walked to her car. There wasn't a bitch on this earth that scared me. I don't know where she got the balls to threaten somebody, like she could fight. I had saved her ass from many ass whippings in the past.

Shawn motioned for me to get out of the car, and I obeyed. I'd seen how Shawn got when he was angry, so I definitely didn't want to get on his bad side.

I entered his house and it was beautiful. It didn't look like a man's home. The furniture was light colored, the floors were light oak wood, and the walls were an eggshell color that matched well. It looked like a home out of a magazine.

"This is very nice, Shawn. I'm impressed!" I said, walking around to view the decor of his house.

"Why is that? I'm a stylish nigga, so you should have known my house would be the shit!" Shawn spoke with confidence while walking closer to where I was standing in front of the fireplace.

"Yeah, you're right about that," I said, generously paying him a compliment.

"You might as well get naked, baby," he whispered in my ear, "'cause I'm about to tear that ass up!" Then he took a step back and smiled at me with a devilish grin that was so damn sexy.

Knowing that I couldn't resist, I still had to play the game.

"Well, what if I say no?" I asked playfully.

"You've been chasing this dick for years now! After I let you touch it, ain't no way you gonna say no!"

He looked me up and down and licked his sexy-ass lips before he kissed me. I was in heaven. I'd been kissed by a lot of dudes before but never like that. I wanted to explode right there. You know it's meant to be when a kiss has that effect on you.

Noticing that I had already come once, he took total control by ripping my shirt off and popping every button. I could count them from the sound of every one of them as they hit the hardwood floor. He pulled my left breast out of my bra and ferociously began licking and sucking on it. After about two minutes he picked me up and started to kiss me again. *Damn, he's the best kisser ever!* I thought. He carried me upstairs to the bed and laid me down. Luckily I wasn't wearing any panties because he would have ripped them too. He lifted my skirt and smiled after noticing I was panty-less. He licked and sucked for what felt like an eternity, causing a never-ending orgasm. He stripped off his clothes and stood in front of me naked, fondling himself and asking me if I wanted a taste. Knowing my head game was tight, I sat up and without saying a word, I went to work.

Loving every minute of it, he called my name, reassuring me that the job was well done. I wanted him inside me and I let him know it. He turned me over and entered me from behind. He was a thug, and he showed it by the way he worked it in bed. He went harder and faster than anyone I'd ever been with. He then pulled out, grabbed some oil from the bedside table, and poured it all over my back and butt. He licked it, so I assumed it was edible, plus I could smell the cherry aroma. Before I could say stop, he rammed his dick in my butt so fast that I screamed from the excruciating pain. He didn't stop, only telling me it would get better. I grabbed the pillow and buried my face in it. I didn't want to tell him to stop because I wanted to please my man. And it did actually start to feel good after about ten minutes.

We continued in many positions until he reached his climax. He lay next to me on the bed. I was exhausted and in pain. But it was all for him, and I wanted him to know that I would do anything to make him happy.

"That was good! I know you're probably in pain right now, but it will get better. Trust me!" He rubbed my back and kissed me on the shoulder.

"I'm glad you liked it. I'll do anything to make you happy," I assured him.

"That's good to hear, baby. It's hard to find a girl like that. That's the kind of girl you hold on to. As long as you stay down for me like that, you'll never have to worry about anything. I guarantee that."

We lay there for a few minutes and then we both showered and got dressed. Since Shawn had ripped my shirt, I had to tie it in a knot and let my bra show. He thought it was funny, saying I liked to be half naked anyway. I laughed, but I also made him give me the eighty dollars that I paid for it, so I could buy another one. He dropped me off a block away from my house so that Daddy wouldn't see that he dropped me off. He told me he would call me later after he handled all of his business.

I walked the block to my house and noticed that my dad's car wasn't in the driveway. Shit, he wasn't even home. I walked that block for nothing! I went in the house and ran a hot bath. I had to soak because my butt was killing me. After I finished my bath, I decided to lie down.

I lay on my bed, smiling, because I was so happy. I had wanted Shawn from the first day that I saw him. I had loved him for years. There was just something about a thug with money that turned me on. Shawn was the finest thug I'd ever seen. He was tall, about six-two with light brown skin and perfect teeth. His hair was always braided to perfection. I was sure whoever the chick was that did his hair was paid well, because his braids were always neat and redone once a week. The way he dressed was flawless. He didn't dress like the average thug. He always wore tailor-made clothes. He had a chick named Mimi that sewed only for him. He was her one and only customer. He wore a new outfit every day, and every weekend he would be fitted for his next week's worth of clothing. I couldn't wait until I could wear tailor-made shit every day. I had money, but not like that. My dad wouldn't let me get my hands on that kind of money. He said that my mind wasn't ready for it.

At that point I didn't have a problem with my dad's policy because Shawn was here and I knew that he would look out for me. The only thing was that we had to figure out how we would tell Daddy the news. My dad was crazy, and if any dude even looked at me in his presence, he would be dead or close to it by the end of the day. I didn't know how he would react to me and Shawn being an item. For one, Shawn was his partner and that was a no-no. Secondly, Shawn was twenty-five and I was eighteen. And finally, Shawn dealt with a lot of girls, and my dad knew it. I really didn't care, as long as he took care of home. Any other chick that he dealt with was definitely not a threat to me.

Later that night, Shawn called me and told me that he had just gotten off the phone with Daddy and that he would be coming home soon. We made plans to meet after Daddy made it in the house. I was so excited. I loved the thrill of doing sneaky things. It always gave me a rush when I did something that I knew was forbidden.

I picked out a pink Baby Phat dress and sandals. I took a nice, hot bath and waited for Daddy to come home. Just as I was about to take a nap, I heard the door open downstairs. He was home. I got up off the bed and ran downstairs to see him. I was always nervous when Daddy went on out-of-town business meetings. I always worried that he wouldn't make it home. After greeting my dad, I made up a story about going out with Toya and Shay. He believed me, of course. My father thought that I would never lie to him. What a joke!

I got in my car and drove over to Shawn's house for round two of what I received that morning. He was waiting for me with roses all over the bedroom. I had the biggest smile on my face, and so did he after he saw how impressed I was. He had on a T-shirt that was fitted like the ones worn by the rapper 50 Cent, showing off his muscular build. Damn, I felt like I had hit the jackpot or something.

Shawn instructed me to strip off my clothes and dance for him. Dancing was definitely my forte, so I didn't have a problem with doing that at all. I removed every article of my clothing, performing a sexy routine that I had practiced at home. I always wanted to dance for my man, but I never had the opportunity. I could tell that Shawn loved my routine. He just sat there, licked his lips, and stared at my every move. Once I was finished he grabbed my hand and pulled me down to the bed. He began kissing me all over my body, sending chills up and down my spine. He turned me over, rubbed some warming massage lotion all over my back, and gave me the best massage that I'd ever received. I was definitely in love. Shawn made love passionately to me that night, and I was in heaven. If this was a dream, I wanted to stay asleep forever.

I couldn't stay the night because Daddy didn't allow me to spend the night out after I snuck over to Tyrone's house one night and my father found out. So Shawn kissed me goodbye, and I made my way home. I felt like I was on cloud nine. I made it home in record time, about five minutes short of my curfew. My dad asked me if I had a nice time, and I told him that I had. I sat in the kitchen and talked to my dad for a few minutes. It was the first time in a while that we had a good conversation. I missed our talks, but lately he'd been so busy that he never had time. I wished that I could share my happiness about Shawn, but I knew that I couldn't. Eventually Daddy would find out, though, when the time was right.

CHAPTER 17

James: The Closer I Get

2000

I was shook for days after killing Big T's wife. I dreamed about that day over and over again because the shit went totally different than I had planned. I wanted to rob that nigga blind so that he would have trouble trying to re-up, but his wife was there yelling and screaming. About a week after the murder I hooked up with Mark to go over our next move. It was too late to turn back now, because we were in too deep. I drove to Mark's apartment and stood at the door for what seemed like an hour before he opened it.

"What the fuck took you so long?" I yelled.

"I was in the shower!"

"Are you here alone?" I looked around the apartment.

"Yeah. Neisha left a little while ago. Why are you all paranoid and shit?"

"Nigga, I'm not paranoid. I'm just making sure it's cool to talk," I said, sitting down at the table.

"Everything's cool. Are you sure you're OK?"

"Look, we have to move on to plan B."

"OK, so what's that?"

"We can use the Columbian connect to entice Big T. I want to tell this nigga that we have this connect that could save him a hell of a lot of money. I know he's going to do some research, but he'll trust me because him and my dad used to run together back in the day. Then I'll throw the partnership card out on the table. Since Shawn is my middle name, I'm going to use that shit instead of James, and you should think about changing your name too. Once I get him to be partners with us, I can start learning the shit I need to know to take him down. I want his rep on the street to depreciate so much that niggas will laugh at him when he throws out an order. I want all of those same niggas to answer to me."

"Well, the plan sounds cool, but I'm not changing my name."

"Well, suit yourself. I'm planning on stepping to that nigga tonight at his club to leave him a number to call when he wants to meet."

"So you really think it's going to be that easy?"

"I'm not saying it's going to be easy, but I don't think it'll be extremely hard. This nigga just lost his wife, so he's not going to be thinking his sharpest. I think this is the perfect time to get in."

That night Mark and I were our way to Big T's club to initiate contact with him. The club wasn't all that packed since it was still early. Mark went up to the bar while I made my way to the door that obviously led to T's office, because of the security that was standing guard in front of it. I had to think fast since I knew these thick-ass niggas weren't going to just let me walk through to the office. As I got closer, the two men zeroed in on me.

"Can I help you?" the larger one asked in a deep tone.

"Yeah, my name is Shawn. I'm here to see Big T."

"See him about what?"

"About a business proposition."

"Does he even know you, nigga?" the other guard quizzed.

"No, but he knows my pop. Tell him Big Mike's son is here."

"Big Mike?"

"He'll know him."

"Wait here!" the tall, black-ass dude said before entering the office.

The shorter one stood there staring at me, as I stared back. This was the ugliest nigga I had ever seen. He reminded me of the dog from *The Jetsons*. He was short and bald with fucked-up teeth. About a minute later, the tall one emerged and motioned for me to come into the office. I walked in to find Big T sitting at the desk, looking at a gun magazine. I stood still as he looked at me as if he was trying to see through me.

"So, Shawn, that's your name?"

"Yeah, that's what they call me."

"So, Big Mike was your pop, huh?"

"Yeah."

"I never remember him mentioning a son named Shawn. Are you sure you're not lying to me?"

"I'm positive. He wasn't around me much, but he was my dad. My mom's name is Marie. You might do better checking up on that."

"I'll have to check up on that, but what is it that I can do for you?"

"I have a business proposition."

"Business? What the hell do you know about business?"

"I know more than you think. I've done a lot of research, and I know how to save you some money."

"Why would you want to do that?"

"Because my dad used to talk about you and he always said good things." I lied because in all actuality, my dad never said one good thing about Big T. I just heard through the grapevine that they were tight once but had a falling out and whatever it was, Big Mike never forgave him for it. Big Mike wasn't one to talk about his relationships, whether they were personal or business, but I figured that Big T would possibly feel sorry for whatever it was that he did, and work with me on the strength of that.

"Really?"

"Yeah. I'm just trying to help you and help myself at the same time."

"Now we're getting somewhere!" he said as he sat up in his chair.

"Of course, there would be something in it for me."

"Oh, I knew that. But what is it, exactly?"

"Look, I have this Columbian connect that can get me the same shit you buy from your connect, at half price. I'm trying to hook you up with them and all I ask is that you make me and my boy Mark your partners, so we can take this shit over together."

"How the fuck do you know what I pay for my product?"

"I told you, I did my research."

"I can see that. So, I'm supposed to trust you? Why?"

"Because you were my dad's best friend. I wouldn't stab you in the back. It should be him standing next to you running this shit, but he's not here. So who's better to be there by your side, than his seed?"

"That was a long time ago."

"I know it was, but that doesn't change anything. I'm trying to do big things, and this is what's going to get me there."

"I have to get back to you about this. I need to check out your story first. Leave your number and I'll hit you up when I'm satisfied with what I find out."

"No problem. It's all love, man. I know you got to check up on me first," I said, passing him a business card.

"I'll give you a call in a couple of days," he said, looking at the business card that I had just placed in his hand.

"All right, I'll be waiting," I said as I made my way to the door to leave the office. I found Mark at the bar and signaled for him to come on so we could leave. Once we were in the car, he immediately began questioning me.

"What did he say?" Mark asked anxiously.

"He said he'd check up on my story and give me a call."

"Do you really think he'll call?"

"I know he will. I could tell by the look on his face. That shit about Big Mike hit a soft spot."

"Damn, I hope this shit works."

"It'll work. It's just going to take some time."

I waited patiently until Big T called three days later. I was sitting in the house with Mimi and the baby when my cell rang. I didn't recognize the number, so I stepped outside to answer it.

"Hello!"

"Is this Shawn?"

"Yeah, who's this?"

"Big T."

"Oh, OK. I was waiting on your call. Did you find out what you needed to know?"

"Yeah, I did."

"So can we meet to talk?"

"Yeah. You can meet me at the club tomorrow at five."

"I'll be there."

"See you then," he said before disconnecting the call.

I dialed Mark and told him about the meeting and I informed him that we would meet up around twelve to go over the script for the meeting. He agreed and I hung up and continued spending time with my family. I could barely sleep that night because I was so anxious to get to the meeting.

I prepared for different scenarios all day. I wanted to know what I was going to say and how I would react to anything that he said. I wanted him to see my sincerity and determination. This was no bullshit for me, and I wanted it to show. That evening I walked into his club with seriousness on my face. Mark and I were searched at the door. We walked over to the bar where Big T was seated in front of a flat screen TV, watching ESPN. Mark and I sat down on the barstools beside him and waited for him to speak.

"So, tell me a little bit more about this connect that you have," he said without ever turning to look at me.

"Well, I told you that I can set you up with them. Since I've been doing business with them for a while, they'll trust you. They'll give you the same price that they've been giving me. Now I know that you've got a sweet deal with the connect you already have, but half of that is better."

"So you're saying I'll pay half of what I already pay for the same weight?"

"Exactly!"

"So, what exactly do you want from me? I know you've mentioned being partners."

"Yeah. With all three of us together, we can buy more weight and turn that shit over more quickly. The three-way split is still going to have you coming out with more than you're getting now. I've done the math and the research. This shit can really work out, if you're down."

"If you're bullshittin', man, I'll make you wish that you were never born. I've been stabbed in the back too many times, and I don't take that shit lightly. It's a lot of niggas buried for trying to test me. I'm going to give this shit a shot, but one false move and that's the end. I pay close attention when it comes to my money."

"Oh, I'm going to prove myself to you," I said, reaching out my hand to shake his.

He stood there and stared at me for a second before he returned the gesture. That handshake sealed the deal. After shaking my hand, he followed that with a handshake to Mark. We were on our way, and the closer that I got to the top, the better the air tasted. I couldn't wait to reach the top. I was ready to embrace success with open arms.

CHAPTER 18

Giselle: On and On

2003

My relationship with Shawn began to progress, and I was so happy. We often went out to dinner and the movies. It was so hard to hide things from my father. There were many times that we would be in the same room with my father and Shawn would blow kisses and things, being sneaky. Shortly after the incident with Gina I began getting hang-up phone calls, and I knew that it was her. I would definitely catch up to her. I conned Daddy into letting me start to spend the night out again, so that I could have long nights over Shawn's house. The lies I told were random, like a girls' sleepover, girls' night out that ran late, and other things of that nature. We had so much fun on our nights together. Many nights we role-played, using handcuffs and every freaky thing imaginable. It was a wonderful thing.

Gina began spreading rumors that I was still sleeping with Tyrone. Shawn knew that she was lying. He never even fed into it, and I was happy. I searched for her on many days, but she was never around. I guess that she knew that when I caught her, it was over. Although Shawn told me to leave it alone, I couldn't let it slide. She was asking for an ass whipping.

For the next six months, Shawn and I kept our relationship a secret from Big T. Even our many out-of-town trips were hidden. But soon Shawn decided that it was time for him to tell Terrance because he wanted our relationship to progress more, and there was no way that could happen if no one knew about it. He never told me that he loved me, but I knew that he did. There was no way that he could do all the things that he did for me, if he didn't love me. I hadn't been spending a lot of time with Toya because Shawn didn't care for her that much. He didn't trust her. I told him that I needed friends, so he took it upon himself to introduce me to his cousin, Neisha. She was in college at the Philadelphia University, majoring in fashion. She was really close to Mimi, Shawn's tailor, and Mimi influenced her choice with her major.

Neisha was about five-six and very thin with shoulder-length black hair. She had very slanted eyes, sort of like an Asian. She dressed nice, but I assumed that was because of her cousin's money. We began to get real close and although I missed Toya, I did like being around Neisha. Every day when she was done at school, she would come over to my house and we would go to the mall.

During another one of my dad's out-of-town ventures, I spent the night over Shawn's house for the entire weekend. I came home that Sunday just in time to wait for Terrance to get home. I grabbed the cordless phone from my room and dialed Toya's cell phone. She answered on the first ring.

"What's up, ho? What the hell happened to you calling me? What's been going on? I miss you!"

"Girl, I've just been spending so much time with Shawn. You know how it is when you get a new man!" I said happily.

"Well, I'm happy for you, G, but I miss you! Well, what are you doing tonight? Are you going out?"

"I don't know. Shawn said we might get together, but we can go hang out if you want. We can go to the bar and get a couple of drinks if you want."

"Yeah, that's cool. What time do you want to go?"

"Like eight-thirty so that if Shawn wants to get together, I can still get with him before my curfew."

"OK, that's cool. I'll be ready."

I heard Daddy come in shortly after that. As soon as I went down to say hello, he began to question me about my weekend.

"Hey, Daddy, what's up?" I asked, hugging him.

"What's going on? How was your weekend?"

"It was cool. I wish you could have been here."

"Why were you at Shawn's house this weekend? You know they told me you were there."

"We were just chillin'," I responded quickly.

"Yeah, that better be all you were doing. I'm surprised you're in the house. Not going out tonight?"

"Yeah, me and Toya are going out at eight-thirty."

"Well you know you better be back in here by one. Don't make me have to come and fuck nobody up."

"All right!" I said as I ran upstairs to get my phone to call Shawn.

I dialed his number and he picked up on the second ring

"What's up, Shorty?" he asked.

"My dad just came home and I just wanted to let you know that someone told him that I was at your house this weekend."

"Don't even trip on that. I'm going to talk to him in a few

anyway. I got a surprise for you, and I know your dad will approve."

"OK! Shawn, I just wanted to tell you that I've loved you for years now, and I'm so happy you finally gave me a chance."

"That's cool, Shorty, and I know you love me. I'll holla at you in a little while, though, alright!"

"OK!" I said and hung up the phone.

I wondered what the surprise was, and how he knew that Terrance would approve. Anyway, I trusted my man. That's how shit was supposed to be.

I lay down for a little while and watched some TV before getting up to find something to wear out to the bar. I picked out a pink-and-white Christian Dior shirt, and a Seven denim skirt. I didn't really feel like overdressing tonight to sit in a bar. I took a long shower and got dressed. I kissed my dad good-bye and made my way over to get Toya. When we walked into Broad Street Eddie's, it was packed. We always hung out there, so that's why they allowed us to drink underage. After about an hour I noticed Gina in the back of the bar, talking to this dude named Black Sam. Black Sam was a big-time drug dealer in Philly, and he was also Daddy's enemy. They had a few run-ins back in the day, but were now able to co-exist.

I tapped Toya on her shoulder and pointed to Gina. She just laughed. It was funny that after that bitch shined on me, she had the heart to come out to the bar alone. I damn sure didn't forget all that shit she said before, nor would I forget the hang-up calls or the rumors. She sat back there laughing and giggling with Black Sam, obviously trying to get with him for his bank because Black Sam was the blackest, ugliest dude I'd ever seen in my life. I'd heard he had a big dick, but looks meant a lot to me, and he was hard on the eyes, for sure.

After about a half hour she got up and made her way to the bathroom. I alerted Toya and we followed. Once we reached the bathroom we went in and locked the door behind us. As soon as she noticed it was me, instantly there was fear in her eyes. I punched, kicked, and stomped her damn near dead. I spit on her and told her not to ever threaten me or next time I would finish where I left off. Then Toya and I calmly walked back out to the bar and had another drink. Gina stumbled out of the bathroom and made her way through the bar. People just stared, but no one even attempted to help her, because everyone knew what kind of person Gina was.

About fifteen minutes later my cell phone rang. It was Shawn.

"Yo! Why the hell did you do that to Gina? She just called me and told me what happened and why the hell are you out with Toya? I told you I don't like you around her! I also told you to drop that shit with Gina!"

"Look, she was disrespecting me. Plus she was in here talking to Black Sam. She could have been trying to set you up or something."

"Look, come outside. I'm on the corner."

"All right."

I told Toya to wait for me inside and I would be right back. I went outside and saw the anger in his face.

"Next time I tell you to leave some shit alone, that's what you need to do."

"OK! I'm sorry, but I was looking out for you too."

"All right. Go drop your girl off and meet me at my crib in an hour."

"OK. I love you."

"Ditto. I'll holla," he said before getting in his car and driving away.

I obeyed. I drove Toya home and was sitting outside his house in my car, waiting for him, in exactly one hour, like he said. He pulled up about five minutes later, parked, and motioned for me to get out and come up to the house. We went inside.

"So what's up? You know that they are going to tell Terrance that I came over here again."

"That's cool. I already talked to him. I told him that you are going to marry me, and he ain't got nothing to worry about."

"Marry you? What the hell are you talking about, Shawn? I'm only eighteen."

"You want to be with me, don't you?"

"Of course I do. But marriage? Isn't that a little extreme?"

"Look, that's the only way I knew Big T would approve, so I told him that we were going to get married. He was pissed off at first, of course, but he called me back and told me that he would rather it be me than any other nigga, because he trusts me. He looks at me like a son. He doesn't want anything to happen to his Baby Girl, but I've always made good on my promises. He always ends shit with a threat, but I assured him that it would never have to come to that. So tomorrow we are going to pick out a ring and then we are going to Vegas to get married."

I stood there in shock.

"Are you serious?" I asked once I was able to speak again.

"As a heart attack!"

I couldn't believe it. I would be Mrs. Shawn Wilson. I had always dreamed of being married, but just not at such a young age. I wanted to be with Shawn, though, and if this was the only way possible, then I was down for it 100 percent. Shawn snapped me out of my trance by kissing me. He laid me on the floor and made love to me right there in the living room. For the first time I didn't have to rush home. I could spend the night out with my future husband. We went up to the bedroom and fell asleep. The next morning I woke up and he was gone, but he left me a note.

What's up, Shorty,

I left you an envelope with two thousand dollars in it. Take one thousand of that to my tailor, Mimi, on Twenty-third Street and she'll hook you up for next week. Every week you'll be able to go and get new shit made. My wife is only going to wear the finest like me. No more of that hooker shit, either! Take the other grand and go buy some shoes and shit. I talked to Terrance about you moving in, and you can leave all your old stuff at his house and start new here. I'm going out to handle my business and I'll be home by ten. I expect you to be here by then too. No more late nights, unless you are with me, so tell Toya that shit is a wrap. Y'all have to hang out in daylight. I don't trust these niggas out here in the street, and I need you to be safe. Around two I need you to go down to Jeweler's Row to my jeweler. I wrote his name on the envelope. Pick out what ring you want, and he'll size you up. I'll go pick it up tomorrow. I need you to change your cell number, too. I don't want none of them niggas calling your phone. The key to the house is in the envelope with the money. I'll holla at you later!

I read the note and laughed. I loved a man who took control. I got up and got dressed. I drove over to Daddy's club first to talk to him. When I got there we sat in the office and talked.

"So, you really love him?"

"Daddy, I do. I've loved him from the moment I saw him."

"I can't believe that I am allowing you to do this," he said, placing his hand on his head.

"I know how you feel, and no matter what, I'll always be

your Baby Girl. I'm growing up now and I know you didn't think I would be the same little G all my life."

"I know. I trust this guy, and that's the only reason I'm letting him live. I've almost killed many niggas over you. He's the only one that came correct, and the fact that I look at him like a son is what's winning me over. I'm not going to let anybody hurt you. You know that, right?"

"Daddy, I know. But just so you know, it wasn't him that was chasing me. I was chasing him."

He laughed. "So, my Baby Girl is persistent, huh?"

"That's how you raised me," I said, joining in his laughter.

"You are really turning into a woman."

"I know, right!" I said, standing up and twirling around.

"You let me know if anything, and I mean anything, that he does is out of line, and I'll take care of him. You understand that?" he said as he stood up to hug me.

"Yes, I do," I said before wrapping my arms around him. "Well, Daddy, I have to go. I'm going to visit Akil today. You know how long it takes me to drive up there."

"OK. I'm glad that you're going. Tell him that I'll be sending some money in a few days."

"Will do!" I said, blowing him a kiss. "See you later, Daddy," I said as I walked out of the club.

I made my way up to the prison to see my brother. I made sure that I went to visit him once a week, although it took me forever to drive there. I had made a promise that I wouldn't break. It was hard being locked away from your family, so I had to make sure he knew that I loved him. I entered the prison and after being checked in and searched, they led me to the visiting room, where my brother awaited me. I was so happy to see him and tell him my news.

"Hey, Li'l Sis! What's up?"

"I got some good news. Shawn and me are getting married!" His smile instantly turned to a frown.

"What? What the fuck you mean you are marrying him? That muthafucker is foul. I heard a lot of shit up in here. Shit that goes back to before he even popped up on the scene three years ago. You need to leave him alone. He's out for blood."

"What are you talking about, Akil?"

"I can't get into all of that, but I'm telling you that he's the reason a lot of shit's happened, and I mean a lot of shit. Word is bond, when I get up out of here that nigga is mine, and that's for sure. I would hate to do that to you, but I'm telling you that nigga has to get his, and when you find out why, you'll feel the same way."

"I don't understand, Akil. And how do you expect me to feel the same way? You won't even tell me what the problem is. That's my man and we are getting married, and unless you can tell me the reason you feel like that shouldn't happen, then I'm moving forward."

"You're supposed to trust me, and obviously that nigga means more to you than me. All I can say is watch your back, and I'll holla." He signaled to the guard, letting him know that he was through with the visit.

I sat there for a minute, stunned. I didn't understand why my brother was so upset. Nor did I understand what Shawn could have possibly done that was so bad, that my brother would have so much hatred toward him. I knew that you heard things in prison, most times quicker than the people on the streets, but what was it? He could be talking crazy because he was in jail. He always wanted to be the man on top, and since Shawn was Daddy's right-hand man, Akil was probably jealous. Anyway, I never listened to my brother when it came to my life because he had no room to comment on anything that I did. His ass was in prison.

I left the prison upset that Akil could make accusations and not tell me the details, but I dropped it. I went down to the jeweler and picked out a five-carat, platinum ring. The cost was unknown to me, and I didn't really care. I knew that my man would get me anything I wanted. Then I visited Shawn's tailor, Mimi, and gave her the money.

Surprisingly, to be a tailor making all this money, one wouldn't know it by looking at her. She was dressed so average. She had a pretty face, though, but her hair was not done. I always thought that he must have been having sex with his tailor to hook him up like she did. But by looking at her, I knew that I had nothing to worry about, and I was sure glad of that. She measured me and laid out a plan for outfits for the next week. She told me that I could come to pick up one every day for the following day, and I was cool with that. Mimi seemed real cool. We sat and talked for a few minutes, and she briefly told me how she started working for Shawn. She said that when she was in high school he hired her for her co-op job and she had been working for him ever since. She said he looked out for her when she got pregnant at a young age so she wouldn't have to go on welfare.

After I got a little more info from her, I made my way to the mall. I was tired as hell, but never too tired to shop. I bought so many pairs of shoes that I spent every penny of the $1,000 that Shawn gave me, plus a couple dollars of my own. I was so ready to shine on these bitches big time. I was already a princess, but now I would be a queen, and I wanted every bitch in the world to know that, as well as the fact that my man was mine, and they would never have the pleasure of walking in my shoes; not even for a minute.

CHAPTER 19

Mimi: So Far Away

2003

I felt like James and I were growing apart since he began his new "role." James had even bought a house that only he could live in. I still stayed at the apartment we shared. I was so unsure about our marriage. It felt like this thing wasn't an act. It felt so real, like he was really living the life of his alias. I hated it, and I let him know it every chance I got.

Our relationship was fading. I felt like all I had become was his slave, not his wife. I tried harder and harder to make things work with James, but he pushed me further and further away. I had been trying to contact James all night because Alyia was sick and I needed to take her to the emergency room. Of course, James was nowhere to be found. I got dressed and took her to the emergency room all alone. At five she was released and I drove home, barely able to keep my eyes open.

Entering the apartment, I found James asleep on the

couch. I was angry. I swung my purse and tapped his legs to wake him up.

"What the hell is wrong with you?" he asked, startled.

"What the hell is wrong with you? Why the hell didn't you answer my call last night? I called you ten times. You daughter was sick, and I needed you to go with me to the emergency room!" I yelled.

"I was working, and who the hell are you yelling at? You know that I would have been here if I could have."

"I'm sick of this shit, James. I want out!"

"That's not an option. We are in this shit till death do us part. Did you forget those vows? This is my job. Your ass don't work. How the hell do you think that you can take care of yourself? You've never even had a damn job before!"

"Fuck you, James. I didn't ask for this!"

"Look, you wanted the money, and I'm giving it to you. You act like you don't appreciate that shit. It's other bitches out here that would love to be in your shoes."

"I doubt it!" I yelled.

With that, he smacked me, causing me to land on the floor. I cried. Realizing what he'd done, he began to apologize.

"Why?" I yelled, covering the side of my face that was now throbbing in pain.

"I'm sorry, baby. You're driving me crazy. Come on, get up," he said, grabbing my arm to pull me up from the floor.

"Get off of me, James!" I yelled.

"I'm sorry, baby, I love you. I'll never hit you again. I promise. I just get so angry sometimes," he said, wrapping his arms around me.

"Damn, James, now my face is going to be all swollen and shit."

"I'm sorry. Let me go get you some ice," he said, going into the kitchen to retrieve the ice from the freezer.

I accepted his apology because I knew that he only

wanted the best for us. I knew that somewhere under this mask was the man that I fell in love with, and I was waiting for the day that he would resurface.

He didn't stay home that day, which I expected, but he did have some flowers sent to me to show how sorry he was for hitting me. I wanted my life back and at that point I was determined to get it. All I had to do was stick by my man, like a good wife should.

Giselle was the new chick that I would have to sew for every day. She was young and beautiful, and had a perfect body and a beautiful smile that I envied. I didn't really care for her personality, though, because of her stuck-up attitude. Having the best of everything all her life without ever having to lift a finger had created a monster.

I felt that she didn't care for me much either, but I didn't care. This was a job, and I, in no way, wanted her to be my friend. She arrived that first day with an envelope of money. The envelope read: To my future wifey, From Shawn. I laughed because these young girls just didn't know what this life would get you.

It was hard for me to sit and smile in her face, knowing the detrimental effect that she could have on my life. I felt threatened by her, and I wasn't sure why. Never in my life had another woman made me feel like I would have to fight for what was mine. I measured her and laid out a plan for clothing. My ideas didn't really matter to her since she had her own ideas and could care less about my opinion. I hurried through the uncomfortable small talk to make the final cuts for her week's worth of wardrobe.

"So how did you meet Shawn?" I quizzed.

"I met him while I was in high school through Neisha. I started sewing for him then."

"Oh, OK. That's cool. I know that was nice to start getting money so young."

"I guess so, but it never really made me that much money, though."

"Oh. So what school did you go to?"

"Mastbaum."

"Cool. Well, Shawn is the bomb. I've been trying to get with him for years. I'm so glad that we finally got together."

"Oh."

"Yeah, he's the shit in bed, too. I ain't never had a dude do me like him."

"Well, that's good. So are these designs OK for you?" I asked, cutting the conversation short.

"They're fine. Thanks, Mimi. I can't wait to shine on these hoes!" she said, smiling.

"I'm sure you can't," I said in a sarcastic tone.

I did as James had asked and lied to Giselle about how I met him. It was extremely hard, but I knew that if I had screwed things up for him I would suffer. James was a controlling man and I had to do as he said if I wanted to continue living the life that I did. I loved him with all of my heart and each time I thought about how bad things were going I thought about the end result, where he would succeed in getting to the top and I would be right there by his side. To get to the top there is always a struggle, and as his wife I had to struggle with him.

When Giselle finally did leave, I sighed with relief. I was so glad when she left. I was so sick of hearing her brag about Shawn that it was beginning to make me sick. I knew that it would get harder and harder every time I had to meet with her, but I had to be professional and I had to hold my composure. James would flip if I ruined any part of his plan and knowing how upset he could get, I had no other choice but to sit and fake as if I really liked this stuck-up bitch, Giselle.

CHAPTER 20

Giselle: Until You Came

2003

After leaving Mimi's, the last thing on my list was to call and have my cell phone number changed. After I did that, I sent Shawn a text message letting him know that I did everything that he asked me to do. He never responded, but I sent him another text just to make sure that he received it. I went to my new home and began placing my new shoes in the closet that he had assigned to me. I dialed Toya on my cell.

"Hey Toya, It's Giselle!"

"Hey, girl! What's up? What happened after you dropped me off last night?"

"I went to his house, and, girl, guess what?"

"What?"

"We are getting married. Can you believe it? And Daddy approved."

"What? Are you serious? Married? Why the hell would you marry him and y'all just got together not long ago!"

"Because I love him, girl, and I want to be with him. I just need you to be happy for me."

"OK, but I hope it's the right thing, G. I don't think you should go through with it, but if you are happy, so am I."

"Thanks, girl. So have you heard anything more about Gina?"

"Yeah. I heard she's in the hospital with two broken ribs. You whooped her ass for real, girl."

"Well she deserved it, but I gotta go. I just heard Shawn come in. I'll talk to you later." I hung up and quickly erased her number from my outgoing call list. I didn't want any drama about me calling Toya. I went downstairs to greet him.

"Hey! Why didn't you respond to my text?"

"Because I was busy, and don't be questioning me, all right? Anyway, I'm glad that you did what I said. It shows me that you can follow directions. I'm about to take a shower right quick and when I get out, I want you to be ass-naked so I can dig your back out, because I'm horny as hell."

"OK," I answered. I made my way to the bedroom, stripped off my clothes, and lay down. When he came out he was already erect. He told me he wanted to hit it from the back, so once again he grabbed the oil and rubbed it all over my butt, as well as his erect member. This time he made me ride him, which hurt even more than doggy-style. This sex in the butt was something that I had to get used to. I had to please my man, so I took the pain and rode him like he was a horse and I was the jockey. After the love session was finished, we both fell asleep.

I awoke the next morning from the sun glaring through the window. I turned over and noticed that Shawn was gone. I got up and went to the bathroom to shower. My body ached from the previous night's events. I got in the shower and let the hot water run all over my body. I closed my eyes and my brother came to my mind. I knew that he probably would reject my visits since he was upset about Shawn and me. I wasn't sure what I would do. I needed Akil in my life. He was my sanity. There were so many times growing up when I was upset and he was always there to give me that pep talk that brought my sprits up. I wanted him to be happy for me, happy that I was about to marry the man of my dreams. I felt like the luckiest girl in the world, and I wanted the whole world to share in my joy. I figured that I would give my brother some time and eventually he would come around. He couldn't stay mad at me forever.

After I showered I threw on a pair of Seven jeans and a Roberto Cavalli shirt. I decided to go over to see Toya, since I would be leaving the following day to get married in Vegas. I wanted to spend a little time with her before I came back a married woman. Things changed once you got married. I got to Toya's house in what seemed like seconds. She opened the door after a few knocks and let me in. We sat in her living room and talked.

"So, you know I'm leaving tomorrow for Vegas, right?" I asked, excited.

"Why so fast? Don't you think you need to a least check his background before you marry him? Marriage is serious, G. I know you've had a crush on him since forever, but don't you think it's strange that after all those years he put you off and now all of sudden he gives you a chance? And then months later he says he's going to marry you. I just find that really strange, like he has some ulterior motive."

"I don't know why everyone is against it. I don't find it strange. Maybe he had feelings for me the whole time and was just waiting for me to get older."

"Why would that be the case, G? He was with Gina, and y'all are the same age."

"I don't know, but none of that matters now."

"I heard that Gina's trying to press charges on you for that fight."

"What? She's crazy as hell, and I'm not stressing it. By the time I get back at the end of the week, it will be a new life for me. She's just mad that I have Shawn now, and ain't nothing going to change that."

"Well, G, all I can say is, good luck."

We sat and talked for a little while longer before Shawn called me and told me to meet him at home ASAP. I got in my car and rushed home. He was waiting for me on the sofa.

"Hey. I got here as quickly as I could. What's up?"

"I'm ready to leave for Vegas tonight. I want to get married and get back. I got a lot of things to handle and I need to be back by Thursday morning."

"OK, I'm ready. I just have to call my dad and let him know we're leaving."

"I already told him, so go ahead upstairs, get your bags, and let's go. Time means money, baby!"

We were on our way shortly after that. I had never been on a plane before, so I was really nervous. We flew first class and it was nice, totally unlike what I'd heard about the coach seats. We arrived in Vegas and it was so hot. I'd never felt that kind of heat before in my life. We went to the Viva Las Vegas hotel, and then after dropping off our bags, we changed and went straight to the wedding chapel, which was located in the hotel. Shawn did seem to be in a hurry with the whole wedding thing, but I overlooked it because maybe he just wanted to marry me that badly. The ceremony was fast, and I was now Mrs. Shawn Wilson. I couldn't have been happier. We went up to the honeymoon suite and made love like never before. Shawn told me that I was guaranteed to have his baby after that. I totally wasn't looking forward to kids anytime soon, but I had to do my wifely duties, and if that included giving him his first child, then that's what I would do.

After we showered, we went out to dinner. I really enjoyed the quality time we were spending together. I knew that once we got back to Philly he would be busy working and I would have to get in where I fit in. We did a little shopping before retiring to our suite. Once we lay down, we were so tired that we fell asleep within minutes after hitting the sheets. I woke up in the middle of the night from a bad dream, luckily not waking Shawn. The dream was really weird. It took me back to the night that my mother died, and instead of killing just my mother, the intruders killed me too. I didn't know if it was some sort of sign or what, but it upset me to replay that whole scene again. After tossing and turning for some time, I finally fell back to sleep.

In the morning Shawn tapped me on my shoulder to tell me to get dressed so that we could make our way back home. The trip to Vegas was short-lived, but we accomplished what we came there for. I got dressed and we made our way back to the airport, got on the plane, and returned to Philly.

I felt differently once we stepped off the plane. I guess being married will do that to you. I wanted to call Toya, but I knew that Shawn would flip, so I would wait until later. We went to see Big T first, who was at the club. I was so glad to see my dad. He told me that he was happy for me, and that being married put a certain glow on my face. After talking to my dad for a while, Shawn dropped me off at home and went back out.

Things began to change between Shawn and I after we returned from Las Vegas. Shawn began staying out more, never spending much time at home with me. Girls began calling the house for Shawn, and I was pissed off. We argued a lot because when I approached him about it, he cursed and walked out of the house. I didn't understand how he could wait until we were married to act this way. I threatened to leave many times, and all he said was that if that's what I wanted to do, then I could go right ahead and leave. I never wanted to leave, though. I just wanted my husband home with me. It hurt that the many times that I said I was leaving, he never fought to make me stay.

The women continued to call and disrespect me, he continued to stay out late, and we continued to argue about it. All I did was stay in the house. The next couple of months went by very slowly. I was bored as all hell. Shawn didn't want me around Toya, saying that she was a bad influence. I had no other friends except Neisha and Mimi, who were always busy, so my days consisted of me staying home, watching TV, and eating. I put on a few pounds and Shawn joked, saying that the extra rolls were good. I would get my hair done twice a week, and my nails done once a week. The only other time I really went out was when I was with him, or when I went to Mimi's to get fitted for clothing.

I would sit and play with Mimi's daughter, Alyia, while she sewed. Alyia was the prettiest little girl I had ever seen. She looked like Mimi in some ways, but I guess the rest of her looks came from her father. Mimi never really talked much about Alyia's father, only saying that he made sure that she was well taken care of, whatever that meant. I enjoyed my time at Mimi's because it was a chance for me to get outside, which I really wasn't able to do otherwise.

About four months after our wedding, I took a home pregnancy test that came back positive. *Damn!* I thought. I wasn't ready for that. I told Shawn, and he was excited. He said that he would hire an interior decorator to design the baby's room. My father was happy, too, since this would be his first grandchild. Akil had a couple of chicks that claimed that their children were his, but since he didn't claim them, neither did my father. I told Toya about it when I snuck and called her on the phone, and she acted happy for me, but I could tell by the tone of her voice that it wasn't genuine. I wasn't really all that happy myself, but a child was a blessing, and I had to believe in that.

CHAPTER 21

Mimi: Mr. Big

2003

Sitting home every day became a bore, and I felt like I needed to get out. James was out having all of the fun while I suffered, and I was sick and tired of it. I decided to put on one of my sharpest outfits, you know the type that makes niggas fall down at your feet. My breasts were pushed up high, my abs were showing, and my pants were extra tight, pushing my butt up in the right direction. I hadn't been dressed up in so long. I usually lounged around in pajamas most of the day. I got in my car, unsure of my destination. I was just excited about going out since it had been such a long time. After riding around for what seemed like hours, I pulled up in front of Ballers Extraordinaire. At that moment I remembered that I had heard this name before. This club was owned by Big T, the man that James had so much hate for. I sat in my car, contemplating my next move. I was sweating just thinking about meeting the man that

James despised. I turned the air conditioner on high and relaxed for a few more minutes before I decided to get out of the car. I switched into the club, which was surprisingly crowded. In a way I was nervous about meeting Big T, but I was also so excited that my panties were getting wet just thinking about him. I wanted to find out what all of the fuss was about. I wanted to see firsthand what all of the neighborhood girls were raving about.

I prayed that I wouldn't run into James, but if I did, I would tell him that I came out to get some air since I was tired of sitting in the house alone. He would probably still be pissed, but at least he wouldn't know that I only entered the club in the first place to see exactly who Big T was.

I walked over to the bar and sat down to wait for the bartender to make it back down to the end of the bar, where I had pulled up a stool. Within a few minutes the fine-ass bartender made it over to me.

"Hey, what can I get for you?" he asked, leaning in close so that I could hear him over the loud music.

"Alize, please!" I said, smiling at his sexiness. I was trying not to be obvious that I was all over his ass. Besides, I was here looking for Mr. Big.

"Here you go, sexy. That's on the house, OK?"

"On the house? Who paid for it?"

"The owner. He loves to treat a pretty woman!" he said, walking away. I was stunned. Compliments of the owner? Where the hell was he? And what the hell made him buy me a drink? I sipped my Alize slowly, swaying to the music. I ordered a few more drinks before I decided that it was time to go. I didn't want to stay any longer since I hadn't run into James yet, and I wanted to get the hell out of here before I did. I had noticed that there was a different bartender, and I couldn't ask him about Big T. I was drunk as hell anyway from all of the free alcohol that I had consumed. I got my balance together and made my way to the exit, but before stepping out of the door, I felt a strong arm around my waist.

"Excuse me?" I said, turning around and noticing the presence of the sexy bartender from earlier.

"Are you OK to drive home? Those free drinks are taking effect, I see."

"I'm fine, but thanks for asking. What happened to the owner? He never showed his face after buying me all of those drinks. You would think that he would at least get my number, or something."

"I'm Big T, baby. I'm the owner. I wasn't going to let your fine ass out of my sight. I was watching you from the minute you stepped into the club."

"Nice to meet you, Big T. I'm Mimi."

"Mimi, huh? I like that. It's sexy."

"So why do they call you Big T?"

"I can show you better than I can tell you, baby," he said, displaying a devilish grin.

"Well, unfortunately I'm married, so I guess I'll never find out!" I said, smiling as I turned my back toward him and began walking out.

"Wait. Let me drive you home. I wouldn't feel right knowing that I got you drunk and let you drive home alone."

"I'll be fine. I'm a big girl!"

"I know, but just let me do that and I'll leave you alone."

"OK," I agreed after a little more hesitation. T drove me home, with one of his friends following us in another car. Once we reached my apartment, he parked my car and turned off the ignition.

"So, can I walk you upstairs just to make sure you get in the door OK?"

"I'm fine," I said as I stumbled out of the car. After regaining my balance, I leaned on the hood of the car to wait until he got out.

"Look at you. You are tore up," he said before scooping me up off my feet.

"What are you doing?" I asked.

"I'm taking you upstairs," he said sternly.

I closed my eyes as he carried me up the steps to my apartment. Once we reached the door he opened it and carried me inside. I was almost asleep when he placed me on the sofa and took my shoes off. I opened my eyes when I felt his warm tongue on my toes. I didn't resist because it felt so good. I had never had my toes sucked before, and I was enjoying the chills it was sending up my spine.

"I just wanted to relax you, ma. Give you something to dream about. I'm not trying to take things any further because you're not sober, but I will leave you my business card and you can call me when you are ready."

"What? You get me all hot and now you are going to leave?"

"I'll be back whenever you want me. I'm going to go now, and when you need me, just call."

"I need you now!"

"No, you don't. You need to get some sleep," he said, kissing me on my forehead. "Your toes were delicious. I can't imagine what the rest of you will taste like!" He smiled before opening the door and disappearing into the night.

I was so upset that Big T had left. I was horny and ready to get busy before he had stopped. I had to resort to using my vibrator to settle my hunger for more. I had recently purchased a vibrator when I was tired of being left horny while waiting for James to come home. My vibrator had been my man and my best friend lately, two positions that my husband was not filling.

The next day, when I was sober, I decided to give T a call. I had just dropped Alyia off at pre-school and made my way back home. I found the number and after a few seconds of hesitation, I dialed.

"Hello!" He spoke in the sexy, deep-toned voice that turned me on immediately.

"Hi. Is this T?"

"Yeah. Who is this?"

"It's Mimi. How are you?"

"I should be asking you that. You were pretty drunk last night. How was your night?"

"It was fine, although I tossed and turned thinking about you."

"Oh really?"

"Yeah. You opened the flood gates and left me there to swim all alone."

"I wasn't trying to take advantage of you," he said, laughing at my comment.

"That's cool."

"I can come see you tonight if you want me to."

"I definitely want to see you," I said, smiling. Noticing James's car pulling up in the driveway, I decided to end my call with T. "Just come past after nine. I'll be waiting," I said seductively.

"No problem. I'll see you then," he said before hanging up.

I quickly placed the cordless phone on the base and ran to the sofa to sit down. I flicked on the TV just before James made it to the door and used his key to enter the apartment. I gave him a fake smile as if I was happy to see him.

"What's up?" he asked, nodding his head.

"Nothing," I said quickly.

"You went out last night?"

"Yeah, I was bored. I'm tired of sitting in here all alone, James."

"Well that's the way shit is, so stop complaining about it. I came here to spend some time with you, so if that's all you have to talk about, I can turn my black ass right back around."

"You know that's not what I want, James. I just miss you, that's all."

"I know you do," he said, coming over to the sofa and sitting down next to me. "I miss you too, believe it or not. It's hard being away from you and Alyia."

"So how long does this charade have to go on, James? It's killing our relationship."

"Not too much longer, I promise. I'm so close to the top I can taste it. It's almost over for sure," he said before moving in closer to kiss me. I missed his lips and his touch when he wasn't around, and the feelings that his kiss gave me made me realize exactly how much I needed him. He began to fondle my perky breasts through my Victoria's Secret tank. I moaned in anticipation, since it had been months since he'd touched me this way. The aroma of his cologne flowed through my nostrils, sending chills through my body. He sucked on my earlobes, causing my inside to erupt and creating lubrication for his entry.

"I love you," I whispered in his ear as his hands moved down into my shorts and massaged my labia through my French-cut panties.

I began to grind my hips into his hands and I could feel the juices running out of me as I climaxed. "I want to taste you," I spoke softly before unzipping his pants and taking him into my mouth. I could feel his hands on the back of my head, guiding me up and down his pole. I enjoyed this show of affection as much as he did. After he had enough, he removed my shorts and panties and pushed my legs up in the air. He began to make sweet, hot circles with his tongue.

"I miss you so much!" he said, sticking his fingers deep inside me and licking my clit at the same time. I rubbed on my breasts ferociously as the lustful feelings intensified.

I wanted him inside me and I couldn't take the waiting any longer.

"Fuck me, J, please!" I moaned in excitement. He used the head of his dick to massage my clit, and I could feel my body start to shiver as I came.

"You like that?" he asked.

"I love it!" I moaned as he slowly and deliberately pushed inside me. A moan escaped him as I contracted the walls inside my juicy tunnel. The sound of him moving in and out of me, along with my moans, boosted his stamina.

"Harder, J, harder!" I screamed as he rammed his stick inside of me with force.

"Awww, baby, this pussy is the best!" he moaned, driving deeper inside me. I locked my legs around his waist as I felt the throbbing of his member deep inside me.

"Oh shit, I'm cumming, baby!" he moaned in delight as I held him inside me and milked him until there was nothing left.

"Damn, that was good!" he said before leaning in to meet my lips with a deep, passionate kiss.

James got up to get a shower. As I watched his naked body walk toward the bathroom, I became horny again. I decided to join him in the shower for round two before he decided to run out again.

After heading to the market to pick up a few things for my meeting with T, I made a quick stop at Victoria's Secret to pick up something sexy to wear. After debating for a while, I decided on a sexy Brazilian crotchless panty-and-bra set that was sure to turn T on. I cleaned up the apartment to remove the aftermath of the earlier sexual encounter between James and me.

I went to get Alyia from school and take her over to Mrs. Marie's house. I told her that I wasn't feeling too well and needed a night of rest. I would pick her up the following morning to take her to school. I was still anxious to see Big T, and I figured that if I rested up for a few hours before he came over I could be ready later on. After my nap I got up and soaked in a hot tub of water to tighten me up a little since I had just had sex earlier that day. I cooked dinner and lit candles while waiting for T to arrive. After dressing in my new lingerie, I put on my silk robe. At 9:05 the doorbell rang and I was excited as I opened it to see his fine ass standing there in all white.

"Hello, Mr. Big!" I said, smiling and leaning up against the door while motioning him to come inside.

"It's smells good in here. You cooked?"

"Yeah."

"Damn, a fine-ass woman that can cook. That husband of yours is a lucky man."

"Only if he knew how lucky he was!" I exclaimed. "Come on in and have a seat so we can talk over dinner!"

"Cool," he said, making his way over to the table and sitting down.

"I'm really glad that you're here. It's not that often that I have the pleasure of entertaining."

"Well, although I appreciate the food, we can dine later. I'd rather you entertained me first," he said, licking his lips.

"You want entertainment?" I asked while making my way over to the stereo and putting in R. Kelly's *TP-2* CD. I began to dance as "Strip For You" played. I hummed to the chorus. "Sit back in the chair, my baby, 'cause I'm about to go there, my baby . . . do you mind if I strip for you?" I moved slowly to the music, sensually removing my red, silk robe to reveal my lingerie. I rubbed my hands all over my body, moaning as I hummed to the music. I could see that his shaft was hardening through his linen pants, which excited me even more. I revealed my breasts one at time, taking each nipple into my mouth.

"Take it out and play with it!" I instructed. T pulled his pants down around his ankles and pulled his pole through his boxers. As he began to stroke his member, I continued my dance, watching him at the same time. I got down in a squatting position, revealing my crotchless panties. I took my index finger and began pleasuring myself as he watched me from the chair.

"Come taste me," he instructed, and I didn't waste any time taking him in my warm mouth. I flickered my tongue around the head, causing him to moan.

"You like the taste of it, baby?" he asked.

"Ummm, yes!" I moaned, enjoying the taste of the precum in my mouth. He used his hips to move his member in and out of my mouth. My mouth was completely filled as I finally learned why they called him Big.

Although my walls were still sore from earlier that day, I couldn't wait to have Big's thickness inside me.

"You want me to fuck you?" he asked as he noticed me pushing two fingers in and out of my wetness.

"Yes!" I exclaimed with a moan.

"Come on and sit on it," he instructed. I straddled him and used my hands to guide his large shaft into my tunnel.

"Damn, this feels good, T!" I said, grinding in a circle to create friction on my clit. I continued to move up and down on Big, increasing my tempo. T turned me over and I arched my back to give him an easy path of entry. I screamed in ecstasy as his balls pounded against my clit and the sounds of him moving in and out of me reached my ears.

"Oh, shit, T, I'm cumming!" I yelled as my body began to

shake uncontrollably. He soon followed with his own orgasm as he exploded inside me. I lay there on the floor, exhausted. I was definitely satisfied, and I knew that it wouldn't be the last time I had a piece of Mr. Big!

Over the next two weeks, T made a stop past my house almost every night, and every night I was happy with what I received. I was falling in love with T, and I knew that it was wrong. I was a married woman and although my husband was sleeping with other women, two wrongs didn't make a right. One day, as I waited anxiously for T to call me, I was startled when I heard James enter the apartment.

"Mimi!" he yelled. "Where the hell are you?" He slammed the door.

"What's wrong, J?"

"You fucking that nigga, huh?" he asked, slapping me and causing me to fall down to the floor.

"James, please!" I cried.

"Get the fuck up, Mimi! You didn't think that I would find out that you were fucking him? Is the dick good?"

"James, please!"

"Answer me! Is the dick good?"

"No!"

"No? Then why are you fucking him every night? You're fucking lying to me!" he yelled before slapping me again, causing me to fall back down to the floor. "Get the fuck up!" he yelled, grabbing me by the arm. "Now tell the truth. Is the dick good?"

I spoke as tears rolled down my face.

"Yes!"

"Is he better than me?"

"No, James."

He slapped me again.

"Stop lying to me!"

"Yes," I cried.

"Well since you went behind my back and fucked that nigga, you're going to keep sucking and fucking him until I tell you to stop!" he yelled.

"What?"

"You heard me! Keep fucking him until I say otherwise. Now go clean yourself up. I know that nigga is on his way over! I'll talk to you later!" he said before exiting the apartment.

I sat there, crying and scared. I had betrayed James, and now he was going to use me to his advantage. My telephone rang as I was in the bathroom washing the tears off my face. I ran out to grab the cordless.

"Hello!" I said, shaking.

"Hey, babe. I'm outside, so open the door," T instructed.

"OK!" I said, turning off the faucet and walking to the door. I opened the door, trying to avoid looking T in the eye.

"What the hell happened to you?" he asked, concerned.

"I had a fight with my husband, but I'm OK!"

"You don't look OK."

"I'm fine."

"Does he hit you all the time?"

"No, just when he's pissed."

"What pissed him off?"

"Nothing big. He just has a bad temper, that's all."

"Come here. Let me hold you," he said while wrapping his arms around me as a tear escaped my eye. I was scared, not only for me, but for T as well. I loved him and I knew what James was planning. I also knew that James was responsible for his wife's murder. I felt guilty loving him, because I knew that my husband was planning to destroy him. T held me that night without sex, and it was then that I knew what it really meant to love someone. I thought that I loved every man I'd ever been with, but none compared to

T. He truly cared about me, and he showed it in everything that he did. I lay there in his arms crying until I fell asleep.

Before leaving he kissed me softly on my forehead.

"I love you, Mimi," he whispered in my ear, and with that I had a good night's sleep.

I continued spending time with T and began loving him even more. James hated to see me with him, but it was now a part of his plan of attack. James wanted me to keep T occupied, and I did what I had to do. One day soon after James discovered my affair with T, I went to CVS to pick up a home pregnancy test since I had been feeling sick and fatigued lately. I wasn't surprised when the test results were positive. I was scared the moment I saw the two pink lines displayed on the screen. I knew that it had been a while since James and I had sex, but I'd been sleeping with T on the regular.

I sat in the house, unsure of my next move. James would probably want me dead once he found out that I was pregnant and unsure of whom the father was. I knew that I couldn't tell T, but I had no choice but to tell James. I dialed his cell phone number in tears, and I froze for a second before responding to his hello.

"Hello!" he shouted for the second time.

"J, I have something to tell you."

"What the fuck do you have to tell me?"

"I'm pregnant."

"What?"

"I'm pregnant."

"How far along?"

"I don't know. I just took a home test."

"Is it mine?" he asked

"I don't know."

"You don't know? What kind of shit is that?"

"You told me to keep seeing him, J!"

"Bullshit, Mimi. You wanted him, and you weren't even smart enough to use protection."

"I didn't use protection the first time I had sex with you, either."

"Well I guess I better go get tested for HIV since I'm married to a ho!" he yelled.

"Look, James, you are not innocent here, either."

"Whatever. You need to look in the phone book and call an abortion clinic, because you are getting rid of that baby. Do you hear me?"

"It could be your baby, James."

"I don't give a fuck. I said you are getting rid of it, and that's that. You need to contact that nigga T and end that shit too. No more fucking around, Mimi, and I mean it. I better not hear that you fucked that nigga again!" he yelled. "I'll kill that nigga if you fuck him again!"

"OK."

"I'll be there later so we can finish this conversation!" he said before hanging up.

The tears began to flow as I contemplated calling T to end it. I didn't want to end it with him. If anything, I would end it with James if I had a choice, but I didn't. I was in love and I was afraid of what would happen to me. T had been so good to me, always positive. I couldn't remember one bad time when I was around him. Everything about him was sincere from the way he spoke his feelings, to the way he made love to me.

I had never dreamed of dealing with someone that was so much older than me; Big T was at least 20 years my senior, but I was happy that I had the experience. I wished that I didn't have to give it all up, but I knew that I wouldn't be able to deal with it if I was the cause of Big's death. I dialed his number as the tears continued to run down my face. I was hoping that the answering machine would pick up so I could leave a message and be done with it, but he answered on the second ring. I sat there in silence for a second before I said hello.

"Mimi, what's up?"

"T, we have to end this relationship," I said, sobbing

"Why? Did I do something to you?"

"Not at all. You've been the best thing that's happened to me in a long time."

"Well, what's the problem?"

"My husband knows about us, and I can't go on any longer hurting him."

"After all of the things he's done to you, you care about his feelings?"

"I love him, T."

"I thought that you loved me."

"I do love you, T, with all of my heart, and that is the reason why I have to let you go."

"What do you mean?"

"I mean that I took a vow when I married my husband, and I have to honor that. I enjoyed every minute that I had with you, and just know that I love you."

"Mimi, don't end it like this."

"I have to."

"No, you don't."

"Good-bye, T."

"Mimi!"

I hung up, sobbing as the receiver hit the cradle. I hated the fact that when James found about my relationship with T, he forced me to continue it. I cared about T back then, but not nearly as much as I did now. I hated the man that James had become, and I also hated the person that he had forced me to be. I thought about my past, and I thought about the fact that before James, I had a good man. I wished that I had been smarter and stayed faithful to Maurice. I even wished that Tony had never hurt me, and maybe I would not have been so quick to hurt Maurice. Although it was too late to turn back, I hoped that the future would be different. I prayed that if I did everything James's way, he would return to the man that he used to be.

When James entered the apartment, I was lying on the couch, still crying. I tried to pretend that I was asleep, but James knew that I was faking. He probably didn't care, anyway.

"Mimi, get your ass up!" he yelled. "Did you do what I told you to do?"

"Yes."

"You better not be lying to me. Tomorrow you are going to make that appointment to get an abortion."

"James, please don't make me go through that," I pleaded.

"What I said is final, Mimi. That baby could be his, and there is no way I'm going to raise another nigga's baby."

"James, please," I cried.

"There's nothing that you can say to make me change my mind. I want you to go wash your face and get naked. I'll be in the room in a minute."

I decided that it was a losing battle, and I did as he had instructed. After I stripped off all of my clothing, I washed my face and laid down in the bed. A few minutes later James entered the room, naked and erect. He forced me to give him oral sex as I continued to cry. I was in no mood for sex, but I didn't want to upset James anymore than he already was. He forced his hardness in and out of my mouth for the next few minutes as he instructed me to stop crying because I was messing up his concentration.

After he was satisfied with the oral sex, he bent me over and rammed his pole inside my asshole, forcing me to scream in agony. It felt as though my insides were ripping to shreds. I begged him to stop as he continued to force himself inside my tight hole. I tried to move away, and every inch I moved, he moved with me. He was angry and he showed it with every hard stroke. I continued to cry as he pounded me. Soon he stopped, and I was glad. He turned me over and stroked his member over me until he exploded all over my face. I felt so degraded by the whole episode, which was exactly how James wanted me to feel.

I was in so much pain as I sat there and cried. He yelled at me to stop, and told me that I needed to go shower and get ready for bed. After I did what he told me to do, I fell asleep praying that the following day would be a better one. I called and made an appointment at the abortion clinic the following week, and James accompanied me to make sure that I went through with it. I cried the entire ride home because he had forced me to go through with the abortion. From my first experience with an abortion, I knew that things would only get worse.

James promised me that things would be different, and he did appear to change in the following weeks. I didn't believe him because he still spent more time being his alias than he did spending time with me. I was so lonely, and I missed T. T made me happy, and I wished that he could take me away from this madness called life.

CHAPTER 22

Giselle: Baby Makes Three and Four

The pregnancy went fast since I found out at four months. On March 15, I gave birth to Shawn Jr. He was perfect, and I fell in love with him instantly. When I went into the hospital to have my son, Shawn didn't even come up to the hospital for the delivery. When Toya came up to the hospital to see me, she told me that she had seen Shawn around the way driving by with some girl in his passenger seat. How could he be fucking some chick while I was there, giving birth to our son? I hated him so much at that point, and I didn't know how much more I could take. I stayed in the hospital for two days, and then went home. The first couple of months were the worst because Shawn was never around to help me with the baby. At times I was so depressed, and since I didn't have any friends that Shawn approved of, I couldn't count on any help from anyone. I had a little help from his cousin, Neisha, who watched the baby for me when I did go out. I was getting close to her, but I needed more. This was a time when I needed my mother around. And I missed her even more now than ever.

Periodically I would call Toya to get a heads up on what was going on in the neighborhood. On one particular day she had so much to tell me that it would change the way I looked at things from that day forward.

She told me first that Gina was still dealing with Black Sam, which wasn't a surprise. Gina needed a dude like that to survive. She also told me that Gina was talking greasy about me, saying that I was all happy with my life with Shawn, and how I would find out that he was no prize. Toya told me that she heard a little while after I had the baby that Shawn Jr. wasn't Shawn's first child, and that, in fact, Alyia, Mimi's daughter, was his. I couldn't believe my ears. How could both of them not reveal such a secret o me? Why would he tell me that he had no children? And why wouldn't Mimi ever reveal that to me during my many visits?

I thought that it was a lie and that people were just throwing salt in the game to see where my head was at. I wouldn't allow them to ruin my life. I was still fighting to make my marriage work. With the little bit of time Shawn and I did spend together, we were either having sex or arguing, and that was not the way it was supposed to be. I didn't change my last name for nothing!

I thanked Toya for the information, but I informed her that I didn't believe any of it, although I would do some research. I couldn't bring myself to believe that it was true. I played it cool and didn't confront either of them. On my next visit to Mimi's house, I told her that I would watch Alyia while she ran to the fabric store. When she left, I began my search. I looked everywhere for anything that would reveal the truth. In her office there was a locked file cabinet. I used a safety pin to pick the lock. Inside was a lot of paperwork, including Alyia's birth certificate, and the father's name was James Wilson. So Shawn was not the father of her child. I was relieved; it was the same last name, so it could have been one of his brothers since I didn't know any of them. I looked through some other papers and found a previous address for James Wilson. I wrote the address down for my records. Although Shawn wasn't the father, I was still curious to find out who was, since she never talked about him. I stashed the address to use at a later time.

In the weeks that followed I tried my best to make things better between Shawn and me. I was still unsuccessful in every attempt. I hated being a failure, but it wasn't totally my fault. Shawn wasn't trying. I felt like a prisoner. I hadn't seen my brother. I hadn't even seen my father that much and I missed them both. My life had turned into something far different from what I had imagined. I always thought that being married to a drug dealer would be the best life anyone could ask for. I looked at the life my mother had with my father and somehow, I was blinded by all the material things. My mother never went out. All she did was go get her hair and nails done, go shopping, and take care of my brother and me. I never thought that things would be that way for me. I always thought that she wanted to live the way that she did, and she always seemed happy with it.

It was nothing like you saw on TV. I had all the glamorous clothes, but I never went anywhere to wear them. I had the nice cars, but I never went anywhere in them. I had the nice house, but I never had friends that could come over to enjoy it with me. When Shawn Jr. turned one, he didn't even have a birthday party. Shawn just took him to Chuck E. Cheese's, not exactly what I had hoped for.

About two months after Shawn, Jr.'s first birthday, I found out that I was pregnant again. I was not happy at all, but I hoped that this new baby would bring Shawn and me closer together. Shawn was much more attentive when he found out about the baby, and he began to make love to me on the regular. This pregnancy seemed to be turning Shawn into the perfect husband. Many nights I lay there next to him, smiling because he was mine. I was glad that I had a man that loved me the way Shawn did.

He even allowed me to spend a little bit of time with Toya. I was so happy because I felt like things were changing for the better. Toya and I began to catch up on all of the time that we had lost. Surprisingly, Shawn didn't object. I needed Toya in my life just as much as I needed him, and I finally had them both.

My birthday came that year when I was six months pregnant. I was home lying down since I hadn't been feeling too well that day. Shawn came in and I smiled when I saw the roses and large gift box that he was carrying. I sat up and waited for him to reach the sofa.

"Shawn, what's that?"

"I got something special for you. Open it."

I opened it and found a smaller box, which led to an even smaller box. I looked at him and smiled once I reached the smallest box that contained a princess cut, pink diamond ring. I hugged him as a tear fell from my eye. He told me that it was a thank-you for being a good wife. He also told me that he had planned a big party for me at my father's club. He gave me an envelope full of money to go to Mimi's and have her make me an outfit for the party.

She didn't seem too excited about making the outfit, but I contributed it to her being lonely. One thing that I noticed about Mimi was that she never had a man. For all of the time that I had known her, I had never seen her with a man. I often wondered if she was gay. I couldn't begin to wrap my brain around how any woman could do without a man. That was just not an option for me.

After leaving Mimi's I had my hair and nails done. I also

made a stop and had my makeup professionally done. I even went as far as having eyelashes applied. My makeup, along with my pregnancy, made me glow, and I was sure that with the outfit I had I would glow brightly enough to light up the club. After I was dressed I made my way down to the club and was knocked off my feet by the surroundings. Shawn and my father had the club decorated for a queen. The color scheme was pink and white, from the balloons down to the tablecloths. The centerpieces were silver candleholders with pearls wrapped around them. The lights were dim, and the candles set a romantic tone. They even had a special chair for me, which was similar to a throne. I couldn't believe that they went out of their way to find a chair for me to sit in that emulated my thoughts of being a princess. Shawn even had a tiara made for me, with "princess" spelled out in rhinestones. I had never seen anything so beautiful in my life, and I knew I'd remember that day for a long time to come.

I knew that this party was going to be another huge step on the road to happiness for Shawn and me. We had been getting along so well that it was almost hard to believe my life wasn't a dream. I had been getting so used to being disappointed by his actions that I was scared to believe that life with him could be good. During the entire party he gave me his undivided attention. He was making sure that I knew that he loved me.

I had plans of making love to him that night like I had never done before. I wanted to show him that I loved him just as much as he loved me, if not more. I wanted him to know that I had forgiven him for everything that he'd done, and that we could make it work. Unfortunately my plans were derailed when I returned from the bathroom and noticed Shawn in a heated argument with Mimi. I didn't know what to think. Why was Mimi even here? And I couldn't think of any reason Shawn would be arguing with her. I had to know what was going on. I had to find out once and for all what his ties were to Mimi. I had to know if everything that Toya told me was the truth, since this scene definitely played out something more than a friendship or tailor/client relationship.

CHAPTER 23

Mimi: Fed Up

2004

I tried my best to hold off from snapping on Shawn. James was long gone, and Shawn never loved me the way that James did. James walked out on me the day that Shawn arrived, and I hadn't seen James since. Even though he was the same man in body, his mind was totally different.

It hurt that Shawn loved Giselle, and I knew from the moment I met her that sooner or later she would ruin my life. I agreed to his affairs because he didn't give me any other option, but we never agreed on babies. He told me when Giselle was pregnant with his first baby that it was a terrible mistake, and it would never happen again. But now she was carrying his second child, and to add insult to injury, he was giving her a party, flaunting her around like I didn't even exist.

I decided that enough was enough and it was time for him to make a choice, and if he couldn't make a choice, I would leave. I had to. I could no longer stand being his wife and staying in the background like a jump-off.

I drove down to Giselle's party with all intentions of ruining it. I had to make my presence known, not only to him, but to every other person that thought I was just his tailor.

I entered the club, and after greeting a few people with the only smile that I could produce under the circumstances, I found James standing alone with a drink in his hand.

"What are you doing here, Mimi?"

"Look, I can't deal with this shit anymore, Shawn. If you want to continue your life with her, then please let me go so that I can move on."

"Why don't we talk later? I told you not to come here and fuck this shit up for me. She's already suspicious."

"Fuck her, Shawn. I'm your wife! Remember me? You're playing me and I'm not going to stand for it anymore!"

"Whatever, you need to go home and I'll talk to you later. I told you about this hothead shit. This shit is important to me, and you don't give a fuck. So fuck you. I'll talk to your tired ass later!"

"Fuck you!" I yelled, slapping him. I stormed out of the club, crying. I got in my car and sped home to the apartment. That was the longest drive I had ever taken in my life. I thought back to the first time I was hurt by a man, and that made it even worse. How did I let myself get played by another man, as if the first time wasn't enough of a lesson?

When I pulled into the parking lot I sat in the car and let out a scream. That scream released all the tension that had built up inside me since the day Shawn met Giselle. I hated her even more now than I did before. She had ruined my family, and I was pissed at myself for allowing it to happen. Sometimes women can be so blind, and I was blind for sure. I thought that after all of the trouble that James went through to get with me, he would never do anything to ruin that, but I was fooled. I got out of the car, staggering because I was so upset, and made my way up to the apartment. I went in and begun to cry again as I eased down on the hardwood floor and rested my back against the wall.

CHAPTER 24

Giselle: It will come to light

2004

I couldn't take the view any longer. I wanted to see what was going on. I made my way over to Mimi and Shawn. Then Mimi slapped Shawn and stormed out of the club. I walked up to Shawn.

"What the hell was that about, Shawn?"

"Nothing!" he yelled.

"Obviously it was something. People don't just slap people for nothing."

"Giselle, we need to talk about this later at home. People are starting to stare."

"I don't give a damn about these people! Are you fucking her, Shawn?"

"Giselle, I said we'll talk later!" he said, walking away.

"Shawn, don't walk away from me!" I said, grabbing his arm.

"Get the fuck off me, Giselle," he said, pushing me away.

"I'll talk to you later." Then he walked away and left the club.

I was fuming mad. Why the hell did my night have to be ruined with this bullshit? I hope he didn't think it was over. I told Toya that I was leaving, and I said a few other good-byes before I left. I assured my dad that everything was fine, because he had noticed the commotion and asked if I was OK. I left the club and made my way over to Mimi's house. I wasn't surprised to see Shawn's car in her driveway. I sat out there for about an hour, but he never came out. I drove home, crying and upset. What the hell was happening? Here I was, loyal, six months pregnant with his second child, and he was acting this way. I didn't know what to do. I went home and told Neisha, who was babysitting, that she could go home. She noticed that I was upset and asked what was wrong.

"Nothing. I'm just a little emotional. You know how it is when you're pregnant," I said while putting my purse down on the table and sitting down to take off my shoes.

"Well, how was the party? You're home so early."

"It was OK!"

"Giselle, you don't have to front for me. What's wrong?"

"Everything!" I said, starting to cry again. "I don't know what's going on. I thought things were getting better with our marriage. Mimi came to the party and they had some type of argument, and she slapped him and stormed out of the club." I paused to catch my breath.

"Baby mama drama, huh? I know how that is."

"What? What do you mean by that?"

"Nothing. I was just talking about me," Neisha said quickly, attempting to cover her mistake.

"Neisha, if you know anything, please tell me," I pleaded.

"G, I'm sorry I even asked, but Shawn would kill me, so I can't tell you anything. I'm sorry."

"Why did my life have to turn out this way? I thought that

I was going to be happy, and look what happened. I should have listened to my brother. I feel like a damn fool." I put my face in my hands and the tears started to pour out. Neisha rubbed my back.

"G, I'm sorry. I have to go. Call me tomorrow if you need me to watch Shawn Jr."

"OK."

She grabbed her bag and left. I couldn't be mad that she didn't tell me anything, but I knew that something was definitely up between Shawn and Mimi. She gave it away by saying that it was baby mama drama.

I sat there on the couch and fell asleep. I woke up at two A.M. when I heard Shawn Jr. crying. I went upstairs and noticed that Shawn still wasn't home. He was probably still at Mimi's. I was going to give him a piece of my mind when he did get here. I went and rocked Shawn Jr. back to sleep. When I was done I went to my room and started to put some clothes in my suitcases. I wanted to get packed because I getting the hell out of this house.

There was no way I was going to continue living like this. My children and I would be fine without Shawn. No man was worth all the stress I'd been through. I knew that once I got the chance to tell him how I felt, it would take a load off of me. I would have a new beginning, and even though I loved Shawn with all of my heart, I was done loving a man that didn't love me. No longer would I be the fool. Situations like these were the reason why they created divorce!

CHAPTER 25

Mimi: Too Much To Bear

2004

I knew that it wouldn't be long before Shawn arrived to kiss my ass. At this point I was ready to let him kiss it, but this time he would be kissing it good-bye! He came in still drunk and angry that I came to the club and put him on Front Street. I didn't care. I wanted him to realize that my life was not a joke, and it was important to me. I just wished that I had realized that before now, because it was damn sure too late. I was still sitting on the floor, crying, when he arrived.

"Mimi, what the hell is wrong with you? You know you almost fucked everything up for me tonight!" he yelled.

"I don't care anymore. I married you because I believed that you would never hurt me, but that's all you've done since the day I met you. I left a good man for you, and this is what I get in return!" I cried.

"You didn't leave a good man. Did you forget that he left you? Did you also forget that you fucked that nigga Big T! I knew from the beginning that you weren't to be trusted, but I trusted your lying ass anyway. I should have let your dumb ass have that baby so you would be alone, once I kill that nigga."

"Whatever. You act like you are a saint in this. I only slept with Terrance because of you!"

"Bullshit, Mimi. You slept with Terrance because you are a ho!"

"Fuck you, Shawn, or whatever the hell your name is now. Just leave, OK? We both already know that this is over."

"I'm not going anywhere until I'm ready!" he yelled before he pushed me all the way down to the ground and started to rip off my clothes.

I screamed for help, but no one could hear me, and if they did hear me, they probably just wanted to mind their own business. He slapped me repeatedly and I continued to cry as he yelled obscenities, spitting his liquor-filled saliva all over my face. He was much too strong for me to push him away, so I was forced to lie there while he raped me. I couldn't grasp the idea of what was happening. My husband, who I took vows with, was raping me. I screamed in agony and all he did was smile. The entire act lasted about five minutes, but it seemed like forever. Once he was finished, he stood up and fixed his clothing.

"You better be here when I come back tomorrow. If you try to leave with my daughter, I'm going to kill your ass when I find you!" he threatened.

I didn't respond. I just lay there and cried. I felt so degraded and I was in so much pain. As soon as he walked out of the apartment I got up and fixed my clothing. I gathered up a few things and left the apartment to pick up Alyia from Shawn's mother. I knew that I had to move fast before Shawn returned. If I stayed he'd probably kill me. I wanted to warn Terrance about Shawn's plans, but I knew that I couldn't. Although I did have love for him, I loved my life more.

I fell for Terrance, and not because of the money. His personality was unlike anyone else I knew. He was strict but sweet, and you could tell that it was genuine. I walked away from him because I feared for my life, but I decided to give him a call once more before I disappeared.

"Hello."

"T?"

"Yeah. What's up, stranger? I haven't heard from you in a while."

"I know. I've been thinking about you all the time, though."

"Really?"

"Yeah. You know I love you, T."

"I can't tell the way you dropped me like a hot potato!"

"I didn't have a choice. My husband threatened to take my daughter away from me."

"I know, but I haven't stopped thinking about you."

"I'm glad. I called to tell you that I am taking my daughter and leaving. I'm not coming back."

"What?"

"I have to leave, T. I can't take it anymore. I just want to tell you that I'll never stop loving you."

"So that's it? You're gone just like that?"

"Could you tell me that you love me one more time before we hang up?"

"I love you, Mrs. Mimi. Take care of yourself!"

"I love you, too, Mr. Big. I'll miss you," I said as the tears began to flow down my face. "Good-bye!" I said before hanging up.

Although I wasn't sure, I had a feeling that I would never talk to Big T again, and I wanted to make sure that he knew how much I cared for him I also wanted to know that I was loved by someone, which made leaving a little easier. The love that he had for me, along with the love that I now had for myself, was enough to give me the strength to leave this life behind.

I prayed that he would be OK as I drove to pick up my daughter and make my way to a new city to get away from this madness. I had to survive. I couldn't let Shawn take me down. I'd made it too far for that.

CHAPTER 26

Giselle: Back Home

2004

Shawn dragged himself in the house around four A.M. I was sitting in the living room in the dark, waiting on him. I startled him when I called his name.

"Shawn, what the fuck is going on?"

"Look, I'm tired and I don't feel like this right now."

"You know what, Shawn, I don't feel like it either. You don't even have to give me an explanation. I'm taking my son and we are leaving!" I said, rising from my seat.

"Whatever, Giselle. You'll be back! You need me. Your dad is about to go down, and you ain't going to be able to have his money, then. So trust me, you are going to need a nigga. You can go 'head and leave, but you ain't taking none of the shit I bought you!"

"What the hell are you talking about, my father is going down? If he goes down, so do you. You're his partner! And I'm never going to need you, Shawn. You'll need me!"

"I don't think so! You'll learn, Shorty. It's every man for

himself." Then he turned his back to me and walked up the stairs.

I went upstairs, got Shawn Jr. and my suitcases that I had stashed, and left. I went to my father's house and found him in the dining room, counting money.

"Hey, Baby Girl, what are you doing here?" he asked, kissing my forehead. "I'm surprised to see you. Is everything okay?"

"Daddy, I had to leave Shawn!" I said, crying.

"Why? What happened? Did he hurt you?"

"Emotionally, Daddy. I can't take it anymore. I've been a prisoner in my own home. He's been lying to me and I know it. I just can't take anymore. I tried my best to make it work, but he didn't. It was a losing battle. I told him that I was leaving and he didn't even try to stop me. He told me that I'd need him one day, and that you were going down."

"What? I'm going down? Fuck that, nigga. I'll kill his ass first. Ain't no way I'm going down. I've been on top for too long, and ain't no young nigga gonna take that away. You don't even have to worry about that shit. You know this is always your home, so you'll never have to worry about a place to live. Now you go upstairs and get some sleep. You don't need to be stressed like that. You have a baby on the way, and one already here to think about. I'm sorry I let you marry his sorry ass!"

"It's not your fault, Daddy."

"Go ahead up to bed, Baby Girl," he said, hugging me and kissing me on my forehead again.

"OK!"

I went up to the bedroom, put Shawn Jr. in the bed with me, and held him close. We all learn from our own mistakes, but I never knew that marrying Shawn would be the biggest one of my life. I knew that Gina was probably laughing her ass off because of how my relationship with Shawn had turned out. At least she was smart enough not to get pregnant by his ass.

I could barely sleep that night, but I tried my best. When I work up in the morning I had a missed call from Toya. I called her to see what was up since she never called me that early in the morning.

"Hey, Toya, what's up?"

"G, what the hell happened last night? Are you OK? Where are you?"

"I'm cool. I'm at my dad's house."

"So you left? What was the deal with Shawn and the chick Mimi?"

"I don't know. I don't really care. She can have him. I'm tired of going through that bullshit with him. It's no longer worth it to me."

"Well now do you believe me about that little girl being his? I told you to check his background before you married him. Girl, I heard that Shawn isn't even his real name. The niggas around the way said that's an alias. His name is James or some shit like that!"

Toya continued talking, but I was no longer hearing her. What the hell was Shawn hiding? Why was he using an alias? Then I remembered that James was the name I saw on Alyia's birth certificate. So maybe it was true. This was getting crazy. I had to find out what he was hiding, especially because of what he said about my father. I had to get in touch with Neisha. I knew she knew something, and somehow I had to get her to talk to me.

I called Neisha on the phone and asked her if she could meet me at this park by my dad's house, and she agreed. I dropped Shawn Jr. off at Toya's house and I went to meet Neisha at the park. When I reached the park she was sitting on the bench waiting on me.

"What's up? I'm glad you could meet me here."

"It's cool."

"Look, I know Shawn is your cousin and you are really loyal to him, but I need your help. I would never tell him that you were the one who told me anything, but I just need to know what the hell I got myself into. "

"What is it that you want to know?"

"What is Shawn's deal? I don't know what's up with him and Mimi. Apparently I don't even know his real name."

"Look, you have to promise me that you won't tell Shawn what I tell you."

"I promise!"

"Shawn isn't his real name. His name is James Wilson. He and Mimi are married, so your marriage to him is really just a front. He got out of jail about five years ago, and that's when he met Mimi. She was young, he ended up getting her pregnant, and that's when he married her. He changed his name because he said his plan to be on top included hurting a lot of people, and he didn't want it to lead back to his past. He took the social security number and past life of some dude that he killed. Shawn is crazy, and he will kill without hesitation. He and Mark used to do robberies and things like that, until he got caught up with your dad. Then they got into the drug game heavy. Mimi agreed for him to deal with Gina, and to deal with you. But she never agreed for him to marry you or get you pregnant twice. That's probably why she was so pissed, because he has you pregnant again and was giving you that party and showing you off as his wife, when really she's his wife. The plan wasn't going the way they had mapped it out. That's really all I can tell you. I shouldn't have told you that much, but if I tell you anymore, it could be my life. I like you, Giselle, and I feel bad that you have to go through this, but all I can say is be careful and watch yourself." Neisha rose up from the bench and gave me a hug.

I was so shocked. What the hell had I gotten myself into?

Was my dad in danger? I wanted to know what their plan was and how the hell I was a part of it.

After I left the park, I decided to drive past the address that was listed for James Wilson. It was a little house in West Philadelphia. I went up to the door and knocked. No one was home. I looked in the window and I didn't see anyone. I went around to the back of the house and to my surprise the back door was unlocked. I went in to find a fully furnished house. It looked like someone lived there because there was a fully stocked refrigerator. I saw a stack of mail and most of the mail belonged to a Marie Wilson. *This must be Shawn's mother's house,* I thought. He did tell me once that her name was Marie.

I went upstairs and looked in all of the bedrooms. When I came to the last bedroom, I opened the door and there wasn't any furniture inside. The room was full of just boxes. I quickly looked through some of the boxes, which were just full of bank statements, medical papers, receipts, and other important papers. I got up and headed out the door. There was nothing there to help me out with what I wanted to know.

I got in my car and drove back to Toya's. I went inside and told her everything that Neisha had told me, and she was just as shocked as I was. She told me that she would always have my back and she would be there to help me with anything I needed. I was so angry now. All of my sadness was gone. I asked Toya to keep Shawn Jr. a little while longer. I called Daddy's cell phone and he told me he was on his way to the club to meet with Mark and Shawn. I told him what Neisha told me, and he was pissed. He told me that he would handle things and not to worry. I was so scared because I didn't know what my father planned to do. I knew that I should just leave it up to him, so that's what I did. I was sitting outside of Toya's house when my cell phone rang.

"Hello!" I yelled, not recognizing the number.

"Can I speak to Giselle?"

"Speaking. Who is this?" I asked

"It's Gina."

"What do you want? And if you are calling to say I told you so, I'm not in the mood for it."

"No, that's not why I'm calling. Look, I know that we've had our problems in the past, but there's a lot of things that I've done that I am not so proud of. There's a lot of things that I know that I wish I didn't know. Although you may hate me, I don't hate you, even after you put me in the hospital. I feel like I deserved it in a way. Everything happens for a reason, and I called you because I still care about you and I want to help you. I feel like that's what I'm supposed to do."

"So why now, Gina?"

"Because I realized that I should have never let a man break up our friendship. It wasn't worth it. I'm with Black Sam now, and although he's not Prince Charming, he treats me a lot better than Shawn ever did. I wish I could have warned you, but I was silly then."

"Well, I have a lot going on right now, and I need to find my dad to make sure he's OK. Just call me tomorrow and we can talk then."

"I really have a lot that I need to tell you, so I will definitely call you tomorrow."

"OK," I said, then quickly hung up.

That was a really weird phone call, one that I was definitely not expecting. I wanted to know what she had to tell me, so I figured that I would have to act civil when she called back just to get the information that I was searching for.

CHAPTER 27

Shawn: Takeover

2004

I didn't know who Giselle or Mimi thought they were fucking with, but I wasn't one to play games. I had to put Mimi in her place to let her know that she would always belong to me. I also had to let Giselle know that leaving me wasn't as easy as it looked. When her old man was long gone, she'd need me. Her young ass wouldn't know how to take care of herself, even if there was a book on that shit. All she'd ever known was her daddy, who paid for everything, and that was soon to be a wrap. I called Mark and told him that tonight was the night, no more bullshittin'. I was tired of dancing around this shit. I needed to be the man on top, and this nigga Big T was making it difficult.

Everything had gone wrong. I knew that if I had never fucked with Giselle in the first place, I could have stayed focused. I planned to ruin Big T's reputation. I had been cutting the product so that his customers would begin to be unsatisfied. The plan worked at first until he found out. How the hell he found out what I was doing, I never knew. I had everything mapped out, and now I didn't know what I was going to do. I was losing my grip on everything, and hurting more people than I had ever wanted to.

I had a meeting set up with Big T at the club that he owned. Mark and I drove down to the club and waited for him to arrive. I had nothing to talk about with this nigga, although he thought that I did. I was through talking, because niggas never listened. I had already told him that he needed to get out the game and turn it over to me, but he didn't want to listen. He was pissed about what was going on with Giselle and me. I would speak loudly and clearly tonight, because I wasn't going to give him any other options. Either he gave this shit up, or he gave up his life.

Once Big T arrived, we all entered the club and made small talk to pass some time. I put another offer on the table, giving this nigga one more chance to stay alive. Of course he didn't want to hear it. He was still pissed about what had happened between Giselle and me.

"I'm not going for that shit, Shawn. I got too many years in this to throw it away. I knew that I should have never trusted you."

"I should have never trusted you. Nigga, you fucked my wife and got her pregnant!"

"Your wife? Who the fuck is your wife? Giselle's your wife!"

"Yeah, Mimi, nigga, that's my wife. You were fucking my wife! I knew you were a slimy nigga; that's why my dad stopped fucking with you!"

"I see. So you got pissed over that? I really did care about her! And as far as your dad, we fell out because he didn't want a partner. He wanted the limelight all to himself. It wasn't about anything that I did to him; we were best friends before the money went to his head. If you would have done more research, you would have known that."

"And if you would have done more research, you wouldn't be sitting here in the predicament you are right now, nigga!"

"So what do you plan to do now? The gig is up. You young niggas should have planned this shit a little better. You could never take my spot! All of your plans are fucked up! You ain't never going to be me, so what the fuck are you going to do about that?" he yelled before pulling his gun from his waist.

"Rock your ass to sleep, nigga!" I said before pulling out my 9-millimeter handgun and firing without hesitation. Big T slumped back in the chair before hitting the ground. Blood splattered all over Mark and me.

"What the fuck, man!" Mark yelled, jumping up from the chair. "What are you doing?"

"I had to get rid of that nigga. Nothing was going as planned, man. I had no other choice!"

"I'm through with this shit, man! You're slipping. You can't just keep killing people. None of that shit was part of the plan!" he yelled.

"Fuck the plan! We're doing this my way!" I yelled back.

"I'm doing shit my own way. I'm through with this shit, J. I mean it!"

"You can't be done with this. This is a marriage, nigga. Do you understand that shit?"

"Fuck that. If it was a marriage, then take these words as a divorce!"

I didn't really care if Mark abandoned the plan, because killing Big T was a victory for me. There was a new king in town. After I basked in the glory for a few minutes, Mark and I left the club and went out to the car. Once I reached my house, I changed and burned up the blood-covered clothing in the fireplace.

Mark went home a little shook. He was always shook when it came to murder, so I brushed off the remarks that he made after the shooting. This was something that had to be done. I knew that I would have to get away and lay low until everything blew over. The cops would definitely suspect me. I packed up a few things and got in my car to begin my escape. I called Mimi's apartment and got no answer.

You can run, but you can't hide, I thought. *We'll meet again, Miss Mimi, and when we do, only one of us will come out alive.*

I wasn't sure of my destination, but I knew that I had to get there fast, wherever it was. I hopped on I-95 and continued to ride, blasting the radio the whole way.

CHAPTER 28

Giselle: Losing It All

2004

I made my way to Daddy's club after getting off the phone with Gina. I was two blocks away when I saw all the yellow police tape, and I screamed in fear. I got out of my car and ran up to the police tape. They wouldn't allow me to get through. I told them that it was my father's club, and finally they told me that my father had been rushed to the hospital with multiple gunshot wounds. I broke down as the officer tried to console me. Once I got myself together, I ran back to my car and drove to the hospital, which was ten minutes away. I cried so hard during the drive.

What have I done? It's all my fault. Please, Daddy, be OK! Please be OK. I can't do it without you.

I reached the hospital and ran through the emergency room door. At the registration desk I told them who I was and they led me through to the back trauma room where my father was barely clinging to life. I couldn't lose another parent, not like this. What did I ever do to deserve this? I sat down and prayed out loud, holding on to my father's hand.

"Dear God, I am so sorry for every wrong thing I have ever done in my life. Please don't take my father away from me. I need him in my life. I know that it's all my fault, and I wish I could take his place right now. If I hadn't dealt with Shawn in the first place, maybe I wouldn't be in the situation I'm in right now. Please, Lord, I love my father so much. I don't know how I can go on without him. I know that you never put more on a person than they can handle, but I don't know how much more I can take."

Just then my father's heart monitor beeped and his heart rate went flat. I cried so hard as the nurses and doctors did all they could, but their efforts fell short. My father died of six gunshot wounds, the fatal one collapsing his lungs. After they unplugged all of the machines, I sat there next to him. Everything in my world was going wrong. I loved my father so much, and now he was gone. The detectives came to talk to me and I told them everything I knew about Shawn. They assured me that they would catch up with him and that there were witnesses at the scene that had pinpointed Shawn as the shooter. They also said that they had Mark Bowers in custody and he was being very cooperative with their investigation. They gave me their business cards and allowed me to sit with my father a little while longer before they came to wrap him up.

"Damn, Daddy, why did this have to happen to you?" I asked myself. Then I told him that I loved him, kissed him on the forehead, and assured him that his Baby Girl would be OK.

I called Toya and told her what happened and she cried with me. I told her that I had a few things to handle. I drove past Mimi's house and saw that her car was gone. When I went up to the house, the door was open, and it appeared that she left in a hurry. I got back in my car, angry as hell, and drove past the house that Shawn and I had shared, and everything was still there but he wasn't anywhere to be found either. It was all a setup, and I was the sucker! They had this all planned. All I could do was sit there and cry.

I went up to the prison the next day to tell Akil the news. He wouldn't accept my visit, so I told them to relay the message that our father was dead. He probably already knew, and didn't accept my visit because he was still mad at me. I needed him to talk to me. He was all I had left besides my son and the baby that I was carrying.

I made arrangements for Daddy's funeral, which was that Saturday. I had never seen a funeral so crowded in my life. It was like a funeral for someone famous. The cops escorted my brother to the viewing in shackles. It was so hard to see him like that. I told him I loved him as they took him away. The following weeks were the hardest, and I ended up being hospitalized for dehydration. I was so depressed that I failed to eat or drink properly. I knew that I had to get myself together for the sake of my children. And I knew that if this baby I was carrying was going to survive, I had to take care of myself.

I never heard from Gina that next day. I wasn't really all that stressed about it either. I had a lot of other things I needed to worry about. I sold my father's house because I couldn't bear to live there after losing both of my parents. I bought a house in Willingboro, New Jersey for the children and me. It was a four-bedroom house in a nice, quiet neighborhood. I tried to get as far away from the drama as I possibly could. Toya and me became closer than ever in the following months.

I delivered a baby girl three months after the death of my father. She was so beautiful. I named her Alexis Tajay Doran. There was no way I would give her Shawn's last name.

Toya was by my side through all the pain of the delivery, which was much more painful than the delivery of my son. It was very hard, especially not having any family to gather around me to share in my joy. I went home two days later, and Toya practically moved in to help me take care of the baby, along with helping me with Shawn Jr. As time passed, I was able to look at my future in a different light. Although Shawn was on the run and the police had no idea where he was, I couldn't continue to live my life as his prisoner.

I started going out more, and I even got a job working as home health aide for a nursing agency. My life was changing for the better. I even began to date, but after dating another drug dealer, I realized that I wasn't into drug dealers anymore. Shawn had turned me off. I moved on, but I didn't give up on men, just on drug dealers.

I knew that there had to be someone out there for me and I found him shortly after my breakup with the drug dealer. It was a Friday and I decided to stop at the mall after work to pick up a few things for the kids and me. As I walked from the parking lot, this fine, dark-skinned brotha with a nice build called out to me.

"Excuse me, miss, how are you? My name is Kevin. I know you don't know me from a can of paint, but when I saw you step out of that car, I had to stop you. I just wanted to let you know that you are a beautiful woman and I would like to get to know you; that is, if you don't have a man and you are willing to give me a chance." He extended his hand.

Reaching out to shake his hand, I then responded.

"Hi. My name is Giselle and no I don't have a man, but I just got out of a bad relationship not so long ago, and I'm not sure if I'm ready to get into something new."

"I understand that, and I'm willing to just be your friend, if that's OK with you."

Taking a second to think about it, and looking him up and down once more, I agreed.

"OK, here's my number and I'll be waiting to hear from you," Kevin said while passing me his business card. I glanced at it and noticed that he worked for a real estate agency.

"OK." I took the number, waved good-bye, and went on my way. I shopped for about an hour before returning home. Toya was at my house, playing with the kids in the living room when I came home.

"Hey, how was work?" she asked as she picked Alexis up and walked toward me.

"It was OK. Sorry I'm late, but I stopped at the mall and I met this guy named Kevin. He seemed really nice."

"So, what happened?"

"Nothing! He gave me his number and I told him that I would give him a call."

"That's good, girl. You need to get a man and stop stressing. Life doesn't end because of one crazy dude. You have to move on. You can't let Shawn control the rest of your life."

"I know, and I'm not going to do that. I'm definitely going to give him a call."

"OK. Well I'm about to get out of here. I have to get home to get ready for work tomorrow, but I'll call you in the morning," she said, grabbing her bags.

"OK," I said, hugging her and walking her to the door.

I took the children upstairs and gave them both a bath. I noticed that I had a letter from my brother on the table. After I put Shawn Jr. and Alexis to bed, I went downstairs, opened the letter, and read it.

What's up, Li'l Sis,

I know that I have been acting like a nut, not accepting your visits and not replying to any of your letters. I am so sorry, G! I love you more than life itself, and I was just upset that every-

thing went down the way it did. I knew that nigga was up to something, and I feel bad because I didn't warn Big T before it was too late. Now he's gone. I never even got to say good-bye. I hadn't even seen him since before I got locked up. I heard a lot of things in here and I tried to warn you. I didn't know that he was going to do what he did, but I knew that it was going to be bad. I'm glad that you are doing well now, and I know it's hard, Baby Girl, but keep your head up. You have to move on! Thanks for the pictures of the kids. Damn, I still can't believe that you have two kids now. There are a lot of things that I want to tell you, but I'll wait until the time is right. I know that things are going good for you now, and I wouldn't want to upset you all over again. I'll be home soon, G. Six more months and I'm out of here. And don't worry, that nigga Shawn is going to get his. His boy Mark has already paid for his sins. But enough of that, Baby Girl. I love you and I'll see you soon.

Akil Doran

I was so happy that my brother finally got in touch with me, and even happier to hear that he would be released from prison in six months. I took a quick shower, climbed into bed, and fell asleep. The next day I woke up, fixed breakfast for the kids and me, and went out to the park for a while. I dialed Kevin's number while I sat on the bench. He answered on the second ring. I didn't know what to say.

"Hello, hello!" He repeated his greeting when I hesitated to say anything.

"Hello," I finally replied. "May I speak to Kevin, please?"

"Speaking. Who's this?"

"It's Giselle, the girl you met at the mall yesterday."

"Oh, yeah! How are you? I'm glad that you called."

"I'm fine. How about you?"

"I'm good. I really want to get to know you, and I wanted

to know if you wanted to go out tonight so we can talk over dinner or something."

"That will be fine. I just have to get a babysitter."

"Oh, you have kids? How many?"

"Two—a boy and a girl."

"Oh, that's cool. I have a son. He's eleven I haven't seen him in a few years, though. His mother had full custody and she moved down to Atlanta"

"Oh, OK."

"So, do you want to meet me at the restaurant, or do you want me to come pick you up at your house?"

"I can meet you at the restaurant. Just give me the directions and let me know the time, and I'll be there. "

He gave me the directions and told me to meet him there at eight. The time couldn't have gone by fast enough for me. I decided on a short black dress and some black strappy sandals. I put my hair up in a bun and was on my way to meet him. When I reached the restaurant, the hostess took me to the table where Kevin was waiting for me. He looked even better than he did yesterday. We sat and ate, which was nice. That day led to the beginning of a promising relationship.

Five months passed and we were still going strong. At that point he knew everything there was to know about me, and I knew everything that there was to know about him. We got along so well, and he got along great with the kids, too. I felt so safe with him. He wasn't a drug dealer or a thug, and I truly loved him. This was the way that life was supposed to be. It was a shame that it took me so much time and so much heartache to figure that out.

The time was coming near to my brother's release date, and I couldn't have been happier until I finally received that phone call from Gina. She told me that although she still needed to talk to me in person, she wanted to give me a heads up and let me know that Shawn had surfaced back in

Philly. She also said that his cousin Neisha was found dead shortly after that. She thought I should know because he was looking for me. I thanked her for the information and told her I would be contacting her soon so we could have that talk.

When I hung up the phone it was as if all of those bad memories had happened yesterday. What was I going to do now that he was looking for me? I notified Toya, and she immediately gathered some of her things and came out to my house to stay with me. I told Kevin about it and he told me not to worry. We contacted the local police, and they assured me that they would catch up to him.

Two weeks later my brother was released and I was there with open arms waiting for him. I ran to him and gave him the longest hug ever. This was the first time I was able to hug him in years without having to be told to let go when we hugged for a few seconds too long. I told him that Shawn was back in Philly and that I wanted him to come stay with me. He told me that he couldn't do that and he had to handle Shawn. I pleaded with him to let the police handle it, but I knew he wouldn't listen. I introduced him to Kevin, and Akil approved. He said that he was the kind of dude I needed to be with. Akil stayed with me for about a week and then I dropped him off in Philly at my father's club. I never closed the club. I felt like I owed it to Daddy to keep it open. There was a condo-type apartment over top of it, and that's where Akil chose to live.

I talked to him every day over the next few weeks. I wanted to make sure that he was OK. I also made arrangements to meet with Gina. I drove down to Philly to meet with her, and while on my way I spotted Mimi going into the fabric store. I waited for her to come out. She got into her BMW and drove away. I called Gina to let her know that I would be a little late. I followed Mimi, which led to an apartment building in the Northeast. She parked, and I pulled up next to her and jumped out of my car.

"Damn, girl, you scared me," she said, stunned.

"What's going on, Mimi? Long time, no see. How did it feel to set me up like that?"

"Look, you were never supposed to be involved. I liked you, Giselle. I don't understand why Shawn did what he did."

"But you knew what he was doing and you just went along with it. He killed my father and you ran away with him."

"No, I didn't, Giselle. I left him. I don't know where you are getting your information from, but it's all wrong. That night after the party I told him that I couldn't deal with him anymore. He was never supposed to get serious with you like that. I guess somewhere deep down he really had feelings for you. I had to escape to get out of there; he wanted to keep controlling me the way that he'd controlled you. He never really loved me, and he never really loved you. He only loved himself. I am glad to be rid of him because he only brought me heartache and pain anyway."

"But I don't understand why he's looking for me now."

"I wouldn't know that. All I know is that I'm done with that part of my life, and I've moved on. I'm sorry that you had to go through all of that, but it wasn't my fault."

I couldn't listen to any more of Mimi's lies, so I got in my car and drove away. I didn't trust that bitch as far as I could throw her. I knew that she was lying, but I let it go for the time being. I drove to the club to meet Gina and she was sitting in her car waiting for me. I motioned for her to come in the club and we sat down at the bar and talked.

"So what's up, Gina? What is it that you wanted to talk about?"

"Look, I know that I hurt you really badly when I started dealing with Shawn behind your back, and I'm really sorry.

Truthfully, that was the biggest mistake I ever made in my life thus far. I didn't realize it until I met Black Sam. I didn't know how I was really supposed to be treated. Anyway, I really want us to be friends again. I know that it will take some time, but I'll wait as long as I have to."

"I thought that you said that you had some things to tell me?" I asked, ignoring her comments for the time being.

"I do. I don't know how else to tell you this, but I think that Shawn had something to do with your mother's death."

"What? How do you figure that?"

"Black Sam told me that before it happened Shawn tried to cut a side deal with him. Shawn offered him a lot of money if he would help Shawn take over your dad's empire. Although Black Sam and your dad were enemies, Black Sam turned down the offer. He just wasn't into that grimy shit. A little while after that, your mom was dead and Shawn and your dad became tighter than visegrips. Black Sam said he knows that Shawn and Mark had something to do with the murder. If they didn't do it personally, then they paid someone to do it." A tear fell down my cheek as I listened to Gina.

"So he planned this all along from day one. Damn, Daddy, how could you not see it coming?"

Gina reached in to hug me, and although we weren't the best of friends, I needed some emotional support at the time. I was so hurt. My mother was killed all because they wanted to take over my dad's empire. How crazy was that? My dad used to be much sharper than that. I don't know how he could have missed that.

"Also, that chick Mimi, she's just as foul. Black Sam said that she was having an affair with your dad during the time that Shawn was dealing with you. In fact, I heard that at one point in time she was pregnant by your father and Shawn made her get an abortion."

This was too much for me to take in all at once. What the

hell happened? That bitch Mimi must have messed with my dad's head. Daddy would have never been caught slipping like that. I knew that I had to get back at her. I didn't know when, and I didn't know how, but it was sure to happen sooner or later.

I thanked Gina for telling me everything she knew. I may have never known all these details if it wasn't for her. I told her that we would get together and talk soon, and maybe one day we could be friends again.

After Gina left I went up to the apartment and noticed that my brother's things were nowhere in sight. I called him on his cell phone, but the number had been disconnected. Where the hell was he?

I began my drive back to New Jersey and my cell phone rang. I didn't recognize the number, but I answered it anyway, hoping that it would be Akil.

"Hello!" I yelled into the phone.

"What's up, Shorty?" Shawn's voice made me cringe.

"What the hell are you calling me for? And how did you get my number?"

"Don't worry about all that. I called because I wanted to talk. I want to see my kid!"

"Please. You better take me to court, because it will be a cold day in hell before I ever let you see my children."

"Look, I'm trying to do this the nice way. I'm not trying to hurt you. I still love you."

"Shawn, that's bullshit. You never loved me. I was just a part of your plan. I hope it was worth it to you."

"Oh, it was well worth it! Look, this is my cell number, so holla at me when I can see my kids," he said before hanging up.

I was really angry, but afraid at the same time. I knew what Shawn was capable of, and I didn't want to experience any more pain from his hands. I cried because I was so unsure of what the future held for my children and me. I knew that Shawn didn't care about my children or me, and as a mother I had to find a way to protect them as well as myself.

When I reached my house, Kevin and the kids were out in the yard playing.

"What's up, babe?" he asked after kissing me. "How did everything go?"

"I talked to Gina and she told me a whole lot about Shawn and my father. She told me that Shawn had something to do with the murder of my mother. And she said that my dad had an affair with Mimi. It's just all so crazy. I can't find my brother and to top it all off, I'm on my way home and Shawn calls my cell phone asking me when he can see the kids. I told him he was crazy."

"How did he even get your number?"

"I don't know."

"Well, what do you want to do? We can get away, if you want. I don't trust that dude, and if he got your number, then he's bound to find out where you live sooner or later."

"I just don't know. I'm scared, Kevin, and I don't know where Akil is."

"He'll call. I'm sure of that. He's knows how much you care about him, and he wouldn't leave you like that." I began crying.

"I thought everything would be better, but it seems like it's getting worse," I said.

"Look, why don't you start packing and we can get out of here for a while. We can go down to Florida and you can meet my family. We can take the kids to Disney and just leave all of this drama here. It's time that you start enjoying your life."

I was afraid to leave the environment that I had just started becoming comfortable with, but after thinking about Kevin's offer, I knew that it was best for me to just go. I packed up some things for the kids and me, and I called Toya and told her my plans. I also told her if by any chance she saw Akil, to let him know where I was and to also tell him to contact me ASAP. I told her that I loved her and I would see her soon.

We were on our way to Florida that night. I hoped that this would be the start of a new life, but I needed to know that my brother was OK. I kept in contact with Toya while we stayed in Florida. She still hadn't seen my brother during the four months we'd been gone. I was so scared that I had lost him too.

In Florida I met Kevin's family. His mother, Mrs. Lisa, was so nice. She was very easy to talk to, and was very comforting during the times when I was upset. I really got to know her and it was good to have some sort of mother figure in my life.

On one particular day, Mrs. Lisa had a big barbecue and invited the whole family. It was really nice to finally meet them. It was good to be around such a close family, since I didn't have too much family of my own. At the party Kevin surprised me when he got down on one knee in front of his entire family and asked me to marry him. It was so beautiful. I cried like a newborn baby when he put the ring on my finger.

After going through everything that I had gone through with Shawn, I felt that I deserved a man like Kevin. I'd never been so happy in my entire life. I couldn't wait to tell Toya, and when I did she was ecstatic. I told her that I would be returning north the following month because I wanted to get married at home.

CHAPTER 29

Shawn: Back to Business

2004

I had to put a little fear in Giselle's heart to let her know who was boss. Shit, Neisha was my blood, but I had to cancel that bitch when she couldn't keep her mouth shut. Family or not, it was about loyalty, and she was far from that. I did a little research and found out that Mark had snitched and told the cops everything, so now he was under police protection.

I had to come back to Philly to make my presence known. My stay in Mexico was just what I needed, but I was back now with a vengeance, and the next nigga on my list was Black Sam. I followed this nigga for weeks until I got the perfect opportunity to step in. I noticed him finishing a meeting with some thug-looking nigga. I'd never seen that guy around. He was thick like he had just come out of jail or some shit! Anyway, after I watched him drive away, I walked toward Black Sam.

As I got close to him, suddenly I was grabbed from behind.

My gun dropped to the ground, and Black Sam turned to me and spoke.

"I knew you were coming, nigga. I was just giving your sorry ass a chance to get close. What the fuck did you think you were going to do?"

"Fuck you, nigga!"

"Fuck me? I think you are the one that's fucked right now. You wanted to be the man but you weren't smart enough to get what you wanted and keep it. Your shit is sloppy, nigga. That's why I'm on top now, because I use my head. I've been waiting for this day for a long time, the chance to blast your ass away. No more Terrance to guard your ass. You killed your fucking protection. How fucking stupid was that?" he asked, laughing.

"I don't find shit funny! If you are going to kill me, then kill me now, nigga!" I screamed.

"No problem!" he said before raising his gun.

I soon felt a warm feeling all over my body as I fell to the ground. I lay there gasping for air as Black Sam stood over me. I soon closed me eyes and went home. This was different than the way my father went out, which was always the way that I thought I would go too. I didn't even get a chance to shoot back. Damn!

CHAPTER 30

Giselle: A Breath of Fresh Air

2004

About a week after Kevin proposed, I received a phone call from Akil. The call that I had been waiting on finally arrived, and I was ecstatic to hear his voice.

"Hey, Baby Girl."

"Akil! Oh my God. Where have you been? I was so worried about you."

"I told you I had to handle a lot of things. I saw your girl Toya and she told me that you were out in Florida living it up. Congrats on the engagement. You deserve it."

"So where are you now?"

"I'm in Philly at the club. I've been doing some remodeling on it. I want to reopen it. So when are you coming home?"

"Soon. I'm just scared. I don't want Shawn to find me."

"Baby Girl, he's a done deal! Black Sam handled that nigga. You don't ever have to worry about him again. Now you can come back to Philly and help me with the club."

"OK, Akil. I love you. And I'll see you soon."

I ran to Kevin and told him the news. Shawn was dead and my children and I never had to worry about him again. But it was a bittersweet victory. The father of my children was dead, and although I didn't wish death on anyone, I sure was glad to have Shawn out of my life for good. Kevin decided that we could leave a little sooner since Shawn was out of the way.

We took a flight back to Philadelphia the following day. When I reached the club I immediately went inside. It was so nice. Akil had turned it into an upscale club. He also told me that in the office was a letter that my father had left for me. I decided not to open it just yet. I wanted to enjoy the moment with my brother in this beautiful club.

"Akil, this club is beautiful! I love it."

"Thanks. I had to make some changes. I don't want all those ghetto niggas up in here. Just people with top dollar! You know what I mean?"

"Yeah, I do. Akil, I want to ask you, on a serious note, what ever happened when you were away and I couldn't find you?"

"I was doing some research on that nigga, Shawn. I was pissed that he killed Mom. I had heard rumors of this while I was in jail, but it wasn't confirmed until after he killed Dad. I felt like I should have been here to protect you. That's what I was supposed to do, as your brother. I knew that he wouldn't be satisfied until he got to you, but I found out that the next nigga on his list was Black Sam, so I warned him. I had a couple of meetings with Black Sam and explained to him everything I heard up in jail about Shawn, and how his plan for takeover meant that he had to get rid of Black Sam too. Black Sam didn't take that lightly and he thanked me with a couple stacks. That's where I got the money to fix up the club. The day that Black Sam paid me is the night that Shawn was killed. The next day I received a call telling me that it was done. That's when I knew that it was safe to call you."

"I thought that you had something to do with his death, or even that you had killed him yourself. I was so scared for you. I didn't want you to end up back in prison," I said, crying.

"Don't cry, Baby Girl. This is a happy time. You no longer have to look over your shoulder everywhere you go. You can live, Baby Girl. Continue to be that princess you were born to be."

"I love you, Akil. You remind me of Daddy so much. You always know how to make me smile when I'm down, and I really appreciate that. I wouldn't know how to live without you," I said, hugging him

"Well, enough of the mushy shit. Let me show you the rest of the club. I got a VIP section just for you," he said, smiling and grabbing my hand to lead me to the stairs.

Each part of the club was better than the next. Each table in VIP was labeled with a theme. He showed me to the back and the table that was mine was named "Ghetto Royalty." I laughed.

"This table is all yours. No one will sit here unless you want them to," Akil told me.

"I love it, Akil. Thanks so much." I hugged him again.

Life was so good during the following months. Kevin and I were married on January 31. It was a beautiful wedding. My brother gave me away, and Shawn Jr. was the ring bearer. I loved my new life, and I was extremely happy. I let Gina back into my life and she was becoming the best friend that I remembered her to be. It took Toya some time to trust her, but she eventually came around. We were the closest that friends could be. I loved them both so much.

I was reminded of the good old days, long before Shawn

came into the picture and ruined it all. I was once a happy, young girl with everything I wanted within my reach. It was a shame how a man could come in and ruin my childhood, forcing me to become a woman long before it was time.

I spent a lot of time in Philly, helping my brother with the club, and Toya and Akil became really close, eventually starting a relationship. I was happy for them. Toya was my best friend, so if there was anyone that I wanted my brother to be with, it was definitely her. I thought that my life had taken a turn for the better. Unfortunately, all good things don't last forever. This breath of fresh air wouldn't last very long.

CHAPTER 31

Mimi: Last Breath

2005

After leaving James, I spent most of my time going from state to state, staying at random hotels and trying to survive. It was hard wondering where your next meal was going to come from. I wasn't going to go to my mother's; I'd rather struggle than knock at her door for a handout. I hated dragging my daughter around while I worked at random jobs, but at the time I had no other choice because I knew if James would've found me, I would be dead.

I received a call from Ms. Marie, James' mom, telling me that James had been killed. Even though I cried, because I did love him, it was a relief. I could now go back to Philadelphia and relax without worrying about him chasing me and trying to take my daughter away. The following week I got on a plane to go back to my home. I prayed that it wasn't wrecked, because Shawn was a petty person.

I felt good when I stepped off the plane. I planned to start a business, tailoring for men, women, and children. No one could stop me now. I had to make a better life for Alyia. I wanted her to see that a woman could survive on her own without a man. The one thing that I felt that I had to do was visit Terrance's grave. I still had love for him. I kind of blamed myself for his death. In a way, I wished that I had kept that baby, so I could have always had a part of him with me. I dropped Alyia off at Ms. Marie's before going to check my apartment. I couldn't risk Alyia seeing it a wreck if James had destroyed it. I didn't know what to expect when I got there.

Surprisingly it was the same way that I had left it, just dusty as hell. I smiled and thanked God that it wasn't ruined. I could now start my business. I took this time alone to clean up: I put fresh sheets on the beds, vacuumed, and mopped the rooms. It was back to normal in a matter of hours.

After going food shopping, I dropped the food off at the apartment and made my way back to Ms. Marie's to get Alyia. I thought that my life was about to take off. I was happy and I smiled as I got out of the car. That smile quickly turned to a frown when Giselle pulled up in the driveway behind me.

CHAPTER 32

Giselle: Light At The End Of The Tunnel

2005

Since I was spending a lot of time in Philly, I thought about Mimi constantly, and it took everything in me not to hunt her down and confront her. I tried to stay away but I ran into her, driving through the neighborhood where Shawn's mother lived. It was late and I almost drove past her. I backed up and stopped in back of her car when she was parking in the driveway. She got out and that was my cue. I jumped out and instantly all the anger and rage that I had built up came rushing out.

"You little lying bitch. I knew I would come across you again!" I said, walking closer.

"Look, Giselle. Shawn is dead now, so why do we need talk about anything?"

"We need to talk about the fact that you were fucking my father, and you are part of the reason that he's dead now!" I yelled, frustrated. She backed away, trying to move closer to the house.

"Look, Giselle, I had nothing to do with that, and I'm sorry that your father is dead. I really had sincere feelings for him. I was hurt as well when he died."

"You are full of shit, you know that? You didn't have feelings for my father. You and Shawn had the whole thing planned from the beginning. And all for money! Was it worth it?"

"I loved him too!"

Right then I couldn't take any more of her lying. I called her a few names before pushing her and walking to my car. I noticed through the car window that she was coming up to me to hit me from behind. I turned around in enough time to push her down to the ground.

"You want to fight, bitch? Come on!" I said, motioning her to get up.

As she rose from the ground, I noticed the knife in her hand. I reached in my bag for my gun, and as she lunged toward me with the knife, I pulled the trigger and shot her once in the chest. She fell down to the ground, and blood poured out of her body onto the pavement. People began coming out of their homes. I jumped in my car and sped off. Blood was everywhere. What the hell had I done? I drove home faster than ever before and found Kevin asleep. When I woke him up he noticed the blood on my clothes and instantly became scared.

"What happened, babe? What's wrong?" he asked nervously.

"I killed her!" I began screaming.

"Who, baby? You killed who?"

"Mimi. I shot her! She tried to stab me, and I shot her! We have to get out of here." I continued crying.

"You have to turn yourself in, baby. You can't go on the run. You have to or you'll look guilty."

"What? I can't go to jail. I just can't," I cried.

"I'll take care of it, I promise. I'll get you the best lawyer that money can buy."

I believed in my husband. I called my brother, Toya, and Gina before calling the police to tell them that I would be turning myself in. I went to prison that night and it was the worst day of my life.

Sitting in that cell I began to reflect on my relationship with Shawn. When I first met him, I fell in love. I was young, but I knew that I wanted him to be mine, and all that I went through to get him ultimately left me with nothing. I let him take over my life. Now I could end up in jail forever because of him. I spent weeks in jail before a trial date was even set. It was hard. The women constantly bothered me. I could never sleep, and I never ate. I was getting sick on a regular basis, and I was losing so much weight that I began to look anorexic.

Kevin came to visit me every time visiting was allowed. I cried at the end of every visit. I missed him and my children so much. I told him never to bring the children there to see me because of my appearance. I didn't want them to see me the way that I was at that point. I cried every day and every night. Kevin was now out there struggling to take care of two children that weren't even his biologically. There was no number for the amount of love I felt for him. Kevin stood by me every step of the way, even when my emaciated figure no longer resembled the woman that he'd married.

I stayed in jail for six months before the trial came in December. I pled not guilty to murder. It was self-defense and the prosecutor knew that. He just wanted to make me suffer for all of the years that he was unable to lock my father away for anything. It would make him feel good to lock me away for life.

Luckily my lawyer had a few tricks up her sleeve. Mrs. Marie was the surprise witness that saved me from a life-term prison sentence, or even worse, a death sentence. She was the defense's star witness, telling the jury that she witnessed the entire event that took place outside of her home and that it was definitely self defense. I had never met this woman before in my life, but for some reason she saved me, allowing me to be there to raise my children.

She could never truly understand how grateful I was to her for that. I felt so connected to her even though I had never met her. She was my angel, and I now believed that we all have them. The jury found me not guilty and I was released into the arms of my husband and children. It had been a long time since I was able to hug them.

Those hugs were the hugs I needed to keep me alive. I almost gave up in prison, and I almost let Shawn take my life away. I planned to get my life back now and show him that I could make it. I was sure he was looking up from hell, mad that I was even alive.

The next few months were a struggle. I slowly began to gain my weight back and get back to normal. I soon found out that I was pregnant, and Kevin was excited. I hoped that my past eating habits wouldn't affect the life of my unborn child.

Several weeks later I received a letter from Ms. Marie. I was nervous to open it, so I went in the bathroom, locked the door behind me, and quietly sat down to read the letter. Anxious was an understatement for what I felt.

Dear Giselle,

I know that you don't know me, but I have heard so much about you. I just wanted you to know that I helped you because it was the right thing to do. I deeply apologize for any pain that my son caused you. I know about your mother and father, and no one should have to endure that much pain in a lifetime. All I ask is that you allow me to see my two grandchildren. I have been in contact with your friend Gina for the last year or so and she explained everything to me from beginning to end, and it hurts my heart that my son did all of those things to you. So that night when you showed up in front of the house and had that confrontation with Mimi, I knew that it was all in the Lord's plan. You were the one left standing for a reason. I will always have love for you, and you are always welcome in my home. God is looking over you and He's calling you. Hopefully you'll listen.

Ms. Marie

I sat there and smiled. Gina was part of the reason that I was free. She went to Ms. Marie and told her everything about me. She encouraged her to save my life. And I would always be grateful to her for that. I decided to give myself to God. I began to go to church on a regular basis, and I was even baptized along with my husband and children. I now knew that God had a plan for me, and it was for me to be happy. God was trying to tell me something long ago, but it all fell on deaf ears. I was now listening and his words were loud and clear.

I began spending a lot of time with Ms. Marie, and my children loved her. She kind of filled the void that I had been missing since the death of my mother. I remembered my mother—her smile, the way she smelled. I missed her reading to me at night and buying me ice cream when I had a bad day. Everything about her was perfect. She resembled the woman that I wanted to be one day—strong and able to stand alone in this world. She would always be special to me, and I hoped that she knew exactly how much she meant to me.

Weeks passed before I found the strength to open the letter that my father had written, but God was pushing me to do it. I knew that I couldn't really move forward with my life until I knew what it was that my father had to say. Sitting alone in my bedroom on a Sunday after church, I opened the letter. When I did a check fell out onto the floor. I picked it up and blinked twice when I read the amount of one million dollars. I couldn't believe it, but I knew that it was part of my healing. God was trying to tell me that there was light at the end of the tunnel.

Dear Baby Girl,

If you are reading this, then that means that I am no longer there to have your back, and I am so sorry. I want you to know that I loved you and your brother with all my heart, and I only wanted the best for you both. I know by now that you've heard about my run-in with the infamous Mimi, and I'm sorry that you had to find out about it. I never wanted to hurt you in any way. I loved your mother so much, and I would have given my life for hers, but I was lonely without her and there was something about Mimi that reminded me of her. I fell in love with her, Giselle, and I know that you may not believe that, but it's true. It was hard for me when she walked away, but I knew she would have stayed with me if she could. I don't ever want you to hate her for the things that may happen to me; she is not the cause of any of it. He husband was extremely abusive and she feared for her life. She finally got the courage to run and in the midst had to leave me behind. When you came here and told me that you'd left Shawn you made a comment to me that confirmed my suspicions about him. I had only that day found out that he was out to get me, and was sitting in the house figuring out what to do when you walked in. I know that I owe it to you and your mother to protect you and the children. I am writing this letter in the hopes that when I get to the club to meet with Shawn and Mark that I return home, and if not, I leave you every dime that I have. I want you to move on, and know that I am looking over you and I will al-

ways be there in sprit. And I want you to always keep me close to your heart. You will always be my baby girl, and you will survive. Don't ever give up. I love you.

Daddy

I had cried many tears in the last few years, but this time they were tears of happiness. I knew that my father was my angel as well. I knew that he was watching over me and I knew that he was the reason that I was alive.

In a way, I felt sad, knowing that my dad really did love Mimi and what she told me about him wasn't a lie. I would have been happy for my dad to find love again, had it been under a different circumstance. I don't believe they would have been together since she was with Shawn; and though Shawn may have been abusive, she still went along with the plan. I wished that things had turned out differently; maybe if I had read Daddy's letter before I got into it with Mimi, things would be different now.

Every event in your life happens for a reason, so I knew now not to ever question God's plan. I knew now that being young and wanting to live the fast life didn't come without a price, and that price was much more than I could afford. I no longer yearned for that life. I loved the life that I was living now. I learned a very valuable lesson, and the downside of it all proved that living the fast life was not as glamorous as what you see on TV. **I also learned that being the heir to a drug empire doesn't guarantee the life of a princess.**

Daddy, I didn't give up! Daddy, I will survive!

I love you,
Your Baby Girl . .

Acknowledgements

First and foremost, I want to thank God for everything. I know that it is very cliché to do this but without God, I wouldn't have been able to get through the things that I have. 2005 was an extremely hard year for me with writing, going to college and raising my son but as many times as I was ready to give up, God always gave me the strength to move forward. So with that said, I owe everything to God and I will continue to work with all of the talents that he has given me and not let them go to waste.

My son Kristion, it is you who makes me strive to succeed. I know for a fact that without you, I definitely would have given up a long time ago. I brought you into this world and I owe it to you to give you the best that I can. I dedicate this book to you and I want you to know that Mommy loves you and though I may not have been totally prepared to have you, I am a much stronger person because of you.

Mom, I want to thank you for all that you do. I want to thank you for all of the encouragement that you give and for never giving up on me. I thank you for all of the love and for being the best mother a person could ask for.

Daddy, thanks for always listening and for encouraging me to do my best at whatever it is that I do. I'm lucky to have a father as understanding as you and I couldn't ask for a better father.

To my grandfather, who is no longer here. I miss laughing

with you and driving up to see you sitting outside with your friends, relaxing. You were very special to me and I will always have a place in my heart devoted to you.

Curt, thanks for all of the times you've looked out for me. I appreciate all of things you've done for me and my son, and I will never forget any of it.

Grandmom Pat, I know that I don't see you as often as I should but I love you very much, and appreciate having you in my life.

To my Aunt Dimples, thanks for making me laugh constantly. Hope thanks for always being there to talk to. Johnetta, thanks for being there to help me whenever I call you with a million questions and thanks for giving me my little cousin Brianna, who shares my birthday; that is definitely a blessing. Honey, thanks for looking out for me. Audrey and Cynthia, thanks for being a part of my life, I love you all.

To my uncle Sonny, you are hilarious and though we don't always see eye to eye, we have a good time when we are around each other.

To Daryl and Audrey, I love you both. Eric, I miss you and I can't wait to see you soon. I hope your little sister has made you proud.

Hoagie, I love you and thank you for all of the letters you send me. I know that I don't always respond right away but I will get better with that.

To Francis, I love you, girl, and I thank you for listening to me whenever I call to vent. Alicia, you are like my sister and you know I would do anything for you. Najla, though we are not as close as we used to be, I still love you just as much. You are my cousin and my Godsister and you will always be special to me.

Aunt Connie, thanks for all of the encouragement over the years. You have always stood behind me with whatever it was

I wanted to do. Peaches, I love you so much and you keep me laughing. You have always been down to earth, no matter what.

To all of my other cousins: Desmond, Alveata, Anthony, Damon Jr., Ashleigh, Wayne, Crystalle, Ryan, Damon Sr., Bernard, Tracey, and Joi. I love all of you.

To Jennifer H., thanks for being one of the best friends anyone could ask for. We've been friends for a very long time and I plan on keeping it that way. Love ya!

Christine, thanks for all of the encouragement. You are my girl. Jennifer B., thanks for always making me laugh.

Whistle, though I know that things haven't turned out the way that we planned, I will always love you. You helped me a lot when I began writing this story and I will never forget that or anything else that you've done for me. You will always hold a special place in my heart, no matter how things turn out. Thank you for being a friend and giving me our wonderful son to keep me going.

Corey, thanks for hanging out with me and letting me get to know you. You are a really nice person, and I am glad that I was able to experience that.

Mr. and Mrs. Myers, I love you both. Mr. Myers, thanks for being a wonderful teacher and supporting me long after I was no longer your student. You have made a difference in my life and I will always be grateful for that. Lisa, I love you to death and I thank you for being there to talk to, thanks for keeping me laughing all of the time and, let's not forget, keeping me up on the gossip! LOL

Ms. Booker, wherever you are, it was your writing assignment in Vaux that sparked the creative juices in me, and I thank you for that.

Gwen, thanks for being a great friend. I love you and I appreciate all of your support. Rasheeda, thanks for reading all of my stories for me, even though they were never complete. LOL! I love you and you will always be my friend.

To **Mark Anthony**, thank you for giving me the wonderful opportunity of publishing this book and welcoming me to the family. I would have never guessed a few years back that I would be where I am today. I thank you for always listening to me and for being the coolest boss in the world!

Candace K., thanks for raving about my book when I sent the query; I wouldn't have a deal if it wasn't for you. I want to also thank you for all of your help throughout the editing process of this book. I know I may have been a pest sometimes, but I appreciate you being patient with me.

To **Nakea S. Murray**, You have become a great friend and I want to thank you for sharing all of the knowledge that you have with me. I appreciate everything you've done and want to thank you for placing other opportunities in front of me. Thanks for giving my book its name and lending your belongings for the cover! LOL. I can't wait to work with you professionally, since I have a lot of confidence that you will help me succeed, since you have helped me tons already.

Anna J., thanks for telling me the things to look for and what to expect. You have become a good friend as well and I am so glad that we are on the same team.

Erick S. Gray, thanks for critiquing my book your suggestions really helped me out. **Shawna Grundy**, you are so cool to hang out with and I want to thank you for the encouragement you gave me. **Daaimah S. Poole**, thanks for all of the knowledge you shared with me. I hope to do as well as you some day. **Karen E. Quinones Miller**, thanks for displaying your query letter on the site. It was that guide that helped me to write my own. Thanks for being so nice to me when we met and leaving such nice encouragements on my page. **Miasha**, thanks for being so nice in person, it's a good look though I'm sure you knew that already. I hope to sell as many books as you one day. To all of the other authors I've met along the way, **K'wan, Tonya Ridley, Sha and Hickson, Azarel**—thanks for the encouraging words on Myspace, it is so nice to meet so many successful black authors.

To all of my co-workers: Pat, Jackie, Bridgette, Donna—you are a great friend and I'm lucky to have you in my life and Crazy Tony thanks for the laughs and tell Troy I said what's up. LOL!, Pat C.—You are the most thoughtful person I know and I love you. Tracey L.—you are my girl, Lisa L.—thanks for the good talks; you may not know how much they mean, but they mean a heck of a lot. Byron—you keep me laughing, Dottie—thanks for answering all of my many questions. Angel, Lesleon, Audrey, Bre, Joyce, Karen—wherever you are, I miss our talks. Kim, Lishea, Gail—I love you. Nancy and anyone that I've forgotten, I thank all of you for the encouragement and support.

To all of my other friends (there are so many): Andre—you are one of my best friends, remember that! Big Lil—you know I couldn't forget you we will work together soon. Angie, Nikki, Monique, Javon, Derrick, Ambi—I miss you, can't wait until you come home. Mary—you will always be my best friend. Kevin—you will always be special to me, I love you. Terry, Aiasha, Michelle, Basil and the entire Ebauche En Vogue Salon staff, Ebey, Thomas C.-my MySpace literary brother, Vicki—my MySpace friend, thanks for all of the wonderful words. TC, Maine, April—I miss you girl. Lekisha—congrats on your baby! Latisha, Gloria and Steve, I thank all of you for the continued support.

Hydirah and Marquan, Godmom loves you both. Wade, Nadine and Adranetta, you guys are the best babysitters in the world! To my mom's friends, Ms. Gene, Ms. Eleanor, Ms. Pam, and Ms. Betty, you guys have always supported me. Thanks to everyone that stopped by my website, www.Brittani-Williams.com or www.myspace.com/msbgw and left a comment.

To anyone that I may have forgotten, just know that it was my mind and not my heart. I tried to thank everyone that has made a stamp on my life but this list would go on forever. Anyone who has supported me or encouraged me, I thank you with all of my heart. To all of the people that have ever disliked me or doubted me, I thank you too because it's people like you that keep me going.

Ms. Brittani Williams

About the Author

Brittani Williams was born and raised in Philadelphia, PA, where she currently resides. She began writing when a school assignment required her to write a short play. This assignment showed her how far her imagination could go.

She started out writing short stories in play script form until deciding to take a plunge at changing the format to that of a novel. After doing some research and finding out how hard it was to get a publishing deal, she briefly gave up on writing. After attending college and switching majors a few times, she decided to get back to writing when she got an idea for an exciting story.

Next she self published a short story to get feedback and when each response was good she decided to write a novel-length version of it. After more research she came across Q-Boro Books' website and submitted her manuscript. They quickly responded and soon gave her a book deal.

Brittani thanks Mark Anthony and the entire Q-boro staff for giving her the opportunity to show the world what her family and friends have raved about since day one.

She is currently majoring in Education and Fashion Design in Philadelphia. Brittani is the mother of a three year old and is also hard at work on her second novel. Stay Tuned!

PREVIEW

Sugar Walls

By Brittani Williams

Coming in December 2007

Sugar's the Name

It was cold, dark, snowy, and lonely as I lay there tied up with no idea where I am. I could feel each of my limbs freezing one by one. I could barely even speak, let alone scream for help. No one could help me—no one even knew where I was except the bastard who put me here. I could hear random noises in the background: police sirens, horns beeping, music playing; but all of these sounds were distant and too far away for my weakened voice to be heard.

The way that I had mapped out my life, I never thought that it would land me here. I had a plan A, B, and C, none of which included being beaten, tied up and left for dead in the snow. This cold dark night led me to reflect back to how I got there and how it all began. It also made me wonder if I could have done anything to prevent it or done anything different to make my life turn out the way that I had originally planned.

Named Sugar Alise Clark, I was cursed from the beginning. I was born to an alcoholic, crack-addicted mother and a deadbeat, drunk-ass father. I'm surprised DHS even allowed them to bring me home from the hospital! It's amazing how the things you think a child should be taken away for are totally opposite of the things that they are really taken away for.

My mother Elaine was once a beautiful woman, far tucked under the tired appearance that she carried now. Pictures of her were the only proof of her past beauty, because the way that she looked now was the only way that I had ever seen her. I was her firstborn, with my sister Mya to follow. Mya and I were best friends growing up, close as two sisters could be.

Elaine was born and raised in Brooklyn New York, but she moved to Philadelphia after high school to attend Temple University. Her college life was short lived when she dropped out after only one semester. She opted to stay in Philadelphia after meeting my father Ron at an off-campus party. They hit it off quickly but their relationship was anything but perfect.

Ron worked at any place that he could make a quick dollar. He would cut grass in the spring and summer, rake leaves in the fall, and shovel snow in the winter. He was your neighborhood hustle man. How my mom fell in love with him, I'll never know, but I do know that he was a big factor in her downfall. Soon after moving in with him, they began drinking heavily and snorting cocaine on the regular. Neither of them could keep a steady job, so we lived in poverty. Our parents were barely able to feed us because their drug habit was more important to them. I was always ashamed of my mother and father, and there were many times that I wished I had never even been born. No child should ever feel that way.

I wasn't fast growing up; I didn't loose my virginity until I was eighteen. I was never the girl who stood out; the guys in school never paid me any attention. Mya, on the other hand, received so much attention that she didn't know how to handle it. At the young age of fifteen, Mya had her first child. Marlo was one of the unlucky men that my sister slept with, unlucky meaning the fool that got her pregnant. See, Mya had a reputation that was far from good. She was branded the "neighborhood booty", because most dudes in the hood could get some from her anytime.

Marlo was different. He was from South Philly, so he had never had the opportunity of sitting in on any conversations where Mya's sexual favors were the topic. She met Marlo after leaving WOW skating rink on a Saturday night. Marlo noticed Mya and a group of females including me waiting on the R bus to get back home. Marlo drove up in a brand new Mazda Millennia, black with extra-dark tint in all of the windows.

Mya stood about 5'5" at the time, and she wore her hair short and spiked. She lined her lips perfectly with brown lip liner and applied her cherry lip-gloss, making her lips shine. Her body was like Halle Berry's; even at the age of fourteen she mirrored that of an adult woman. There was no way that Marlo could resist her dancing in her short denim mini.

He pulled into the gas station behind the bus stop where we were standing and beeped his horn before rolling down his window. Not calling anyone directly, Mya switched quickly over to the car, automatically assuming that he was beeping the horn for her.

"What's up, sexy? What's a fine-ass girl like you doing waiting on the bus stop? If that nigga you were fucking was a real man, he'd be picking you up, or better yet he'd buy you a car so you wouldn't have to wait on nobody's damn bus!" he spoke

"Well, I don't have a man so that's why I'm out here."

"All of that can change if you want it to."

"Oh, really!"

"Really, if you fuck with a real man and stop playing with these kids!"

"Well, I'm down for whatever! I need a real man in my life."

"Let me give you a ride so we can talk more. I'll tell you all about what I can do for you."

"Cool, let me go tell my girls I'm leaving with you."

"All right, but don't have me waiting too long!"

"I promise I won't," she said before walking back to where we were standing.

I was angry. "What the hell is wrong with you, Mya? You don't even know him!"

"I will know him by the end of the night."

"You are so dumb! Do you even know his name? And how are you going to leave me to go home by myself? It's 10:00 at night."

"You'll be all right. I haven't had sex in a while, and I need a hook-up! Sorry, I'll see you tonight. Cover for me with Mom."

"As if she'll notice you are not there anyway, she'll be too busy getting high. And then be pissed at me tomorrow."

"Well then it's settled, I'll see you later. I promise I won't stay out all night," she said before running off.

"Mya!" I yelled.

Mya entered the car without even turning around to acknowledge me. I was pissed, but this wasn't the first time that she'd left me hanging like that, and at that moment I felt that it wouldn't be the last time either.

That night, I made it home safely, though I ran from the bus stop, afraid I would be attacked. Entering our small, roach-infested two-bedroom apartment, I found my mother asleep on the living floor. There was a glass pipe or a glass "dick" as they call it less than two feet away from her. I went into my bedroom as I usually did, put on my headphones, and drifted off to sleep. I'd learned after many sleepless nights to wear the headphones to block out the drunken arguments between my mother and father, or the loud-ass sexual episodes they would have after getting high. I listened to my music to block out the realities of my world.

Mya never came home that night, and, as usual, I was the one who received the punishment. Being slapped, waking me out of my sleep was something I was used to. Since I was older, and I was responsible, my mother made sure I was aware of the fact that if Mya messed up, then I would be punished for it.

"Mom, what are you hitting me for?" I yelled, shocked by the blow to my stomach.

"Where the fuck is Mya? She didn't come home last night. How many times do I have to tell you to make sure she brings her ass home!" she yelled.

"Mom, I tried, but she didn't listen."

"You didn't try hard enough. Next time you are really going to make sure that she comes home or I'm going to fuck you up for not doing what you were told!"

"Why do I get in trouble for her?"

"Don't question me. I pay the bills in this muthafucker, and until you get your own, don't ask me shit! I make the rules!" she yelled before leaving the bedroom and slamming the door.

I sat there and cried as usual. Mya was never punished for anything. It was always me, and I was the stand-up student. How ironic is that? I came home every night, but Mya maybe came home once or twice a week. Therefore, I was punished five or six days a week. I was slapped, punched, kicked, and spit on for things that I didn't even do.

That afternoon Mya strolled in after twelve when she

knew my mother would be out buying her drug and liquor supply for the night. I was in my room studying.

"Hey, did Mom notice that I was gone?"

"Of course she did, I thought you weren't going to stay out all night. You know she came in here hitting me this morning. Mya, why do you always do that when you know what she's going to do to me?"

"Sorry, Sugar, but I was having so much fun with Marlo, and I didn't want to leave."

"Marlo! So that's his name? Did you have sex with him?"

"Of course I did, I needed some sexual healing!" she said laughing.

"I don't think it's funny, Mya!"

"Well, I do! I enjoyed myself."

"Whatever."

I learned early on that Mya didn't care about anyone but Mya, and it was too bad for me that I cared about her. The following day I went to school as usual and headed to my part-time job at Bloomingdales afterward. I loved my job; it was the only time I was ever able to be around designer clothing. I even tried different outfits on some days, just to pretend that I was actually going to buy them.

I dealt with the rude customers, and it didn't bother me half as bad as the treatment that I received at home. I was constantly looked down on for working in a department store, but I didn't care because I was working to save money for my college education.

I greeted everyone as I clocked in. I felt like today was going to be a long day. I normally worked in the children's department, but due to a call-out, I was placed in the women's shoe department. This day was the day that would eventually change my life.

I was summoned by a customer for help, and I instantly

noticed her beauty. This woman stood about 5'9" with a perfect shape and flawless face. Her make-up was perfect, and it looked as if it had been professionally applied. I tried not to stare, but I was memorized. I jumped at the chance to meet her even if only to get her the shoes that she wanted.

"Hi, how can I help you?" I said nervously.

"Can I see these in a size 7?" she said before passing me three pairs of Marc Jacobs pumps.

"Sure, I'll be right back!" I said, smiling before going in the back to search for the shoes. I rushed because I didn't want her to get impatient. Once I was back on the sales floor she was sitting down waiting for me to return.

"Okay, I've found all three. Just let me know if you need anything else."

"Would you mind giving me your opinion?"

"No. Not at all," I said anxiously.

She tried on each pair, and I told her how good each pair looked on her feet. I wasn't gay by far, but to be honest, she was the prettiest woman I had ever seen. She thanked me and ended up purchasing all three pairs of shoes, totaling $1,195.

"Thanks a lot! What's your name?" she asked.

"Sugar!"

"Is that your real name?"

"Yeah."

"Did you ever think about modeling or anything? You have a really pretty face."

"Not at all! No one has ever told me I was pretty," I said, shocked by the comment.

"Well, here's my card. Call me and maybe I can hook you up with a job, then you can afford to buy the same stuff that you sell!" She smiled.

"Okay, thank you Ms . . ."

"Dyna, the name's Dyna. I'll look forward to hearing from you."

"Okay," I said putting the business card into my back pocket.

I continued work, still in pain from the blow I received from my mother the day before. I caught the bus home and dreaded going in, afraid of what would be waiting on me when I got there. I never knew what to expect going home. Mya went to a different school than I did so I was never sure if she went to school or not. Every night when I would come home from work I was afraid that I would be beaten if Mya had missed school that day. I entered the apartment and found Mya and my father sitting on the sofa watching the television.

"Hey, baby! How was work?" my father asked.

"Fine," I mumbled before walking into my bedroom.

My father, unlike my mother, never abused me. Though he smoked the same amount of crack that my mother did, his attitude was totally different. I loved my father, but was always afraid to show it because of my mother's jealous actions. If my father showed us any attention when she was around, we were sure to be punished for it later. Mya was always closer to my father than I was, but I guess that she wasn't as afraid of my mother as I was because her beatings were never as brutal as mine. I entered my room and followed my daily routine of homework and then shortly after fell asleep.

I went to school the following day as usual. I went to all of my classes and sat and ate lunch alone while I waited for Marissa to arrive. I didn't have many friends; truthfully, I only had one true friend and that was Marissa.

Marissa was normal; there was nothing really striking about her appearance. She was raised by her mother who worked as a maid most of her life. The money that her mother made was never really enough to supply Marissa and her siblings with good clothing. They were forced to wear clothes from random thrift shops and hand-me-downs. I met her in fifth grade, and we had been best friends ever since. There were many times that we were in fights because people constantly picked on both of us. Me, I wasn't wearing thrift shop clothing, but I wasn't pretty and I was overweight. The fact that I always had a bruised face or busted lip from my mother didn't help. Marissa was pretty, but she didn't stand out because of her attire, and she was ridiculed constantly because of it. We would both fight for each other, and never thought twice about doing anything differently. I sat at the table for a few minutes before she decided to show up at lunch.

"What's up, what took you so long?" I quizzed.

"I had to finish up my test. Sorry! No one messed with you, did they?"

"No, I'm fine. You know I got in trouble this weekend for Mya again."

"You know, if I was you I would beat her up every time I got in trouble for her. That's crazy that she doesn't even care."

"Mya only cares about herself. Maybe if I didn't care about her it wouldn't bother me as much."

"Well you need to be more like her, stop caring!"

"It's easy to say that, but she is my little sister."

"I know, but it's a shame. Well, you'll be graduating soon, and you can go to college and be rid of all of their crazy asses!" she said, laughing.

The next three months flew by. My mother and father didn't even attend my graduation, but I didn't care. I was proud of myself even if no one else was. After graduating and returning home to the apartment, my mother said that she forgot all about it. I knew that was a lie, and I also knew that my father didn't come because my mother wouldn't allow him to. I began working full-time during the week after school was over. My daily routine was soon without any incident until Mya decided to get pregnant. I came home from work and found my mother sitting on the sofa. I figured my father was probably out hustling up some more drug money. I sat my bag down and was instantly approached by my mother.

"Did you know that your sister was pregnant?" she yelled.

"What?"

"You heard me, your little ho-ass sister got herself pregnant. Where the hell were you? Too busy worrying about yourself to do what I told you to do!"

"Mom, I am working to go to college."

"Fuck that! You ain't never going to be shit anyway, so you are wasting your time. I told you to be responsible for your sister, very simple and you couldn't do that. How the fuck do you think that you will finish college?" She began laughing.

"I will finish, and I don't find anything funny. Mya is old enough to be responsible for herself."

She smacked me, making me fall to the floor, "Who the fuck are you talking to?" she yelled.

I got up off the floor angry. All of the built-up anger that I carried all the years I had been abused surfaced, and I could no longer hold back. I could no longer be subjected to her abuse for things I didn't do.

I stood there rubbing my swollen lip as she yelled more obscenities in my face. I balled up my fist and after too many "bitches" that she called me, and began punching her repeatedly. She fell to the floor with me on top of her, and I continued beating her until I was exhausted. Her emaciated frame was nothing compared to mine. I jumped up, grabbed my bag, and ran out of the apartment crying. I was hurt because it had been going on too long. I'd had enough at that point, and I didn't care what happened to my mother after that. I wanted her out of my life.

I took a little money out of my bank account and stayed at a hotel that night. The hotel was nothing spectacular, but it was much more than the apartment that I had shared with my family. I took a long hot bath, and I quickly fell to sleep on the queen-sized bed that was much more comfortable than my twin mattress on the floor at home. This was the first night that I didn't have to wear my headphones to block out the noise around me. This was my first peaceful sleep, and I had waited long enough to have it.